Mr. Purley, coming down from the fourth floor, stopped the lift for her. There were two sacks beside him; she had some difficulty in avoiding them.

"More bodies for the students," he said in a hollow voice, making his usual joke.

"You'll end on the gallows yet," said Barbara. The lift stopped with a jerk, and she stumbled against one of the sacks. And as she did so, the mouth of the sack opened. An inert hand slid out.

Barbara, in her novels, had from time to time pierced an odd character or so with a sword. She had several times knocked villains out with a clean left from the hero's fist. But never had she visualized anything so horrifying as this dead hand which crept out and dropped to the floor.

It was, of course, Mrs. Warren's hand. . . .

Also by Charity Blackstock
Published by Ballantine Books:

THE FOGGY, FOGGY DEW

DEWEY DEATH

Charity Blackstock

BALLANTINE BOOKS • NEW YORK

The man of much business or affairs must study every problem in its manifold relations—i.e., must classify and make charts of his results. Without these he is like a sailor in stranje waters, sooner or later shiprekt unless he uzes charts to find safe channels as wel as to avoid roks and shoals.

from
DECIMAL CLASIFICATION
AND
RELATIV INDEX

by
MELVIL DEWEY, M.A., L.L.D.

ISBN 0-345-32509-5

This edition published by arrangement with London House and Maxwell, New York

Manufactured in the United States of America

First Ballantine Books Edition: December 1963
Second Printing: October 1985

CONTENTS

INTER-LIBRARIES DESPATCH ASSOCIATION
(I.L.D.A.)

CHIEF LIBRARIAN
Mr. Ridley

DEPUTY LIBRARIAN
Mr. Latimer

LOCATION DEPARTMENT
Miss Holmes
Mrs. Warren
Miss Barbara Smith
Greta
Maureen
Peggy

MICROFILMS & PHOTOSTATS
Mark Allan

PERIODICALS
Mr. Dodds

REFERENCE ROOM
Mr. Rills
Mr. Wilson

FINANCE OFFICE
Mrs. Bridgwater

PACKING ROOM
Mr. Purley

SCOTLAND YARD
Detective-Sergeant Robins
Police-Constable-Detective Hall

And Charles, engaged to Barbara; and Miss Dorothea
Langdon, a temporary typist

I. MALE AND FEMALE EMPLOYEES
647.22 & 647.23

IT started—How did it start? With a novel. A few words. A chance interview. A silly woman with an interfering mind and an ugly laugh. It started in July and ended in September. At first, one could not bear to remember. Music one could never listen to again. *Sweet Thames, run softly till I end my song.* And sugar ships in the moonlight, and gentle hands grown cruel; kind words and harsh words, loving words and hating words. The ugliness, the terror, that dimmed and faded, to leave the things that mattered, the things that endured. To have entered into a person's mind, and at the end, the very end, to take that mind into yours, so that it was a part of you, to stay with you, stripped of its despair, till the end of your days. . . .

It started then with a novel, a novel accepted for publication. It was something of an occasion. So of course, as he once said, is murder, but then one did not see the black, grim shadow in the corner—

She had told Charles, and that was all; Charles was her fiancé. But now she stood in the office doorway and said, "They have taken my novel."

They turned to look at her.

She added, "I will buy you cake for tea."

For this was an office custom at times of celebration; besides, it ensured an interest in her literary career.

"Smashing!" said Greta, raising her great, dark cow-eyes, hooded by black, mourning brows. She was wearing a new outfit of a white blouse and turquoise-blue skirt; she looked like the heroine of a Middle-European operetta.

Maureen said mildly, "Why don't you tell us the name you write under? Then we could all read it."

Barbara looked down and away. She had never told them her pen-name. Miss Smith worked in the Library, was a reasonably conscientious worker, except when her imagina-

9

tion got the better of her, and led a calm, sedate life. But Miss Allen, Miss Barbara Allen, the creator of handsome heroes who fought duels and made love in the eighteenth-century moonlight, was a different creature and one whose identity she feverishly concealed.

There was Mark Allan, who worked at the Library. It afforded Barbara a foolish amusement that they should meet in the evenings; he would say, "Good-night, Miss Smith," and she would reply, "Good-night, Mr. Allan," and smile to herself.

Later she was to remember that. Later, she was to forget how to smile. But that was still to come.

She said at last, "Oh, does it matter? Perhaps I don't want you to make fun of me. Perhaps I have my pride. Eat your cake and be thankful."

Mrs. Warren said suddenly, "I should like to see what you write. It should be interesting."

'Oh no, you don't,' thought Barbara. 'You, of all people.' She could not quite conceal the dislike in her face as she looked at Mrs. Warren, who had already gathered a vast pile of forms by her typewriter. She would never be able to finish them by twelve o'clock, but she would not part with them, either, even if there were no work for the girls. Mrs. Warren had worked in the Library for seven years, and had come to envelop the department as if she ruled it. Charles, who had seen her once when he called for Barbara, had remarked that she looked like some sinister French *concierge*. She was a woman of fifty, with black hair middle-parted and worn in a bun, a stout little person with a resolute, hard-cut face, black eyes, and determined legs that she planted obstinately one in front of the other. Her voice was guttural and resonant, but it was her laugh that so distressed her neighbours; she laughed loudly and often in a strange, hysterical giggle which she did not seem able to stop.

She began to laugh now. "Perhaps," she said, "you are ashamed of it. Is it so very sentimental?" Her face was alight with glee; the giggling laughter bubbled forth.

"It is not," said Barbara, "the kind of thing you would care to read."

"That I can believe," said Mrs. Warren, "but it seems foolish to me to write books and not let anyone read them."

"Several thousand people do read them," said Barbara in the exaggeration provoked by anger, and turned to the wire basket to pick up such forms as still remained. She had her own little room opposite. She never knew why she had this privilege. It was true that she was older than the girls, but then Mrs. Warren was a great deal older than herself. It was perhaps because she had a degree. Mr. Ridley, the Chief Librarian, was an Oxford man and, because he had spent all his life in the world of books, did not realise that a university degree was an impractical thing with no commercial value. But whatever the reason, Barbara worked on her own, with the addressograph and Gestetner for company. She greatly valued her privacy, and wrote there all her more emotional scenes on scraps of office paper.

Maureen called after her, "The C.S.A. is closed for the summer vacation. So is Liverpool University."

Barbara acknowledged this with a nod, and departed with her pile of forms. There were not many left. Mrs. Warren, now watching her with black, beady eyes, had taken almost everything. She hung up her coat and, sitting down at her desk, made a brief note with regard to Liverpool University and the Cambridge School of Agriculture. The initials did not worry her at all. She worked in a world of initials, as the librarians worked in a world enmeshed in the decimal code. To them, enforced devotees of Mr. Dewey and his decimal classification, 800 signified literature and 900, history. Hell to them was not a fiery furnace; it was simply 237.5, while the mysteries of life, dueling and suicide (Mr. Dewey had his own method of spelling) were summed up succinctly in 179.7. To Barbara, then, B.N.F. stood for British Non-Ferrous Metals Research Association, C. Phil. for the Cambridge Philosophical Society, and H.L. for the Howard League of Penal Reform. It had become an automatic process, and she could now follow the scrawled directions of the Reference Room, without hesitation.

The Inter-Libraries Despatch Association (I.L.D.A.) stood encircled by the universities it largely depended on. It stretched out its hands to the farthest quarters of the globe, to procure books for people who still wished to read. If Mr. X wished to read a Russian periodical on mechanics, he applied to his public library; the appropriate form was sent in to I.L.D.A., who then obtained it. Sixteenth-century books and the latest modern treatises, articles on textiles, sludge, electricity, politics, fashion-designing and T. S. Eliot, all were gathered in from every possible source. Requests went out to Paris (Bib. Nat.), to Rome (Bib. Naz.), to Cologne (Universi-täts-und Stadtbibliothek), to Budapest (Országos Széchenyi Könyvtár) and the Library of Congress (Lib. Cong.). The Reference Room looked up the locations of all books; Mr.

Dodds, who was in his own way a far more genuine eccentric than Barbara, dealt with the periodicals. Mark Allan, who looked alarmingly like one of Barbara's heroes, handled microfilms and photostats, and there was also a vast packing department, usually staffed by Irishmen, and presided over by Mr. Purley, who was crabbed and irascible, who smoked surreptitiously, despite the veto, and who carted down in the lift vast sacks of books deposited in the basement stacks for sorting.

There were some seven thousand books in I.L.D.A. Barbara spent most of her spare time in the history section, wandering from stack to stack. For the most part the Location Department, which was hers, did not trouble about the existence of these books. Their job was to send out to W.I.R.A. (Woollen Industries Research Association) for an article on the combing of fleece, required by Witwatersrand University. It meant little more to them than copying out invoices. They copy-typed in French, German, Italian and Russian, without understanding one word; they applied for English books without troubling their heads about them, either. It was the day's work. Mrs. Warren sometimes made fun of them. "Fancy," she would say, "typing *Wissenschaft* without the capital letter. And how amusing not to know elementary French——" She attended evening classes, and made a great cult of culture. "But of course," she would add to Barbara when she first came and appeared in the light of a soul-mate, "they're all dreadfully common and uneducated, poor things. I don't suppose they really know what a book is. Or anything else, for that matter. That little Maureen said she watched 'Peer Gynt' on the television last night, and turned it off after the first three minutes. Fancy anyone turning off 'Peer Gynt'." And the hysterical laughter would peal forth at this studpendous joke, until she seemed to be scoured by a storm of intellectual merriment. Then she would stop laughing and shut all the windows, and report the matter if the girls protested.

That, of course, was only during Barbara's first month. After that Barbara showed plainly that she preferred the company of the girls, and for this treachery Mrs. Warren never forgave her. She then contented herself with grabbing all the work she could, laughing continually at the stupidity of the fools around her, and reporting to Miss Holmes, the head of the department, any tit-bits of information she thought worth recounting.

Barbara was normally careful not to mingle her two lives. But the starting of a new novel was always a delirious moment in which her sanity left her. And this time it was such a magnificent idea. It was as always eighteenth century, but it concerned an historical incident that no one seemed so far to have considered, and it would involve her hero (A duelling type with a lean, scarred face and a disgraceful past) in the London underworld where she could describe the highwaymen, drabs, thief-takers and sharpers who fascinated her to a point of the wildest excitement.

(Charles, who loved her, forbore to make too much fun of her, but he did once remark casually, "You always make your heroes so tough. It's nice to think they're ever such gentlemen at heart, reelly——")

Mr. Andrews—for that was to be his name—was of course as soft as butter. But he was very attractive, and Barbara, after applying for the *Poulterers' Weekly*, a second edition of Defoe's *Compleat Gentleman* and something which ran, "Akademia Nauk S.S.S.R. Inst. Organicheskoi Khimii", could stand it no longer. Once a week she stencilled a long list for some fifty universities; the discarded pages made excellent rough paper. She pulled out one of these sheets now and, with a great feeling of guilt and excitement, fitted it into her machine. And then she was lost. It flowed from her, and she thought, as she so often did, 'Oh, God, if only the speed of one's fingers could match one's brain.' For that brief time she was out of I.L.D.A. and the world. Her sword was drawn by that of Mr. Andrews. (She had discovered a useful little book called *The Fencer's Companion;* she was very ashamed of this, and kept it hidden), but ripostes and feints and parries flowed easily from her, as her hero, having discovered the heroine in some compromising situation, drove into the attack. A scathing bit of dialogue followed between Mr. Andrews and Mary (Jane? Selina? Elizabeth?) and so engrossed was she that she forgot all caution, and did not perceive Mrs. Warren until that lady was standing beside her.

It was too late then to do anything, and Barbara was too proud to remove the paper from her machine.

Mrs. Warren, her head a little on one side, stood there, quite shamelessly eyeing the paper.

Barbara said coldly, "Yes, Mrs. Warren?" She knew she was hopelessly in the wrong. I.L.D.A. did not pay her to write her novels, and she had not even the excuse of lack of work, for morning was always the rush time, and there was still a pile of forms beside her.

"Are you writing more novels?" inquired Mrs. Warren, her

eyes snapping with amusement. The laughter was already surging up in her throat.

"It is my profession," replied Barbara. "What do you want?"

"I only came in for the Science Library book," said Mrs. Warren, giggling a little, and trying always to read over Barbara's shoulder.

"I'm sorry, I don't have it."

"Oh!" said Mrs. Warren. "Of course you don't like doing the Science Library forms, do you? I notice they are usually left for me to do." Then, beginning to riffle through the pile on the desk, she added, "What forms have you got there?"

Barbara said angrily, "Haven't you enough to do, Mrs. Warren? You seem to have taken more than half for yourself, alone."

"At least it means they get done," retorted Mrs. Warren, and rocked with laughter as if this were the greatest joke in the world.

Barbara could not but recognise the justice of this and, having placed herself in the unhappy position of not being able to reply, could only fit an application form into her machine and begin typing viciously.

Mrs. Warren paused for a moment, then said suddenly, an edge to her voice, "I'm so sorry. Of course, I'm not an important person. *I* don't have a degree. *I* don't deserve a room of my own. Oh no. I apologise for speaking to you, Miss Smith. I'm sure it's *lèse-majesté* to disturb you. You must try to forgive me. I am just an illiterate old woman who's not worth cultivating."

Barbara, shocked, swung round. "But, Mrs. Warren——"

"Oh, don't worry about me," said Mrs. Warren, backing to the door, always giggling as she did so, "I don't mind. I am very thick-skinned. Why, even when Mr. Allan is rude to me, I don't pay attention."

"Mr. Allan? I don't understand."

"Such a clever, clever man," said Mrs. Warren, ceasing to laugh, and looking indeed like a *concierge*, and of the kind that spied for the Gestapo. "So interesting. They are all interesting. Mr. Rills is interesting, too. And dear Mrs. Bridgwater. You should write a book about us, Miss Smith, really, you should."

And here she broke into a shrill laugh, and slammed the door behind her.

"Oh, God!" said Barbara, and sat there for a moment, star-

ing at her typewriter. She supposed they were interesting,
though she knew little about them, for I.L.D.A. was extremely
departmentalised. But she did know, as all the office knew,
that Mark Allan was in love with Mrs. Bridgwater, and that
Mrs. Bridgwater, who dealt with the accounts, wages and
finance in general, had always to have at least one young man
in tow, otherwise she would not be fulfilling herself and
establishing her freedom of soul. She knew, too, that Mr.
Rills, from the Reference Room, with his high, flat voice, his
faint lisp and spiteful humour, was a pest who loved making
mischief. But she had not realised that Mrs. Warren had
come athwart them all, though she remembered now a brief
and unseemly passage of arms between her and Mark Allan,
whose temper was notorious and whose manners were even
more so.

He had said, "I should be obliged, Mrs. Warren, if you
would not re-direct forms on your own initiative. If the
Library requires a microfilm, it is my business."

She had replied gaily, "It only seemed strange to me that
you should send to Paris for a German book that I happen
to know is in Cologne University."

At this he had suddenly gone white, and blazed at her.
It was very noticeable, for he had a wild, handsome face,
and extraordinary light grey eyes. "You damned, interfering
old busy-body——" he had begun, and then, in the horrified
silence that ensued—for this took place in the canteen during
tea-break—had checked himself with an enormous effort, and
flung out of the room.

Mrs. Warren had laughed. It had not been a pleasant
sound, and Barbara did not care much for the memory. It
had all been so dramatic, and drama in real life was not
amusing. She angrily pushed Mr. Andrews and his sword into
a pile of papers at her side, and began to type forms as if
her life depended on it.

She was not surprised when, half an hour later, Miss
Holmes came in. Mrs. Warren had had ample time to suggest
that Miss Smith, when left to her own devices, did not always
do the work she was paid to do. Barbara, dutifully typing,
with an impressive pile of completed forms to the right of
her (Mr. Andrews was well out of sight), could see immediately that Miss Holmes was distraught and wondering
how to deal with the situation.

Their relationship had always been difficult, though not
habitually unfriendly. Miss Holmes was accustomed to be
in charge of a number of teen-agers. She bullied them, ordered

them about, told them off, and protected them against attack from any other department, no matter what crime they had committed. They did not dislike her. She was sharp-tongued, at times unfair, and as sparing in her praise as she was liberal in her blame, but they knew well enough that she would defend them to the last, and this gave them a certain feeling of security.

Mr. Rills, who disliked Barbara, as he seemed to dislike everyone, had once come into Miss Holmes's office to complain that Miss Smith was late with her copy of the university list, thus disarranging the work of the entire Reference Room.

Miss Holmes (this was duly reported to Barbara by Greta, who had been present during the conversation), had glanced with the utmost distaste at Mr. Rills, who was a young man with curling hair and a wide, thin mouth. She had said, "If, Mr. Rills, your department would occasionally take as much concern over their own work as they appear to do over ours, I.L.D.A. would run much more smoothly. I have before me a form from I.C.I. for the *Journal of Pharmacy*. The location given by your department, in your handwriting, I believe, Mr. Rills, is oddly enough for—I.C.I. You cannot expect my girls always to notice these things; they have far too much to do. The result is simply that we are made to look ridiculous. I see, too, that an urgent demand from Imperial Tobacco has been held up in the Reference Room for four days. This won't do, Mr. Rills, you know, it really won't. Instead of worrying Miss Smith for her university list, you would do better to put your own affairs in order."

Mr. Rills, who was spiteful without courage, had slunk out like a whipped puppy, his wide, mean mouth working, but the high voice strangely silent. From that time he avoided Miss Holmes as much as he could, but spoke of her continually as a typical old maid, "my dear, pure, pure vinegar. Swamps all those poor girls with maternal feelings gone sour. She should be psychoanalysed, though, really, one shudders to think what would pop out in the analysis."

Mr. Rills believed that everyone should be psychoanalysed, and, on this subject, for a brief while agreed with Mrs. Warren, and they could be seen discussing Freud in corners, his thin voice contrasting strangely with her giggling laugh.

But they no longer discussed Freud or anything else. Barbara wondered vaguely what they could have quarrelled about. She thought they would both be dangerous enemies, for Mrs. Warren worried everything to death, and Mr. Rills, though a coward, had a tongue of the purest venom, and was in his own way as observant as Mrs. Warren in hers.

She glanced sideways at Miss Holmes as she reflected on this, and sighed. She realised that Miss Holmes had never known how to deal with her. To have amongst her staff a young woman not so far removed from her own age, and an educated young woman at that, had always distressed her. However, Miss Holmes never mentioned this directly, and did not do so now. Indeed—as Barbara saw with some sympathy, for she did not dislike Miss Holmes—her position was a delicate one, as all her information came from Mrs. Warren. She said in a quick, irritable voice, "I want you to type a memo for me. It is extremely urgent, so please put those forms aside. It must go within the next ten minutes, so leave everything you are doing, everything——"

"Yes, Miss Holmes," said Barbara meekly. She saw plainly that this last was as far as Miss Holmes dared go. She waited, with her pencil poised.

"It's to Mr. Dodds," said Miss Holmes, adding bitterly, "Really, he's the most tiresome man. What with him and Mr. Allan.—As I said to Mr. Latimer this morning, how he can expect me to run this department without the slightest co-operation from anyone, what with Mr. Allan flying off the handle at the slightest provocation, and Mr. Dodds making long speeches which have simply nothing to do with anything——"

Mr. Latimer was the Deputy Librarian, a handsome, well-groomed little man, with a tooth-brush moustache; to Miss Holmes he was as the high priest, and she bowed before him.

"Yes, Miss Holmes?" said Barbara.

"The usual heading, and so on. You can compose it yourself. I want you to tell him that we must have the periodical requests in earlier for the bureau and university lists. Mr. Latimer says so, that should impress him. It's simply absurd to expect you and Maureen to get your lists off, if you have to wait till eleven before the forms come in. And would he please print the foreign words, because my girls can scarcely be expected to know Russian or Czech. Do you know them, Miss Smith?"

"No!"

"And, anyway, he writes so large that—— You'd better not say that. Just ask him to print. Make it polite."

Barbara at this looked rather doubtful, and Miss Holmes gave her a thin smile. "Well, after all," she said, "you're a writer, aren't you? It'll be good training for you. And remember it must go at once, otherwise we'll only have the same bother all over again."

Barbara typed out the memo and, as she did so, reflected on the strange fact that over-large writing was as invisible as over-small. Mr. Dodds had a monumental handwriting of a hieroglyphic type, and inscribed vast instructions on all his forms which, like high archways, were simply not seen at all, especially as he invariably wrote over the printed lines so that the two could not be disentangled.

She had once dared to remonstrate with him. He had peered at her formidably over his glasses. He was a man of sixty-odd, with a professorial shock of white hair, and broad, bowed shoulders that filled his tiny office. It was said that he took snuff; he was known to be eccentric, and the girls declared they could never understand a word he said, much less what he wrote, for he talked a great deal, in an academic fashion peculiar to himself. He was said to be very happily married.

"Though really, dears," said Mr. Rills, "he is so old that he simply must be impotent. That taking snuff is terribly significant, you know. Poor Mrs. Dodds. I expect she has a shocking time with him. I expect he writes Russian all over her in simply enormous script."

Mr. Dodds, who had in point of fact a singularly unpsychopathic air to him, had replied to Barbara, "You young ladies should take reading lessons, and writing lessons, too. You dare to reproach me for my writing, you, who have learnt the noble art in a vile and disgusting performance known, I believe, as script, and who either print or produce a microscopic scrawl that the very fly, fresh from the ink-pot, would be ashamed of. Get yourself glasses, Miss Smith, on the National Health, or go back to school. And go away. You are wasting my time."

But that was Mr. Dodds's way of talking, and Barbara, who liked him very much, was not abashed. When an hour later, after her memo had been duly typed and delivered, he walked into her office, she smiled at him with some pleasure. Though he stooped and muttered and cultivated an impression of intellectual absentmindedness, he was always courteous, and she was sure he observed a great deal more than people realised.

He did not at first say anything. He wandered over to the stationary cupboard, and began fingering the things that lay inside.

"I see," he said presently, "that you have various kinds of paper here. I should like a few sheets of it."

"Of course. Which kind do you want?"

"Well," he said, "it rather depends on what you have. What is this used for?"

"That is for my university list."

"Ah. Your university list. You are an important young woman, Miss Smith, to hold such responsibility. And this?"

"For the bureaux list, Mr. Dodds. The North-Western Regional Library Bureau, and so on."

"I see. Most interesting. What would happen if you sent out your university list on bureau paper?"

"It would be the end of the world," replied Barbara. "I should have all my buttons forcibly removed, and would be drummed out of I.L.D.A. It would be a most shocking scandal. It doesn't bear thinking of."

He turned to glance at her. There was a faint flicker in the old, deeply-socketed eyes.

She said, "What kind of paper are you taking?"

"Oh," he said, "I don't mind. I shall only write on the back of it, anyway. I was simply interested in the workings of bureaucracy. By the way——"

He paused, and she looked up at him.

He was gazing out of the window. The muscle in his lined cheek twitched slightly. He said, "That memo——"

"Yes, Mr. Dodds?"

"Very interesting. Very interesting, indeed. I had never expected anything so engrossing." He produced the paper from his pocket; it had been neatly folded into a square. "This obviously comes from you, Miss Smith."

"Well, I typed it, yes."

"Ah, but the inspiration is yours, too. I won't," said Mr. Dodds, still staring down into the courtyard, "read it out to you, because I should hate to embarrass you, but I feel you should glance at it, for, as an inter-departmental memo, it holds most unusual features."

An appalling premonition seized Barbara, and the colour slowly rose in her cheeks. She took the paper, while Mr. Dodds watched in a mournful silence.

Then the colour flared into scarlet. She read:

"He rose with an oath. 'By God, ma'am,' said he, 'do you imagine—can you imagine—that I am the kind of man to be deceived by such a farrago of lies? Where is this fellow? Why, ma'am, you *shall* tell me—— And when I find him——' Mr. Andrews drew his sword, and Mary (Jane? Selina? Elizabeth?) caught at his ruffle with a scream——"

Barbara had never really grown accustomed to office life and etiquette. In the emotion that encompassed her, she spoke now in a way that would have thrown Miss Holmes into a fever. She cried out, "Damn your eyes!" The tears of humiliation were very near her own. "I'll not be made fun of."

Mr. Dodds said mildly, "I particularly like the touch about Mary, Jane, Selina, Elizabeth." Suddenly he laughed. "Come," he said. "Come. Surely you can forgive an old man for taking his humour where he may. You must let me have a copy when it's out. You do publish, don't you?"

"Certainly," said Barbara in a muffled voice, screwing the piece of paper up in her hand.

"There is, I find," said Mr. Dobbs, "such a vast distinction between those who write novels and those who publish them. Don't tear it up, my dear. It sounds to me a fine piece of fustian. We all like fustian. My wife reads nothing else." He reached the door as he spoke. "You remind me of something. Mary, Jane, Selina, Elizabeth—Only, of course, it's Mark, Tom, Dick and Harry—One is never sure of the right name."

"What do you mean?"

"There'll be trouble, one day," said Mr. Dodds, apparently contemplating the infinite. "After all, it wouldn't do if you changed the name of the heroine half-way through the book. It would create an impression of instability. But with a hero of your type, so ready with his sword, it would be even worse if the heroine changed the name of her lover. These d'Artagnan types have not gone out with the eighteenth century. The soldier of fortune is always with us, and he is not an agreeable person to make a fool of."

And with this he shut the door behind him, leaving Barbara still very flushed and quite bewildered.

On due consideration, she did not tear the scrap of paper, but put it away carefully in her handbag. Then, having delivered her completed pile of forms to the general office, she went into the cloak-room to get ready for lunch.

She turned on the hot water and, as she did so, saw that Mrs. Bridgwater was standing by the mirror, arranging her beautiful blonde hair.

Barbara said, "Good morning", and continued rather self-consciously to wash her hands, for Mr. Dodds's strange remarks must refer to Mrs. Bridgwater, even though she could not understand their application.

Mrs. Bridgwater, smoothing back the immaculate waves off her high forehead, said pleasantly, "I hear that you've just had a novel accepted. Lucky girl!"

Barbara admitted awkwardly that this was so. She quite liked Mrs. Bridgwater, who was usually good-natured, but she found her large fairness a little awe-inspiring; besides, she suspected there was a hint of mockery in her tone.

"I write, too," said Mrs. Bridgwater, powdering her nose.

"Oh? What—what do you write?"

"Oh, not commercial stuff like you. Mind you, I only wish I could. I should love to earn some money. But actually, I write short stories with a social theme. Some of them are about my own childhood. I was born in the East End, you know. We were so very, very poor. I remember once that I was asked to a party, and I couldn't go, because I had nothing to wear. How I cried! Even now I can remember it. It's the kind of thing that sears one's subconscious, you know."

"Yes, it—it must do," said Barbara, and wondered why Mrs. Bridgwater, when she said this kind of thing, must gaze so raptly at herself in the mirror. The obvious self-adoration came a little strangely from one who was built on such Valkyrie lines; it was true that she had the most magnificent figure, but one felt that Brunhilde would not be so concerned with her femininity.

"Then there was another," continued Mrs. Bridgwater, still staring at her own delightful reflection, "about a little boy whose father died, and who was left in the charge of people with a lot of money and no heart. I wonder why people who have money lack feeling? I suppose it's the same thing as people who admire the royal family, and who always approve of capital punishment. You must earn quite a lot from a novel."

Barbara, blushing, admitted that she did.

"What a curse money is," sighed Mrs. Bridgwater, "and yet one cannot do without it. At least, not in this greedy world we live in. Mark—Mr. Allan says money is the main essential of life. But then, of course, he's a materialist. Most men are, don't you think?" And here she gave a little laugh. "Wretched creatures! Is your young man a materialist, too? I always think he looks so nice, the kind of person one wants to talk to."

'Oh no, you don't,' thought Barbara, filled with a sudden and purely feminine possessiveness. But she admitted that

Charles was nice, and as she said this, the door opened, and Mrs. Warren came in.

It was natural enough that she should do so. It was five minutes to one. But Barbara saw Mrs. Bridgwater's expression, and was startled to see that it was one of the purest hatred.

"And how," said Mrs. Warren, "is your husband, Mrs. Bridgwater? I saw him again yesterday evening." The giggle was trembling in her throat as she added to Barbara, "Mr. Bridgwater takes classes at my Evening Institute. I often see him there. So interesting," she added, with a gurgle of laughter, "to meet people's husbands. Do you know, Mrs. Bridgwater, I used to think you weren't married."

"And why should you think that?" inquired Mrs. Bridgwater.

Mrs. Warren went into peals of laughter. "Oh," she cried, "how fierce you sound! I'm sure Mr. Allan would rather you weren't married. Or perhaps it doesn't matter, anyway. I never had patience with conventions, myself."

Barbara picked up her handbag and fled. Mrs. Bridgwater had a beautiful face, but at the moment it was not beautiful at all, and the pale blue eyes were blazing fire.

'I wonder why we are all so disagreeable to-day?' thought Barbara, setting off for the canteen. 'Perhaps it's the heat.'

It was July, and very hot indeed. Yet on the whole it was a normal office day. Greta sent off a request to the Institute of Advanced Legal Studies for a book on the 'Law of Tarts'. And Peggy, a blonde, who resembled the young woman in an advertisement for milk, typed a letter in which she referred to 'a fiend I know at the H. Museum'. This particular museum dealt in esoteric lore and ancient cults; the phrase was not inapplicable.

Mr. Latimer, reading this, remarked dryly to Miss Holmes that her girls had more perspicacity than he had suspected.

"My girls all have perspicacity," said Miss Holmes.

II. INFLUENCE OF SEX. 615.55

BARBARA, holding beneath her arm a biography of Charles James Fox, stepped into the lift. She smiled at Mr. Purley, who had stopped for her; he was coming down from the fourth floor with a large red, book-filled sack. He began to shut the gates, when there was an agitated crying, and Mrs. Warren, puffing and giggling, flung herself in, as if it were the greatest joke in the world. Barbara wondered if she flourished on quarrels, for there was a great air to her now of malice and joyous satisfaction.

She disliked the close contact very much. She turned towards Mr. Purley, who, with an illicit cigarette sticking out of the corner of his mouth, winked at her. She said, prodding at the sack with her toe, "More bodies for the hospital, Mr. Purley? I am beginning to think you're a combination of Burke and Hare."

It was the stock joke between them, as automatic as the exchange of good-mornings, and Mr. Purley replied gravely, as he always did, "A nice fresh corpse, miss. None of your graveyard diggings. After all, you can't expect me to live on what I.L.D.A. pays me, can you?"

Mrs. Warren looked surprised. "Bodies?" she said. "Bodies?" Then, examining the sack, "Why, it does look like a body, doesn't it? How very amusing."

Having thus destroyed amusement, she relapsed into silence, and so did Barbara and Mr. Purley, so that the journey was finished without further conversation.

Barbara walked into the canteen, waved to Greta and Maureen, who signified that they were keeping a place for her, and took her place in the queue behind Mr. Rills.

Mr. Latimer and Mr. Ridley, close beside her, were discussing something with what appeared to be distress and anger; it seemed that certain books had disappeared. Mr. Ridley waved his cigarette to demonstrate his disapproval, perceived that it was out, and fumbled for his matches, while Mr. Latimer politely fumbled for his lighter. Match

23

and lighter were lit at the same moment, and then Mr. Ridley, who seemed to be in a great state of excitement, dropped his cigarette.

Barbara, watching this pantomime with some amusement, was startled to hear Mr. Rills announce brightly in his disagreeable voice, "We shall this day, Master Ridley, light such a candle as will never be put out. Fish and chips, please."

Barbara refused to smile, and turned instead to talk to young Mr. Wilson of the Reference Room. It was, she noticed, one of his beardless periods, so that he looked unashamedly what he was, an ingenuous, inoffensive, very young man. It was said that he wore a beard when there was an 'r' in the month, possibly as protection against the cold; on these occasions he stalked the office with a powerful, messianic air, the youth and innocence well concealed. "I suppose," Mr. Rills had once said to him, "we should now address you as Pandit Wilson Singh."

"Drugs!" said Mr. Wilson, waving his newspaper.

"I beg your pardon?" said Barbara, then, "I'm so sorry," as Molly at the counter said crossly, "Your pie, miss. Do you want peas or cabbage?"

"Peas—no, cabbage, please. What do you mean, drugs?"

"Don't you read the papers, Miss Smith? Apparently masses of cocaine is being smuggled into the country. Scotland Yard is very excited about it. I have always wondered why I.L.D.A. doesn't do something like that as a side-line. I'm sure there's endless opportunity. Concealed in book-covers or something. I might consider doing it myself. Wilson, the drug racketeer. The man behind the mask."

"Behind the beard, you mean," said Mr. Rills, carrying his plate of fish and chips carefully, "I suppose that's what you grow that fungus for."

A giggle behind them made them all start. "Bodies and drugs!" cried Mrs. Warren. "How very entertaining it all is. Isn't it, Mr. Allan?"

Barbara saw that Mark Allan was standing just outside the queue, his gaze fixed on the door. At Mrs. Warren's remark he jerked round. His bright, light eyes flickered up and down her. He said dryly in his deep voice that could roar so on occasions, "Most entertaining. One day, Mrs. Warren, you will conceivably laugh yourself into your grave. You laugh too much. You talk too much. You should cultivate moderation."

This was excessive, even for Mark, who was notoriously

rude, and Barbara and Mr. Wilson burst out together with, "Oh, by the way—— Did you——"

But Mrs. Warren cut through them. For once she was not laughing. Her small, black eyes met Mark's light ones without flinching, narrowed a little. She said softly, "Perhaps I even see too much."

At this point Mr. Rills dropped his entire plateful of fish and chips, and then Mark Allan, with a sudden laugh, brought his hand down with a great slap across Mrs. Warren's shoulders. He said, "The trouble with you, old girl, like all women, is that you've not enough to do. You're too emancipated now. You take too much upon yourself." He raised his handsome head—it only needs the scar, thought Barbara, fascinated—and then his eyes met hers, and she to her horror began to blush. "This young woman," he said, "at least writes novels, which probably uses up most of her mischief-making capabilities. Why don't you let us read them? What's the matter with you? Ashamed of them?"

Mrs. Warren had leapt beneath the slap, as well she might; it was unlikely that the late Dr. Warren had ever treated her in such a manner. But now she began to laugh again, and at the sound of that laughter, everyone fell silent, even Mr. Rills, who had been swearing as he grovelled on the floor, picking up his fish and chips.

She said, "They're romantic. They're too clever for us. We're not good enough to see them. They're for the intelligentsia, aren't they, Miss Smith? Not for poor, middle-aged women like me, who just do their work in the office, instead of writing about love and so on."

Barbara turned away. She was aware that everyone's eyes were upon her; Mr. Rills was grinning broadly, and even Mr. Wilson gave an embarrassed laugh. Then Mark took the plate from her hand, said casually across his shoulder to Mrs. Warren, "Madam, you are begotten of a chimney-sweeper and an oyster wife. You cannot read, and therefore wish all books were burnt." Then, "Where are you sitting?"

"With—with the girls over there. I can carry my own plate, thank you."

He ignored this, carried her plate across, and put it down. He said, "For God's sake don't pay attention to that old bitch." Then the whole expression of his face changed. It was as if a light had been switched on inside him. Without another word, and with a startling swiftness, he was across the room.

Barbara saw, with a surprising twinge of jealousy, that

Mrs. Bridgwater had just come in, and was taking off her coat.

"Oh, I say," said Greta, "that would be a penny for the swear-box, wouldn't it, Maureen? Did you hear what he said? Who was he talking about, Miss Smith? Don't tell me. I bet I know. I bet it was Mrs. Warren. The old bag."

"It was," said Barbara curtly.

"What's she been saying to you?" asked Maureen. "You look all upset. What's the matter? You don't have to worry about her, surely. She just loves making people unhappy. I hope Mr. Allan told her off. He looks as if he could tell people off, rather well."

Barbara thought that Mr. Allan did indeed look as if he could tell people off most successfully. But she did not want to think of Mr. Allan, for she found him too disturbing. She was irritated, therefore, when Greta, her mouth full, remarked, "He's fearfully good-looking. Smashing. Don't you think so, Maureen? Maureen! Don't you think he's smashing?"

"I wouldn't like to be married to him," said Maureen unexpectedly.

"Oh, I would," said Greta. "Wouldn't I just! Why on earth not?"

"He looks too bad-tempered. He looks as if he could murder somebody. Are your heroes as handsome as him, Miss Smith?"

"Handsomer," said Barbara, adding deliberately, "Much, much handsomer."

"Smashing," said Greta. "What's he called? The new one, I mean."

"John Andrews. He is," said Barbara, "magnificently handsome, and he has no morals whatsoever. He is a duellist."

"Whacko!" said Greta.

"And a gambler. And—oh, all sorts of things. But he has a good heart, really, and it all comes right in the end."

"Smashing," said Greta, with great satisfaction.

Molly came over at this point, to ask if the lunch were all right. She said apologetically to Barbara, "I'm sorry if I spoke so sharp to you, miss. Only that Mrs. Warren worries one so. She kept telling me that fried food was unhealthy, and that we ought to have more salads. And with everybody waiting, too. It gets on my nerves. But I didn't mean to take it out on you."

"It's all right," said Barbara, smiling at her. "Mrs. Warren worries us all."

"Old bath bun," said Greta.

When Molly had returned to the counter, Greta opened wide her vast cow eyes, and remarked, "How kind she is. Not like some I could mention. She's a sort of mummy-lady, isn't she?"

"Egyptian or otherwise?" said Barbara crossly; the feeling of unease was still knifing within her. Then she instantly regretted her sharpness, for Greta was staring at her in an incredulous way, though a moment later she decided to accept it as a joke, and began to laugh. "You are funny," she said. "Isn't she, Maureen?"

"Am I not?" said Barbara, rather grimly, but one could not speak harshly to Greta, so she grinned at her amiably, and wondered as she occasionally did how such words could come from such an exotic-looking creature.

Greta said presently, "Shall we have some bread and cheese, Maureen? Shall we, eh? Maureen! Shall we have some——"

Maureen thought they should have some bread and cheese, and they fetched themselves large platefuls. "Smashing," said Greta, "and when we've finished, we can go on the roof and sun-bathe. Are you coming with us, Miss Smith?"

"No. I think I shall read for a bit." And Barbara, gathering up her book, walked across the room, careful to sit some distance away from Mark Allan and Mrs. Bridgwater, and avoiding also Mr. Rills, who was on the other side of them.

But she could not help glancing at Mark, and she was startled when Mr. Ridley's dry, academic voice came quietly over the top of his *Times*.

"He was with the Resistance during the war, you know."

"Who? Oh, Mr. Allan. Was he?" She hoped there was just the right note of detached interest in her voice.

"Yes, they parachuted him down into France. I understand he did the most wonderful work, derailing trains, helping British airmen, and so on. He never talks about it. The Germans caught him, but he got away. Blew them up with some kind of grenade he manufactured himself. I sometimes wonder," said Mr. Ridley, with the grave astonishment of a man who had never killed a fly, "how these young men can be expected to adapt themselves to peace. To live your life in a world where you are trained to kill, and then to take a job in I.L.D.A. Sometimes I am glad I was too old for the last war."

He settled himself down behind his newspaper.

Barbara opened her book. But she did not read it. From

time to time her unwilling eyes flickered towards Mark and Mrs. Bridgwater. They were talking in some apparent agitation.

"Do you really think she told him?" demanded Mrs. Bridgwater.

"If she has, she'll be sorry," said Mark briefly. His eyes did not leave her face.

"Oh, you men. You're always so melodramatic. I don't care about her being sorry. What I'm worried about is Henry. He's getting so jealous that it's almost psychological. Do you know, he once actually threatened to put detectives on me? It's all so wickedly unfair. After all, I haven't done anything wrong. Because one's married, it doesn't mean one can't have men friends. Mark, don't look at me like that. People will think it's funny. I'm sure that Smith girl was eyeing us in a queer sort of way just now."

"Why don't you come away with me, and be done with it?" said Mark.

"Oh, darling, must we go into all this again? I've told you so many times. It's not that I don't love you. It's not that I'm conventional, either," said Mrs. Bridgwater. "I'm an artist, and I believe all artists must be free. If it weren't for the boys, I'd go away with you tomorrow, and be proud to tell the world. You know that. But I have two sons, and, believe it or not, they're rather fond of their little mother. We have such a pleasant relationship. Really, it's more as if I'm their sister. They call me by my Christian name, you know. But if that horrid old woman has made up a story for Henry—— I thought he looked a bit strange last night. And you know how people misunderstand things. I hate her. Really I do. Sometimes I feel that if she laughs just once more, I shall throttle her."

He had not really been listening to her words, only watching the way her lips moved, the turn of her head, the curves of her body. But at this he began to laugh. "You! You wouldn't know where to begin. Throttling is a highly skilled business, unless you want the devil of a row, and yourself probably out with a few teeth missing."

"Mark—— Please. *Mark*——"

He gave her his slow, twisted smile. Perhaps he had heard a great deal in his time of this 'Please, Mark', but the hand which touched hers moved away. He said, "Do you want to know how to kill someone, Mona? It's easy enough. I'll tell you exactly what to do. Take something flat with a sharp edge. A folder would do, or a ruler. Then wait till the lady's at her desk, typing. Come up behind her, and hit her with the edge across the back of the neck, just here. It's quick. It's simple. And it makes no mess. She'd never tell Henry anything again. Actually, if you have the strength, you could do it with the side of your hand. So."

"Really, Mark, you're quite dreadful. And don't speak so loud. You know very well that I'm a pacifist." But the colour rose in her cheeks, and her eyes sparkled, for she adored Mark in this mood; the violence within him, so barely suppressed, sent a delicious shudder down her spine.

He said suddenly in a harsh voice, "Give me a cigarette."

"But you've only just put one out, silly boy."

"For Christ's sake, give me one. It'll at least give me something to do with my hands and mouth."

Mrs. Bridgwater, greatly thrilled, gave him one. Barbara saw their heads close together, their hands touching as he cradled the flame of the match she held out to him. Then she turned away resolutely, ashamed of her prying, for the flame revealed a look in Mark's eyes which was not for public view, a look that she had never seen with Charles.

After lunch, Barbara went into Miss Holmes's office to collect what were known as the odd lists—short lists sent out to a variety of places such as the London School of Economics, the Royal Geographical Society, and so on. Miss Holmes was apparently in conference with Mr. Latimer, so she opened the drawer, and was sorting through the forms when she heard the door open.

She saw that it was Mrs. Warren. But she did not turn round, for really in the circumstances she could think of nothing polite to say. To her annoyance, Mrs. Warren came and stood beside her, so close that their sleeves touched.

Barbara, glancing up, met a look so hard and hostile that she nearly dropped the forms she was holding. Mrs. Warren for once was not laughing. She said, her mouth thin as a knife-blade, "Kindly leave something for me. You always take the nicest lists. Don't imagine I haven't noticed."

"The nicest lists!"

"You're trying to push me out, aren't you?" said Mrs. Warren grimly. "But it's not I who'll be pushed out. There are quite a number of people who have tried in their time. But I'm still here. I want those lists. You can help with the filing, if you've nothing else to do, though I expect you've ways and means of passing your time. Give me those lists, please."

"Take them," said Barbara, staring at her.

"Thank you. I will," said Mrs. Warren, grabbing them all in her square hands, then, "Why, if it isn't Mr. Rills——"

Barbara, shaking a little, for the enmity that came from Mrs. Warren had been almost tangible, walked towards the door, to find her way partly blocked by Mr. Rills, who seemed quite unlike his usual flippant self, and who was staring at Mrs. Warren in something like terror.

"Excuse me——" she said, but Mr. Rills, still gazing with the air of a mouse fascinated by a snake, neither replied nor moved.

Mrs. Warren said nothing, but began to laugh again. Her laughter giggled forth in such triumph that Barbara wanted to put her hands to her ears and cry, 'Stop, stop.' She could endure it no longer. She pushed her way past the hypnotised Mr. Rills and ran down the corridor to her room.

There she settled down to the exceedingly sad and monotonous task of filing. It was work that she always resented, for it was so very dull, mechanical enough to let her thoughts rove, and yet requiring a certain amount of concentration. She sighed and returned a form for Die Castings to its proper place. The girls had been instructed that *'der, die, das'* were merely the German definite article; Greta had methodically filed Die Castings under 'C'. She muttered the title with a German accent and, as she did so, heard Greta herself come in, whistling unmelodiously between her teeth.

"Talking to yourself," said Greta. "You know what that means, don't you?"

"Well, if I'm not mad already, I soon shall be."

"So shall we all," said Greta, uncovering the addressograph. "Miss Holmes is in a frightful mood. She's just been in, telling us all off, because Mrs. Warren told her we hadn't enough work to do. And she's just furious with Mr. Allan."

Barbara started, and several forms fell to the floor. She said, "Hell's teeth!" then, "Why?"

Greta said coldly, "That's a penny for the swear-box, Miss Smith. I don't know why you say such dreadful things."

"Well," said Barbara, stung, "you're a fine one to talk, you and your bath buns——"

"And what's wrong with that? It isn't swearing."

"It's a bowdlerised form of it."

"It's *what?* You do use the most smashing words."

"It means that it really stands for something else."

Greta moved towards her, the great dark eyes sparkling. "What, what? Do tell me. Oh, go on."

Barbara looked at her, and gave it up. "It doesn't matter. You say what you like. Only let me say what I like, too, there's a good girl."

"Yes, ma'am," said Greta gaily in an American accent, then danced across to the addressograph, where, for a few minutes, she rolled off envelopes in silence. Then she said, "Would you mind awfully if I asked you something?"

"No! Why should I?"

"I mean, you're sort of clever, and you write books and things. You really don't mind?"

"What on earth is it? Has your boy friend been deceiving you?"

"Oh, Miss Smith——"

"I'm sure you have lots of boy friends, Greta."

"I don't like boys much," said Greta. "They make me feel all shy. It's nothing to do with that, anyway. Miss Smith——"

"Greta," said Barbara, and smiled at her.

"Miss Smith—What's the difference between description, narrative and dialogue?"

"Good God! What makes you ask me that?"

"It was on a form. It was an article or something. The girls said you'd know what it meant."

Barbara paused to consider it. "It's like this," she said. "A black cat with white spots and green eyes—that's description. The black cat with white spots and green eyes jumped on to the window-sill—that's narrative. The black cat with white spots and green eyes said, 'Miaow'—that's dialogue."

"Oh, I think that's good," cried Greta, clapping her hands. "The black cat said, 'Miaow'—isn't that lovely? I must tell the girls. Do you mind if I try it out for myself?"

"Of course not. Go ahead."

"A large, plump woman with ash-blonde hair. That's description, isn't it?"

"Perfectly correct," agreed Barbara, amused.

"And—and a plump woman with ash-blonde hair opens the door. Narrative!"

"Yes."

"And the plump woman with ash-blonde hair says, 'Darling, I know she's told him.' That's—that's——" Greta's voice faltered. She went very red. She began to roll off envelopes again with great vigour, her head bowed so that the mane of black hair hid her face.

"Greta," said Barbara, after a long pause, "where did you hear this?"

Greta said sulkily, "I've got these envelopes to roll off. Miss Holmes will be frightfully cross with me if I don't do them."

"It was Mrs. Bridgwater, wasn't it?" It was none of her business whatsoever, but somehow she had to know.

"Well, I couldn't help it," mumbled Greta. "I was in the packing-room, and it's next door to Mr. Allan's, and she said it ever so loud, and I heard what he said, too. He said, 'For God's sake,' and then he pulled her in, or something, and the door slammed. We all heard it. Mr. Purley heard it. He said it was fine goings-on. I don't think," said Greta primly, "that it's very nice. I don't know what it all means, but anyone can see he's crazy about her, and after all she's married, and she's not young, is she?"

"She can't be more than thirty-five," said Barbara wearily.

"Well, that's ever so old. Why, my mummy's thirty-seven."

"Sometimes," said Barbara, "I think I shall give in my notice."

"Oh, you can't do that," cried Greta, her mercurial spirits soaring up again. "I wouldn't have anyone to talk to while I did the envelopes. We do have nice, cosy chats, don't we?"

"We do, yes."

"Are you feeling sort of fed-up?"

"Yes, Greta, I am."

Greta began to reply, but, before she could do so, Miss Holmes came in again, plainly in a seething state of irritation. "Go on with your work, Greta," she said sharply. "I want all those envelopes done by four o'clock. Miss Smith!"

Barbara looked at her. She was too disturbed to make pretence of meekness. She was indeed on the verge of saying, 'I'm going,' but before she could do this, Miss Holmes went on, "I want you to take all these forms up to Mr. Allan. It's simply ridiculous. How I am expected to run my department, I do not know. They are all requests for microfilms from public libraries. Mr. Allan, of course, has nothing better to do than give the location and receive the parcels. We, as usual, have to do the work. He doesn't even bother to mark on the forms whether the microfilms have arrived, much less if they have been sent off. There are two dozens requests here. I want you, please, Miss Smith, to wait while he checks them up. Don't let him put you off. Say Mr. Latimer sent you."

Barbara doubted whether Mr. Latimer's name would have the magical effect Miss Holmes seemed to expect, and looked mutinous. Miss Holmes noticed this, and unexpectedly smiled. "Well," she said, "I know Mr. Allan's difficult. But I don't suppose he'll shout at you. If he does, shout back. After all," she added coaxingly, "I really can't send one of the girls. He'd frighten them out of their wits. But I'm sure you know how to deal with him. You'd better go after tea."

When she had gone, Barbara grimaced at Greta. "Dialogue," she said. " 'Get out!' Narrative: Miss Smith goes flying through the window—and his office is on the fourth floor. Oh, well, it's nice to have known you all. I hope the department will stump up with a decent wreath."

The Location Department ate Barbara's cake for tea. Mrs. Warren chose the largest cream bun. Barbara, watching her in a morbid fascination, reflected that her way of eating was typical of her personality. The powerful jaws snapped at the bun so that the cream exploded on both sides; with an enveloping motion of her tongue, Mrs. Warren swept the débris into her mouth and, her cheeks distended, chewed with brisk savagery until the whole was forced down her gullet.

When the tea-break was over, Barbara gathered up her forms with the utmost reluctance, and dawdled up the stairs to the fourth floor which lodged Mr. Dodds, Mr. Allan, Mrs. Bridgwater and the packing department. She did not want to see Mr. Allan at all. If Greta's reported dialogue was correct, he was bound to be in a flaming temper, and he was not at the best an approachable man, even on his days of good humour.

She paused to exchange a few brief words with Mr. Purley, who was ramming parcels into one of his red sacks. "Another body, miss," he said cheerfully. "Another corpse for the students to muck about with."

She could only summon up a wan smile. She felt remarkably as if she were going to her execution, as if Tyburn gallows, which loomed so large in her books, were now awaiting her. As she passed the periodical department's door, Mr. Dodds emerged. He gave her his slow, mournful look. "And how," he said, "is the soldier of fortune? Has he gutted his enemy yet? I hope he learnt his fencing in the Italian school. It is so much more effective. The French are spectacular, but do too much pirouetting."

"My heroes," said Barbara coldly, "are always undefeatable."

"That is as it should be," returned Mr. Dobbs, "but the trouble with soldiers of fortune is—if you will forgive my using an affectedly foreign word—*l'amour*. These full-blooded men permit their circulation to be heated on the slightest provocation. And the emotions unhappily play the devil with a cool head and a flexible wrist. Does your hero keep a mistress?"

"Certainly not," said Barbara. "My publishers would never permit it."

"How very interesting," mused Mr. Dodds. "I had no idea that publishers had so stern a code of morality. You are, therefore, unhappily denied access to a large section of the century you write upon—the eighteenth, I believe?—for whoring, adultery and black magic were their favourite recreations."

"Black magic," said Barbara, "is permitted, but adultery and—and the other thing you mention—never."

"Black magic, but not adultery," repeated Mr. Dodds. "An interesting reflection on this modern age. So the fourteen-year-old at the breakfast-table must not read of lechery, but can devour the Black Mass with her rice crispies. I am beginning to believe that your heroes must be of a somewhat effeminate type. But perhaps it is as well. The soldier of fortune who falls for a foolish woman is as lamentable an object as the husband who wears the horns."

And with this he vanished back into his room.

Barbara could not but see a certain personal application in Mr. Dodds's words. He must, of course, have heard the dialogue quoted by Greta. This did not improve her state of mind, and the knock she gave to Mr. Allan's door was by no means worthy of her heroes. She waited, then, as there was no answer, pushed the door open.

Mark Allan was there. His desk was chaos; at that moment he appeared to be unwrapping a microfilm. He jerked up his head as she came in. She saw that he was very pale. He said in a low, furious voice, "What the bloody hell do you mean by coming in without knocking?"

Barbara's spirit at once returned to her. She flushed up. She said defiantly, "I did knock. It's not my fault that you didn't trouble to answer."

He looked at her, then down at the microfilm in his fingers. "Oh, all right," he said in a more normal voice, "I apologise. Sit down, for God's sake. There's no need to stand over me like an avenging school-marm. I'll attend to you in a minute."

She sat down. Her knees were weak beneath her. She studied him as he sat there, his head bent to what he was doing. She wished, as she had already wished before, that he did not bear so startling a resemblance to the heroes of her fantasy. It was troubling and disconcerting. The face was a period face. It might without absurdity have been surmounted by a peruke. A stock would have suited him excellently; the long-fingered hand could have held a rapier, should have been ruffled and beringed. She watched his face, stamped with fanaticism and a kind of weary almost exhausted dissoluteness. An unwelcomed quotation floated into her mind, so apt that when he unexpectedly raised his eyes to hers, she started and flushed again.

"You observe me very closely," he said. "What are you thinking of?"

"Tom Wharton," she said, struck into truthfulness.

"Tom Wharton? Isn't he the fellow who wrote *Lilliburlero?* Why on earth should you think of Tom Wharton?"

She gave him a defiant look, and quoted:

"I prithee, good Lord, take old Wharton away,
That young Lord Wharton should rule in his place,
To drink and to whore, and a thousand tricks more,
With his damned fanatical face."

She had his attention now, and rather more than she desired. He laid the microfilm down and surveyed her, his eyes very wide and bright. He watched her blush more and more crimson, then at last he began to laugh. He had a pleasant laugh. "So I drink and I whore, do I? You use very strong language, my dear. Are you perhaps the representative of some Church society?"

"I was thinking more of the damned, fanatical face," said Barbara weakly, then she added, "I am very sorry. I shouldn't be talking in this absurd way, only you swore at me and you made me angry, and when I'm angry, I say what I think—I mean——" She saw that she was only making bad worse, so she took a deep breath and said in a brisk, official manner, "Mr. Allan. Miss Holmes asked me to——"

"Ah, no," he said. "No, no, no. You don't get away with this. You march into my office, you inform me that I drink and I whore, which, God knows, is true, and then suddenly you change your voice and start some nonsense about Miss Holmes. To hell with Miss Holmes. I am not interested in Miss Holmes. The Library seems to breed Miss Holmeses, and with the temperament you have just bestowed on me, you can hardly expect—— I see you are now pretending to be shocked."

Barbara said in a clear voice, "I should like to give you the message. It's about the microfilms——"

"So my face is fanatical and damned, is it?" said Mark. "Have a cigarette."

"We are not supposed to smoke."

"Ah, for God's sake—what is all this? Take your cigarette and stop playing the *ingénue*. I was just thinking that you were one of the few people here I could bear to talk to at this moment, and now you act like a schoolgirl, and a silly one at that. Take your cigarette or I swear I'll push it down your throat. If I'd whisky here, I'd offer you that, too, and I suppose you'd say"—his voice shot up—"'Please, Mr. Allan, mummy only lets me drink lemonade.'"

Barbara, in despair, took the cigarette. Then she gave him a shamefaced smile. "I really am sorry," she said. "Please forgive me."

"Why should I?" he said. "I never forgive anything."

She thought he must have a remarkably long list of grudges to brood on, for he was by no means popular with his colleagues, but she did not take the remark personally, for his expression was not unkindly. She accepted a light from him, then waited in silence, fingering Miss Holmes's twenty-odd forms that lay before her.

He said abruptly, "You're engaged, aren't you?"

"Yes."

"To a nice, steady young man, no doubt, with a good job and prospects, and so forth?"

It sounded very insulting. But it was true, and she had to admit it, wondering why such obvious virtues should be turned at a word into contempt.

"So you're finely settled? And I," said Mark, "am in the devil of a mess. But of course with my drinking and my whoring—— I don't drink very much, actually. I got out of the way of it in the war. It impedes clear thinking, and I needed all my wits. I still need them. Well, I suppose I'll get out of this mess as I've got out of a great many more. Only some of the excitement seems to have gone. I must admit that I never dreamt I'd end up here. Tell me, Miss Smith—your name's Barbara, isn't it?"

"Yes, Mr. Allan."

"Tell me, Barbara—and don't you presume to snub me, yes, Mr. Allan, no, Mr. Allan, like some bloody skivvy. Why don't you call me sir, and be done with it?—Tell me, Barbara. Do you know Mrs. Warren well?"

"She works in my department."

"Talking with you's like digging a ten-foot trench. Do you know her? Are you friendly with her?"

"I hate her guts," said Barbara candidly.

"There's my girl! So do I. So do I. She talks a great deal, doesn't she?"

Barbara thought she knew well enough what he was referring to. She said carefully, "I don't know. She's very nosy. She likes finding out about people. But whether she talks about it or not, I really can't say. I think myself she's more of a passive mischief-maker. It gives her a feeling of power to know—— I expect she cuddles it to herself, giggling."

"How charming," he said. His face had grown quite blank. "But one day, perhaps, the big mouth will open——" His eyes were fixed on hers; she thought how strange they were, almost cat's eyes, of the lightest grey, with dark, luminous pupils.

She glanced down at her forms, then stubbed out her cigarette. She said nervously—the conversation had been wildly unlike anything she had ever held in the office— "Please, Mr. Al—— Please, Mark, these——" She stopped dead. She did not at all know how to continue.

To her relief he smiled. It was a singularly charming and enchanting smile. She wondered irrelevantly how Mrs. Bridgwater could ever resist it. He said amiably, "Yes, Miss Smith, Barbara. We are talking like catalogues. It is very fitting. Yes? Those forms—— I'll tell you, and spare you the explanations. Miss Holmes is very angry. Miss Holmes quite rightly considers Mr. Allan to be a damned nuisance. Miss Holmes wishes to know which microfilms have been received by I.L.D.A. Come and sit at my side, and I will go through them with you."

She would not sit down again. She stood at his side, while he began to flick through the forms. He said casually, without looking up, "I suppose if I kissed you, you'd shriek for help."

"No, I wouldn't," said Barbara in a small voice, and in that moment learnt that Mark Allan possessed one quality above all others, which was an enormous, compelling power of physical attraction. It came from him in shameless tentacles; it encircled and enclosed her, so that she was caught, besieged, defenceless. He put his arm about her and drew her down towards him. He kissed her without tenderness, almost experimentally.

Then she saw that his other hand was still turning over the forms.

He released her. He glanced at her once, briefly. Then he said, "Lambeth Public Library—*Zeitung für Chimie*— yes. Royal College of Nursing—*Hebdomadaire Psychiatrique* —yes. *Etude* for Bedford College—no. Paris won't send the microfilm. I have no idea why not. There. You may tell Miss Holmes that—that everything is now dealt with."

She walked to the door. She was shaking uncontrollably. She turned and said, "Do you catalogue your kisses, Mr. Allan? Or do you perhaps just make photostats of them for future reference?"

He stared up at her, utter astonishment in his eyes, to be succeeded by another expression that she did not choose to identify. "Come here——" he began on a rising note.

Barbara—it was shocking that something so childish should afford her so much satisfaction—neatly and gently shut the door. And then, alas for heroism, she ran down the stairs, as if for her life.

Mr. Purley, at half-past five, stood waiting by the door. He yawned. It had been a long day. He was thankful to be going home. It was a good job, and he had no desire to leave it, but sometimes the monotony got him down, and he wished vaguely there could be a little more excitement.

Mark strode out into the courtyard, merely glancing at Barbara, who was waiting for Charles. "Good-night, Miss Smith."

"Good-night, Mr. Allan."

Then she saw Charles coming. She ran to meet him, clutched at his arm with a fervour that surprised him. She said in a frantic whisper, "Oh, Charles, I do love you so much." He was taken aback. He said, "All right, old darling, I love you, too. What's all the fuss about?"

"I just wanted to say I loved you," said Barbara, the tears beginning to trickle down her cheeks. Her treachery and infidelity hummed in her ears; she did not even see Mrs. Warren, who gave her a hard look as she passed, and said, "Good-night, Miss Smith," in a grudging and forbidding voice.

Mr. Purley sighed. They were all out at last. The girls from the Location Department, Mr. Rills, Mr. Dodds, Mrs. Bridgwater, Miss Holmes, Mr. Ridley, Mr. Latimer. And young Mr. Wilson, who flew by as if he was making an appointment with his best girl. A nice boy, a nice boy——

Ah, well, to-morrow would be another day. The same old round. Mr. Purley gathered up his coat and switched off the electricity at the main. He locked and bolted the front door, and I.L.D.A. sank into blackness and quiet.

III. DETH. 236.1

MR. LATIMER was a man of dignity, as careful of his behaviour as he was of his clothes; in this last he was a constant reproach to the other librarians, who looked like undergraduates in a left-wing book-shop. When, therefore, he was locked in the lavatory on the second floor, it became a situation that rocked I.L.D.A. to its foundations; no literary crisis could have shattered the staff more.

Mr. Latimer, bitterly humiliated, banged and rattled at the stubborn door, roaring out his protesting fury; his shouts of rage penetrated to every corner of the building.

This was at eleven o'clock in the morning. No one, naturally, had the faintest idea how important this would prove.

Barbara came to work, tired, with a headache, and profoundly disturbed. Her guilty conscience had not permitted her to pass a comfortable evening with Charles. They went to the pictures. It was a French film of Barbara's choosing; it was the worst film she had ever seen. She was dreadfully bored, and so was Charles; they did not quarrel, because it was not their habit, but they were not friendly to each other, and walked in a grey, grim silence to a little Soho restaurant that they often patronised; it was cheap and quiet, and one could eat spaghetti.

They faced each other across the table like strangers. Charles said at last, with a hint of apology in his voice, "It's been a hell of a day."

"It's been a hell of a day for me, too," said Barbara, then, "I didn't mean to be so disagreeable. Tell me about your day."

"Oh, we're worked off our feet. You're looking very pale. I suppose it's the heat. There's some new nonsense about a drug racket, and Scotland Yard's in a grand state of excitement. We've been asked to give it all the publicity possible. You'll see it splashed across the front page to-morrow. It's knocked half the other news off, and the old man's going up in the air as if he were Northcliffe or something, and from the general set-up no one would imagine there were any wars on, hot or cold, or indeed anything except this confounded cocaine business—and the temperature in the eighties. Sometimes I think I'll chuck the whole business and take up schoolmastering or something quiet. I don't think I'm cut out for this racket. After all, I'm a nice, steady young man. What's the matter with you? Hell! That's my trousers!"

"I'm dreadfully sorry," stammered Barbara, for she had upset her entire cup of coffee over him. "I—I——" The tears, which had been threatening for some time, spilled down her cheeks. She dabbed ineffectually at Charles's knee with her handkerchief, until he caught at her hand and held it firmly.

He said, very gently, "You're a clumsy girl, and I love you. We will now go into Soho Square and hold hands. You look as if you need to have your hand held, and I think I am probably the best person to do it. You mustn't cry here. They'll think I'm ill-using you. The waitress is giving me a most old-fashioned look, as it is. Where's your handkerchief?"

"It's s-soaked in coffee."

He began to laugh. He beckoned the disapproving waitress for his bill. "Then I shall have to drag you out, sobbing. Why not? It's a preposterous world, anyway, full of drugs and assaults and sudden death. Perhaps I shall soon take to drugs myself. I wonder how they get the stuff in? Perhaps I.L.D.A. is the receiving station."

"What an idea!" cried Barbara, recovering herself. "I.L.D.A. wouldn't smuggle in babies' rattles. We are all most fearfully respect—fearfully——"

She stopped. Charles probably did not notice the pause. In any case, he said nothing, and presently they sat side by side on a bench in the square, their fingers interlaced. After a while Charles removed his spectacles—"I shall always know when you are wanting to make love to another woman," Barbara said—and slipping his arm round her shoulders, turned her face towards him so that he could kiss her. And so they stayed for some time.

It was ten o'clock.

Mr. Rills, in his room in a young men's club at Earl's Court, had got into bed. He lay there, his hands beneath his head, a cigarette dragging at his lips. His face was twisted and white. It was quite impossible to sleep. He tried frantically to think of some way out of the appalling situation. He could see no solution. He began to fabricate to himself a long tale in which he had Mrs. Warren on her knees before him, sobbing for mercy. He was not a stupid young man, and it did not escape him that in reality the rôles were reversed. He whimpered, "I'm sure I have a temperature." He switched on the light, and fumbled among the various bottles that lay at his bedside, for he was a great taker of pills. He swallowed a stomach tablet for his nervous dyspepsia, and two aspirins for the headache. He thought of taking a sleeping-pill as well, but was afraid this might combine lethally with the aspirin. After this, he felt much worse. His temperature, he was sure, was well in the hundreds. If only there were some way out. It wasn't fair, it simply wasn't fair. The old bitch. The old she-devil. He'd like to gouge her eyes out, wring her thick neck, batter her face in. Old women like that shouldn't be allowed to live. "Oh, Christ!" cried Mr. Rills to the four neat walls that shut him in like a tomb, "I wish she were dead, I wish she were dead."

Mrs. Bridgwater sat with her eyes ostensibly fixed on the television. She was waiting for her husband to come back from his evening classes. The *Radio Times,* in the folder that had been a Christmas present from her eldest son, lay upon her knee. She was dreadfully frightened. She still looked like Brunhilde, but the pale-blue eyes were wandering a long way from the screen, and at that moment she would joyfully have exchanged all the illicit kisses in the world for the comfortable peace of Surbiton. She remembered the risks she had run; her eyes suddenly closed, squeezed up in panic. She remembered with shocking clarity her indiscretion in the office at a time when it did not seem to matter, when it was so new, so exciting, and Mark so wonderful with his passionate violence, his utter obliviousness of anyone but themselves, his way of making love. That had been the period when she had been impelled to go continually into Mark's office, when she had returned his naked glances with looks that were equally unashamed. It had all been quite innocent, of course. No one but a jealous madman like Henry could ever think otherwise. Mrs. Bridgwater enjoyed flirting with passion, but naturally one must preserve one's self-respect, one must not go too far. But Henry would not understand. He had never appreciated his wife's craving for artistic freedom. And now, if he—— He couldn't divorce her. There was no evidence. He couldn't take away from her the security she had fought for, the money, the home, the chintz curtains, the television. The blonde head sank a little lower. After all, what could she have seen? They had kissed, yes, but what were kisses, these modern days? Of course there was that occasion on the stairs. Damn Mark. He'd no sense. The Valkyrie face grew hard and old. It was all his fault, he had always been inconsiderate. She pushed from her wildly the memory of buccaneering hands, of piratical kisses, of wild, drunken words that should never have been spoken. Never again. Never, never again. 'If I get out of this,' whispered Mrs. Bridgwater, folding her hands as if she were praying, 'I'll never be so silly again. I'll be a good wife and a good mother, oh, I will, I will, really I will, only just let me off this time, please, God, and I'll be good for the rest of my life, I promise, I swear it. The old cat! Oh, I could *kill* her.'

Her eyes fell to the folder with its slim, sharp edge. The pale eyes dilated; the mouth drew down at the corners.

Then she heard the sound of her husband's key in the lock.

Mark Allan was not in his room. It was a small, untidy room, a-sprawl with books and papers; he seldom stayed in it. He had had a drink with some business friends, and he was striding along the street in the direction of the river, thinking of Mrs. Bridgwater among other things, and smoking chain fashion as he walked. He also thought of Mrs. Warren, and not to her advantage. He did not indulge in melodramatics. He simply wondered how dangerous she could be, and if, therefore, it might be necessary to remove her. Mona had flown into panics before, but this time it seemed serious, and he knew her well enough to realise that if, as things now stood, she were faced with the choice between him and her respectable little home, she would abandon him immediately. He had no intention that she should do so, and hoped soon to force her into the position where she could not do so. He did not, in point of fact, know her as well as he imagined. He was too possessed by the startling flaxen hair and the magnificent body to think about her very coherently. As for Mrs. Warren, it seemed that in one way or another she knew a great deal more than was good for him, and, if that were really so, it was not going to be at all good for her. His mind was made up by two chance snatches of conversation.

The first occurred in a small café where he stopped for a sandwich. He sat down at the marble-topped table, and in the harsh electric light his face looked so dark and formidable that the waitress, intrigued, said impudently, "What's the matter with you? You don't seem in a very good mood."

"Why the hell should I be?" he said.

"Well, you're alive, aren't you?"

At this he gave her so strange a look that her smile vanished. "Am I?" he said. "My God, am I?"

He came out, and continued his walk east, past the derricks, the cranes and the wharfs, until at last he came to the docks. He stood there for a time, staring across the railing. The smell of the river was in his nostrils. A down-and-out touched his arm. "Give me a tanner, guv'nor," he said. "I ain't got the money for a cup of tea. I'm an old soldier. I done my bit. But now the war's over, they've forgotten all about the likes of us."

Mark stared at him in a bitter contempt. "Surely you know by this time," he said, "that old soldiers are always forgotten. There's nothing like war, God save us all. But," he said, tapping on the parapet with his fist, "there's one old soldier who'll not be forgotten so easily."

And he set off home at a great rate, without offering the man so much as a fag-end.

The rest of the I.L.D.A. staff passed their evenings quietly, as if to-morrow were to be a day like any other. The girls were at the pictures. Mr. Latimer listened to a concert on the Third Programme. Mr. Ridley and his family entertained some friends to dinner. Miss Holmes fed her cat. Mr. Dodds read a detective story and looked sternly at his wife when she threatened to reveal the solution. And Mr. Wilson, who lived at home with his parents, studied all the evening papers, and told his mother that he ought to be a detective, because he was discovering more interesting things about I.L.D.A. than he would have thought possible.

Mrs. Warren, in her comfortable little flat, cooked herself a substantial and appetising dinner and, after the hour and a half that her late husband had insisted was necessary for digestion, took a hot bath and went to bed. She was happy and excited. She had always been observant, and it was surprising how careless people could be, leaving odd bits of their personal lives lying around like cottons from an untidy workbasket. They would find out shortly that it did not pay to be rude to her. Mr. Allan had said things to her that she would not forget. Mr. Rills had been so very witty at her expense, and that stupid little Mona Bridgwater had been grossly impertinent on several occasions. Such a foolish woman—and so uncontrolled. Mrs. Warren believed in self-control. Lying cosily back in her bed, with one window a little open, she thought of that business on the stairs. Fancy behaving like that in public. It was really incredible that anyone could

behave in such a manner, and Mrs. Bridgwater running downstairs afterwards with her hair dishevelled and her cheeks
flushed—but it was all very interesting, though a great shame
that Mr. Bridgwater should be so deceived, for he was a fine,
clever man, who deserved better than such a silly slut. It
was no more than her duty to hint that he should keep a
stricter eye on his wife.

And of course there was the other thing. Mrs. Warren's
face grew secret and portentous, and then she gave a little
giggling laugh. Someone shortly was going to be very, very
sorry.

She opened her book. It was a philosophical work called
The Principles of Justice. She always read for half an hour
before going to sleep. She preferred non-fiction, as it stimu-
lated her mind.

She did not know, naturally, that this was to be her last
night on earth.

Before Mr. Latimer's unpleasant predicament, the morning
progressed rather disagreeably. The newspapers, as Charles
had predicted, were splashed with vast, black headlines, and
lurid accounts of consignments of cocaine which had slipped
past the coastal police. All passengers were being investigated
at the Customs, and various protests had been made by innocent people who had been stripped and searched. All
foreign mail was held up for a day, all foreign parcels were
being opened. The newspaper declared that English liberty
was at stake, and all for a small band of freebooters who
could easily be rounded up, if the police were worth their
salary.

Barbara read this on her way to work. She was not very
interested. She was tired because she had gone to bed too
late, and always at the back of her mind nagged an odd
feeling of unease, with regard to Mark Allan. Being a reasonably honest girl, she admitted that her heart was quickening at
the thought of seeing him again. It seemed, to put it at its
mildest, churlish to Charles, who was, after all, a little
more than a nice, steady young man, and who had last night
kissed her very pleasantly, and shown himself to be understanding as well as in love.

She came into the office, five minutes late, and, her senses
sharpened by fatigue, perceived that Mrs. Warren was aglow
with some suppressed excitement. The black eyes were snapping, the wide mouth emitting a continuous froth of little
malicious quips. The girls were plainly aware of this, and

watched her in resentful silence. Even Greta sat there without a word, her heavy black brows an Indian-ink line across her forehead, her mouth sullen, her head down-bent.

"You have infected us all," cried Mrs. Warren to Barbara, as she collected her forms from the wicker tray. "You romantic writers are as much a menace to the community as drug racketeers." Out burst her giggling laughter. "Of course, really you're a drug racketeer, too, aren't you? Dope for the masses, that's what it is."

Barbara was not in a humorous mood, and resented this attack. She saw, however, that the colour was rising in Greta's swarthy cheek, and stared in some surprise.

"And how is your latest hero doing?" inquired Mrs. Warren.

"Perfectly well, thank you."

"As handsome and debonair as ever?"

"Yes, I suppose so."

"Handsome heroes," said Mrs. Warren, "don't always remain debonair. But we shall see."

This seemed so strange that Barbara wondered if she had heard correctly. But Mrs. Warren was now laughing so convulsively that she could bear it no longer, and went at once into her own room.

To-day she had no desire to continue her novel. Mr. John Andrews could draw his sword if he wished; it was no concern of hers. One day she would write a book with a nice young man for hero. Buccaneers were all very well, but it was doubtful if they would make good husbands. She typed out a request for an article on 'the effect of pre-stressing on the buckling loads of statically redundant rigid-jointed trusses', and noted that a request for the *Private Life of the Marquis de Sade* was made by a student, 'required strictly for research'.

'I bet it is,' thought Barbara sourly, then, struggling through Mr. Dodds's arches with something that seemed to be: 'Byull. Eksperimentalnoi Biol. i Med., U.S.S.R.', heard Greta come into the room.

Greta stood by the window, pleating her skirt with both hands. From the hunch of her shoulders it seemed that she might be crying. 'God knows what's the matter with us all,' thought Barbara, completed her form, then said, "What's the matter?"

"She's a horrid old woman," said Greta in a muffled voice.

"Well, so she is. Never mind. She'll meet her deserts one day. Tell me what's the matter. It can't just be Mrs. Warren.

She's not worth bothering about."

Greta moved slowly round. She had been crying. "Miss Smith——" she said.

"Well?"

"Miss Smith, you know yesterday you said—you said you were sure I'd lots of boy friends, and I said I didn't like boys much——"

"Greta. You've fallen in love. That's it, isn't it?"

"You are clever," cried Greta. "How did you guess?"

"I hope he's very nice, and that you marry and live happily ever afterwards."

"I'm afraid I'm too young."

"Well, you can wait a little while. It's fun waiting when you've something worth waiting for. You're seventeen, aren't you? At eighteen you can get engaged."

Greta looked doubtful. Her dark eyes flitted from Barbara's face to the window, then back again.

"And how old is he?" asked Barbara, wishing she would go, for there seemed to be a great deal of work to do.

"I don't know."

"He's older than you, though?"

"Oh yes. Years and years older."

"Good heavens! Is it someone—is it someone in the office? Greta. Who is it?"

Greta, giggling faintly, whispered, "It's Mr.—Mr. Allan. Oh, Miss Smith, he's smashing, he is, really. It happened yesterday."

"What happened?" Barbara's mouth had grown stiff. It appeared that yesterday had been the hunting season. Then she thought, 'God damn him, is he seducing little girls now?'

"He spoke to me," said Greta in an awed voice. "He said—— Shall I tell you what he said?"

"Do."

"He said, 'Hallo. I haven't seen you before, have I? What's your name?' I told him," said Greta dramatically. "Of course he had seen me before, but I expect he just hadn't noticed. And he smiled at me. Oh, Miss Smith, I do think he's smashing, and I shall always love him, always, always, just like the girl I saw in the film yesterday."

"He's old enough to be your father," said Barbara.

"Oh, don't be so crabby. That old bag in there, she's been saying horrid things about him, that he isn't so clever as he thinks he is, and then the girls were teasing me, and she began to laugh the way she does, and said I was romantic. That's why she went on about your novels. He is the handsomest man I've ever seen," said Greta. "And I'm going up there this morning if I can think of some excuse. I'm going to make him notice me. Do I look all right? There's a stain on my skirt that I can't get off, but I don't think it really shows. I like tall men with nice long faces, don't you? It's funny, isn't it, Miss Smith, you talking about boy friends like that, and then this happens."

Barbara, when she had gone, thought sadly how very unfunny it all was. This was indeed a fine state of affairs. Twenty-eight, engaged to be married, a reasonably successful novelist, and one piratical kiss that meant nothing, nothing at all, and then—— He is nothing but a soldier of fortune. "Damn!" she said aloud, "this is not going to happen. It's sheer nonsense. Just because he kissed me once, just because he looks like my heroes who are utterly undependable types, anyway——" And then she thought, 'Oh, God, I'm so tired, I wish I were dead.'

It was a quarter to eleven.

At a few minutes to eleven, Mr. Latimer went up to the second-floor cloak-room. He shot the bolt on the lavatory door, and presently found he could not unfasten it. He struggled with it for a time, cursing, but it was no use, it seemed to be firmly wedged. It was infuriating and undignified, and he was expecting an important phone-call. He kicked at the door, then raised his voice in an angry shout for help.

Barbara, on the floor above, heard the shouts through the open window. "Let me out!" Mr. Latimer was roaring. "Help! Let me out, I say! Purley—*Purley!*——"

She ran through to the general office, to find the girls, work abandoned, hanging out of the window. Mrs. Warren, who would surely have enjoyed this, was not there, neither was Greta.

They were kindly, well-brought-up girls, but the situation unfortunately possessed a universal humour that overrode refinement. Mr. Latimer's bellows increased in volume, and the girls were beginning to giggle helplessly.

"Someone," said Barbara rather incoherently, "really had better tell Mr. Purley."

The girls by this time were incapable of telling anyone; but Miss Holmes, who had also heard the noise and who was shocked to her soul that such a disaster should happen to Mr. Latimer of all people, had already sent a messenger post-haste to the fourth floor. She had been talking to Mr.

Dodds, but could not continue under such shocking circumstances.

"If," said Mr. Dodds, "the French Institute cannot supply——"

"I'm sorry," said Miss Holmes, "but really I cannot possibly concentrate just now. Why doesn't Mr. Purley do something?"

Mr. Dodds sighed. It was surely not a matter of great importance that Mr. Latimer could not open a door. It was a little unfortunate, perhaps, but from the noise outside, one would believe that a major catastrophe had occurred. He saw Miss Holmes dash out of the room, then crossed his legs, and stared contemplatively out of the window.

"Mr. Latimer's locked himself in the gents," said Mr. Rills to Mr. Purley, adding, "It is the voice of my beloved that knocketh, saying, 'Open to me, my love, my dove——' "

Mark Allan, who was outside the packing-room door, made at this point a comment so unseemly that Mr. Rills, though he detested Mr. Allan with all his heart and soul, burst into a snigger of indecorous laughter. Mr. Purley was shocked at both of them. He gathered up a handful of tools and, with a cold glance at the two gentlemen who really ought to know better, made his way downstairs as fast as he could. On his descent he nearly knocked over Mrs. Bridgwater. "I'm sorry, miss," he said, "but with all this row—— Would happen to-day, of course, when I'm single-handed."

She gave him so wild a look that he wondered if she were unwell. But she only continued her way upstairs, and Mr. Latimer's shouts were now quite hysterical, so he hurried down, calling out, "Coming, sir, coming!", his sense of fitness greatly offended by so disgraceful a happening.

By quarter-past eleven peace was restored. Mr. Latimer, very dignified, and in an extremely bad temper, was back in his office; the girls had stopped giggling, and work progressed as usual.

At half-past eleven Miss Holmes came into Barbara's room to ask if she had seen Mrs. Warren.

"No. Isn't she in the general office?"

"If she were, I shouldn't be asking you," snapped Miss Holmes, then, "Well, it's no fault of yours, of course, but what with all the noise and one thing and another, I do not see how I can possibly be expected to carry on the work of this department. I should have thought Mrs. Warren would have had more sense. Did she seem ill this morning?"

"No. I thought she was in unusually good spirits. Why? What's happened?"

"She's vanished," said Miss Holmes. "She left the room some time before eleven, and nobody's seen her since. It is now twenty-five to twelve."

"But how extraordinary," said Barbara, and was on the verge of adding that she might have been locked in, too, when Miss Holmes forestalled her. "I've tried all the doors," she said. "She's definitely not in the cloak-room. And her hat and coat are still there. I cannot imagine where she can have got to. It's so unlike her to go away like this, without a word. She's such a conscientious worker. Go up to the top floor, will you, Miss Smith, and see if she's in one of the offices there. She might conceivably be with Mrs. Bridgwater, though why she should choose to gossip in office time, I do not know. If she's not there, try all the other departments. I think," added Miss Holmes, "that I am going mad. People can't disappear like that, and unless she's had a brain-storm or something, she surely wouldn't go home without her hat and coat. And if she's had an accident, we'd have heard by now. You can't fall down those electric lifts, anyway—the doors don't open unless the lift is there. I've sent Maureen down to the basement stacks——"

Barbara glanced in at the general office on her way, and saw that Greta was crying again, and being consoled by her friends.

"Mr. Allan's been rude to her," said Maureen over her shoulder. "She's very upset. Hasn't Mrs. Warren turned up yet?"

"I'm just going upstairs to see if she's there," said Barbara, looking sideways at Greta. Mr. Allan, when he chose, could be very rude indeed, but it seemed strange that he should expend his thunder on a little girl who fancied herself in love with him.

She ran upstairs. Mr. Purley looked morosely at her as she passed his door. In front of him lay two of the red sacks filled to bursting point. "What a day!" he said. "What a bly awful day, if you'll pardon my bad French."

"What a day, indeed," agreed Barbara. "You haven't seen Mrs. Warren, have you?"

"I saw her earlier, this morning," said Mr. Purley, without interest. "Talking to Mr. Allan, she was. And," he added in a sudden outburst of confidence, "between you and me, miss, I don't care if I never see her again. Proper interfering old woman she is, and I don't care who hears me say so. Here I am, single-handed, and with twice the usual number of books to cope with, and she's got nothing better to do than tell me that filling them sacks is a waste of time, and that half the books we send downstairs had better be burnt, because if we don't want 'em, nobody does. I ask you! 'Mrs. Warren,' I said, 'I've been in I.L.D.A. for twenty-five years, and if I don't give satisfaction by now, I never will.' And she says to me, laughing the way she does, Mr. Purley, she says, 'I've been here for seven years, and no doubt will be here for the next seven as well, and I think I know more about the workings of I.L.D.A. than all of you put together.' Cheek!" said Mr. Purley savagely, "I hope you've lost her for good."

"She certainly seems to have disappeared," said Barbara. "Perhaps she's in Mrs. Bridgwater's room. I'll just look in and make sure."

Mrs. Bridgwater had a great pile of pay packets on her desk, and a mountain of money before her, for this was payday. She looked up at Barbara. Barbara's first impression of her was that she looked extraordinarily untidy. This was surprising, for she was normally a most excellently groomed woman. The fair hair was falling over her face; her skin was blotched and unpowdered, and quantities of tobacco ash had fallen on to her black skirt.

She caught Barbara's glance, and brushed ineffectually at the ash, saying quickly as she did so, "I know I shouldn't smoke, but I just couldn't help it to-day, I felt so nervous and out of sorts." She gave Barbara a strained, unhappy smile. "You won't tell on me, will you?"

"Of course not. I only wish I could smoke myself. Have you seen——"

"Have one, dear," cried Mrs. Bridgwater, holding out a packet of Players. Her hand was shaking as if she had the palsy. "Oh, do have one. I should love you to. It would ease my conscience, you see, and I do so love corrupting people. Wait. I'll give you a light."

"Thank you, but I haven't time. Later on, perhaps. Look, have you seen——?"

"But you must," insisted Mrs. Bridgwater, leaning forward and taking a cigarette out of the packet as she did so. "You can always pretend you were discussing your income-tax or something. Take it, there's a good girl. And then you can sit down and have a little chat with me. I get quite lonesome in this office, all by myself. Besides, I like talking to you, because you're an artist, too, and I feel we have so much in common. The others just don't understand, but you and I, we feel things so much more than other people, don't we? You must tell me all about your books. I am dying to read one. They sound so exciting. What name do you write under?"

"Allen," said Barbara, before she could stop herself. She was so distressed by Mrs. Bridgwater's frantic, almost incoherent speech, and the desperation in the pale blue eyes, that she was taken off her guard.

Mrs. Bridgwater's flow of speech stopped as if a hand had been clapped over her mouth. Her lips were working, but no sound came from them. Then she broke into a foolish giggle; she was not a woman who normally giggled, and the sound was a little horrifying. "Oh!" she said, "but how amusing! And does Mr. Allan know?"

"No," said Barbara, looking away. "No. And neither does anyone else. Please keep this to yourself, Mrs. Bridgwater. I didn't really mean to tell you. Look on it as a great secret, will you?"

"I'm ever so good at keeping secrets," said Mrs. Bridgwater, still staring, and speaking in a high-pitched, artificial voice. The cigarette was dangling from her fingers, but, instead of offering it to Barbara, she put it between her own lips.

Barbara said, "I really came to ask if you'd seen Mrs. Warren anywhere. We—we've lost her."

She knew this sounded perfectly ridiculous, but she was not prepared for the shrill, hysterical shriek of laughter that burst from Mrs. Bridgwater, who cried. "You've *lost* her! How funny, how funny. Oh, I do think that's funny." And then she broke into a flood of tears.

Barbara stared at her in utter dismay. Oh, God, had the whole world gone mad? She put out a hesitating hand and touched Mrs. Bridgwater's shoulder; she was sobbing now as if her heart were broken, making no attempt to cover her face or hide her tears; she sat there, shivering, staring ahead, the tears flooding down her cheeks.

"Oh, please, don't," cried Barbara. "What's the matter? Are you ill? Can I help? Please do stop crying. I'll get you a glass of water."

Mrs. Bridgwater sobbed, "I'm v-very highly s-strung, you know. It's nothing. Really. I'm a silly girl, aren't I? Just stay a minute, will you? Just one minute. I'll be all right soon, truly I will."

Barbara, bewildered, took the hand that lay on the desk and patted it. Tremors were running through it. Then she felt the hand flinch in hers, and saw that there was a thin, red cut running across the palm, just beneath the ball of the little finger. She said, "You've hurt yourself."

Mrs. Bridgwater snatched her hand away. She had stopped crying. She said in a cold voice, "We can't sit here, holding hands like this. What will people think? I cut myself on a tin this morning. It was a tin of tongue. I was opening it for my husband's breakfast. He does so like tongue, and after all one must indulge the brutes a little, mustn't one? Such greedy, greedy creatures. You'll find that out when you're married. Still," went on Mrs. Bridgwater; a muscle in her cheek twitched like a nervous tic, "it's such fun being married, I always think. And Henry's such a dear thing, and we're still terribly in love, you know. Sometimes I think it's a wee bit absurd, and me with two sons at boarding-school. He's quite besotted over me, really." An accent that she had long cast out was sliding back into her speech. "I says to him only last night, 'Henry,' I says, 'anyone would think we was a honeymoon couple.'" Suddenly she became again very much the aristocrat. "My dear, you must excuse me, but I expect you want your money just like everyone else. I've *so* enjoyed our little chat. You must look in whenever you're on this floor."

She flashed a brilliant smile at Barbara. Behind the smile was pure, palpable terror. Barbara backed to the door. She could think of nothing to say. She was thankful to be out in the corridor again. She turned into the periodical department, where Mr. Dodds was sitting at his desk.

He said, before she could speak, "No, I haven't got her. And candidly, Miss Smith, I do not want her. I shouldn't be at all surprised if she'd been murdered, for that is what she deserves."

"Mr. Dodds!"

"Well? She belongs to that small but distinctive class of persons who must be constantly meddling in other people's business. I have," said Mr. Dodds in a calm, judicial voice, "not the slightest sympathy with her. In the course of a long life, Miss Smith, I have learnt that people are as they are, they will not change, they will not take advice, they will go their own way, and they are utterly irrational in their reactions. Unhappily, women like Mrs. Warren tend to equate themselves with God. They start in a small way by disinterring gobbets from the human rubbish-heap, then grow to believe that they can control the lives of other people. Nobody can control anybody. And the human being, if meddled with sufficiently, is apt to react in a surprising manner. Especially—— However, that is beside the point. You want Mrs. Warren. I cannot imagine why. In any case, I do not have her. You may search this room if you will. The filing-cabinets are to your right. The cupboard holds nothing but stationery, a raincoat and my umbrella. I assume you are not accusing me of a liaison?"

"You have not yet given me a chance to accuse you of anything," said Barbara.

"I always feel," he said, "that as you are compelled by a rigidly Puritanic publisher to write about sexually repressed characters, you must have some outlet for your more lurid imaginings. I thought, therefore, you might assume——"

"I never assumed anything of the kind!"

"You see," said Mr. Dodds. "You see——"

"But you must admit that it's a bit strange. She has simply vanished. She may be all you say, but she's not a witch. Do you think anything serious has happened to her?"

"I think it is more than possible. She has, after all, been playing a most dangerous game. Oh, I have heard things. There is nothing wrong with my hearing. I don't suppose the people in this office are any more dangerous than anywhere else, but the lady seems to have a flair for baring the Achilles' heel, and sticking a dagger into it."

Barbara said, "You speak so remotely that, if this were a detective story and she really had been murdered, I should know at once you were the murderer."

"Oh, do you think so?" said Mr. Dodds, in surprise. "I do not believe I'm likely to commit a murder. I am too old Would you not like to look in my cupboard?"

"No!"

"Well, you must now ask Mr. Allan, must you not? How is your soldier of fortune?"

Barbara said, rather bitterly, "I'm thinking of tearing him up and starting a new novel about a nice, decent, honourable young man."

"It won't sell," said Mr. Dodds. "Virtue in fiction is incurably dull. We are bored by it. I personally read detective stories. I am partial to maniacs. I remember once as a young boy that I accidentally killed a rabbit. We were playing in the garden, and the animal was confined in one of those wire-netting affairs. I lifted the netting to give it a piece of lettuce; it dived out, and I dropped the netting, catching it on the back of the neck. It's a vulnerable point. A useful method of murder, I should imagine. The animal was not quite dead, but dying, and in pain. I wished to kill it, for mercy's sake. I raised my arm. But I couldn't. I could not deliver the blow. My arm was, as it were, suspended in mid-air. Most extraordinary. But with some people, of course, the brain's instructions are obeyed more promptly. I do not feel, therefore, I should make much of a murderer. But of course one never knows. Let me know when you find Mrs. Warren. Good-morning."

Mark Allan glanced up at Barbara as she came in. He said nothing, but waited. He looked much as usual, but the lines of temper were deeply engraved, and the bright eyes hard. It was impossible to imagine that he had ever kissed her.

Barbara said, stammering slightly, much to her fury, "I w-wondered if Mrs. Warren were with you."

"Why should she be?"

"I thought she might."

"You have no reason to think anything of the kind." His voice was harsh. "I detest the woman. I have always done so. I am not likely to seek her company. Perhaps you would like to examine my photostat-room. She might be concealed beneath the table."

"I am sorry," said Barbara stiffly, then, because she would not refuse the challenge, "You are very unco-operative, Mr. Allan. I ask you a simple question, and you have to take it as a deadly insult." She remembered suddenly how Greta had been crying. Her anger flared; her nerves were snapping and flickering like damp electric wires. She said, "You like upsetting people, don't you? You even make little girls cry. I was brought up to believe that it was the meanest thing imaginable to hit someone who cannot hit back."

He shot her a look of sheer amazement, then the bad-tempered lines creased into a broad smile. "Why," he said, "are the swords out, then? *Puisque nous sommes ici, battons-nous!* Come, I'll make bold with one of your nine lives, mistress, and, as you shall use me hereafter, dry-beat the rest of the eight. Come along. Show your mettle——"

"I'll do nothing of the kind," said Barbara, gathering to her such determination as was left; her mouth was unaccountably dry, and her heart pounding shamefully in her ears. She shut the door behind her with a regrettable slam. She was sure she heard him laugh.

On the stairs she paused for a second. Mr. Purley, dragging his sacks out into the corridor, said, mopping his brow, "Cor, these aren't half heavy. Found her yet, miss?"

"Oh, damn her," said Barbara, then meeting his startled

gaze, "Yes, that's what I said. Damn her! She must have gone home, and good riddance to her."

At one o'clock there was still no sign of Mrs. Warren. The Location Department, despite Miss Holmes's injunction that work must go on, could talk of nothing else.

"Could she have fallen out of the window?" asked Maureen. They all crowded to the window and looked fearfully out. But there was nothing to be seen in the courtyard below. They gazed at each other. It was no longer a joke. "If she disappears," said Greta, "we might disappear, too. Perhaps there's some sort of Jack the Ripper about."

Barbara said with a badly assumed briskness, "Nonsense. She's gone home. She probably felt ill."

"She's never ill," said Greta.

"Well, that's all the more reason why she wouldn't know how to cope with it. And perhaps she didn't think about her coat. After all, it's very warm. I expect she'll ring us when she gets home."

"She'd have been home ages ago," said Peggy.

"She might have stopped at the doctor's on the way. There are a hundred explanations."

But they were all frightened, and so was Barbara, who could only say, "Well, I think you're all being very silly. You mayn't want any lunch, but I do."

She could not help but notice that the girls, as they went along the corridor to collect their coats, walked very closely, side by side. She nearly joined them. But it was too ridiculous, and Jack the Rippers do not fit into a library régime. She rang for the lift.

Mr. Purley, coming down from the fourth floor, stopped for her as he always did. There were two sacks beside him; she had some difficulty in avoiding them.

"More bodies for the students, miss," he said in a hollow voice. "Two, this time. A real gala day, this is."

"It's growing on you, Mr. Purley," said Barbara. "You'll end on the gallows yet." The lift stopped with a jerk, and she stumbled against one of the sacks. And as she did so, the mouth of the sack opened. An inert hand slid out, to lie with clenched, pallid fingers on the lift floor.

Barbara, in her novels, had from time to time pierced an odd character or so with a sword. She had several times knocked villains out with a clean left from the hero's fist. She had once even shot a wicked marquis so that the bright blood flooded his cambric shirt. But never had she visualised anything so horrifying as this dead hand which crept out and dropped to the floor like some obscene and monstrous toad. For a second she stared at it in silence. Then the scream came from her in a shrill, whistling sound, and crumpling with face upraised, hands spread out, she fell across the sack which now burst completely open to reveal Mrs. Warren's dead face, twisted at an unsightly angle on her broken neck.

IV. PRIDE, ENVY, ANGER, JELOUSY, HATE, AND OTHER VICES. 179.8

BARBARA said to Charles that evening, "It was like the worst kind of nightmare. Only one didn't wake up." He had come round to comfort her; she suspected he had also come for the story. "The only saving feature was that it didn't seem quite real. Only—only I shall never kill anyone in my books again, unless they are absolutely wicked. I have never liked her, and sometimes I have detested her, but I didn't know that dead people looked like that, so small and so— so very dead. It was indecent, somehow, like seeing a fat, elderly person undressed."

She recovered consciousness almost immediately, to find that she was in Mark Allan's arms. She did not tell Charles this. In any case, it was not romantic, for she felt sick and shaking; he carried her with efficiency and without emotion into her own room, where he set her down on the chair. She was still dizzy, and not quite knowing where she was, and she clutched on to him, begging him not to leave her. Then she came more fully to herself and apologised.

He made no comment on her apology. She raised her eyes to look fully at him. What she saw amazed her so much that she thought she must be about to faint again; she caught the edge of the desk in her hands, reassured by its firmness. His face was as she had never seen it. It was alight and alive, with all the boredom and bad temper wiped clean off it. He looked, indeed, ten years younger. There was a suppressed smile on his lips, his eyes were sparkling, and the dangerous vitality and attraction came from him like an electric current. But even as she looked, his face changed. He said abruptly, "Well? Are you all right now? Do I have to hold your head or something? It has been quite a shock for you."

She remembered again that hand, and the nausea rose in her throat. Her colour must have changed, for he said quite roughly, "Come. Pull yourself together. You're not a Victorian miss, after all, the people die every minute of the day. There's no need to brood on it. And she's not much of a loss, let's face it."

She was shocked by this; he saw it and laughed. "Ah," he said, "the usual clap-trap that surrounds death. Mr. X, when alive, is a swine. When he dies, he is no better than bacon, and probably not half as useful, but no, we clasp our hands, we wear black for him, and up goes the tombstone— a beloved husband, a worthy father, going straight, nonstop, to Abraham's bosom, rest in peace, while the old bastard deceived his wife and beat his children and trampled on the poor every day of his life. Mrs. Warren was a meddling old bitch, and a confounded nuisance. I do not believe there is one person here who liked her, one who will miss her, one who is not thanking God she is dead. There is no need for plumes and crosses. I once thought you were a reasonably intelligent girl. Next you will be putting on the special voice reserved for the dead, hush, hush, *de mortuis*. I'm glad she's dead. I hope she goes straight to hell, with Bosch's demons to stick spikes into her. Here, have a cigarette. I assure you that no one will reproach you. It's a general holiday. Besides, it will help to calm you before the police come, and, as you discovered the body, you will probably be interrogated most thoroughly."

"The police!"

"My dear girl, you can hardly imagine that old ladies, even when they're pests like Mrs. Warren, insert themselves into sacks, then commit suicide, afterwards neatly—though rather insecurely—tying the string over their heads."

Barbara said suddenly, "Please go away. You seem to find this funny. It isn't. It's horrible. I don't care if she was an old pest. Nobody should die in such a manner. I hope they catch the murderer and hang him."

He looked down at her consideringly. "Do you now! I should have thought you one of those enlightened people who don't believe in capital punishment. So you'd hang the murderer, would you? Well, I shouldn't let the murderer know. After all, one can only hang once, and he might decide, like the ancient Egyptians, to take an escort to the shades."

Barbara, repeating a somewhat expurgated version of this conversation to Charles, said afterwards, "It was incredibly stupid of me, but it was only then that I realised she'd been murdered, and that the murderer must be one of us."

Charles said, "Probably that fellow Allan."

"No!" she had cried before she could stop herself, then more quietly, "Why should he? I mean, he's a normal, decent person. People don't do that sort of thing."

"Someone did," said Charles.

Someone certainly did. Mr. Purley, very white and drawn, chain-smoking in bleak defiance, said later to his cronies at the local, "One of them did it. And I've a pretty good idea who it was, too. No, I'm not saying. But I hopes they get him. Fair turned me up, it did. I've seen some pretty ugly things in my time, but that——"

He stood on guard outside the door. It was the Russian Union Catalogue room, converted temporarily into a mortuary. He looked wretched and sick. Despite his crabbed manner, he was a kindly man, and he dearly loved I.L.D.A., though he cursed and swore at it a dozen times a day. Mrs. Warren had irritated him, but he had no real grudge against her, and he did not care to think of her as she lay now on the table, decently covered with a dust-sheet. He had been equally irritated by Mr. Allan, whose language and unseemliness shocked him, by Mr. Rills, who could be as waspish as any old maid, and by Miss Holmes, who nagged at him, and perpetually complained about dust and dirt. But to Mr. Purley they were all I.L.D.A., and I.L.D.A. was his life, and this shameful business was therefore his shame, too.

Besides, he had helped to carry Mrs. Warren in. He had cut the sack away from her, and he had seen her before she was mercifully covered by the sheet. The dead were not pretty. He would never forget the look of anger and astonishment on her face. He was not a religious man, but as he covered the thing up, he had muttered something almost like a prayer, though Mr. Allan, who had helped him get the body out of the lift, had seemed completely unmoved.

He stood there, barring the room against inquisitive sightseers. He was relieved when the police came, the doctor and the photographers. He glanced in once, then hastily away again. The whole scene possessed a theatrical unreality. The doctor had finished his examination, and Mrs. Warren lay on the table, uncovered, in the brilliant flare of the flashlights. There was a great bustle and running here and there. It seemed impossible that so short a time ago she had been alive.

There was naturally no work being done in I.L.D.A. at

all. Miss Holmes, looking ghastly with the shock, exclaimed to Mr. Latimer, "How I am expected to carry on the work of the department, I simply do not know," and then checked herself, for with Mrs. Warren lying dead in the Russian Union Catalogue room, only a few doors away, she really could not in decency's sake continue. But secretly she was thinking that now they would have to engage a temporary, and temporaries were such hopeless creatures, usually actresses who were 'resting', or young students wanting to earn vacation money. They could seldom type, and as soon as they had been taught the work they left, and one had to start all over again.

Mrs. Warren had always been such a dependable worker, never ill, and never, naturally, liable to the distractions of domestic rows and difficult young men.

She looked wildly at Mr. Latimer. She said, refusing to acknowledge the black-lettered word that was printed across her mind, "I just don't see how it could have happened."

Mr. Latimer, who had been compelled by virtue of his position to see the body, and who was feeling very ill in consequence, said harshly, "She was murdered. That's all there is to it. Someone," he added with a crudity normally alien to his nature, "hit her on the back of the head and broke her neck."

"It's not possible," whispered Miss Holmes, and suddenly covered her face with her hands.

"I had a word with the doctor," continued Mr. Latimer, staring out of the window. "He said she could not have been dead for much more than an hour."

Miss Holmes said nothing, but began to tremble. An hour ago—— Then, as Mr. Latimer's silence was prolonged, she said in an over-loud voice, "Some maniac, of course. I've always said that it was far too easy for strangers to walk in. The telephonist never bothers to check. It could have been anyone."

Mr. Latimer said slowly, "No. It couldn't have been anyone. It was one of us. It's no good, Mary." (He had never addressed her by her Christian name before, but neither of them noticed it.) "It's no good. Do you think I haven't tried to believe it was an outsider? Do you think I want to believe that a member of my staff is a brutal murderer? But of course it was one of us. The murder must have taken place on the top floor, and almost certainly while I—when that confounded bolt jammed. And it was someone who knew the routine of the packing-room. Someone who knew that the sacks were taken down to the basement, and left there until the—the contents could be sorted out. She might have lain there the whole week-end if Miss Smith—— How is she, by the way? She'd better be sent home in a taxi."

"She won't go," said Miss Holmes. "She says she'd rather stay with the others. They are all talking about it. There's no work being done at all."

Mr. Latimer said with a faint flush of humour, "Well, we're talking about it, aren't we? What can you expect? Anyway, I think Mr. Ridley is going to close the office down for to-day. He's summoning a staff meeting. To-morrow we shall all have to be in. Scotland Yard is sending a couple of men down."

"It'll be in all the newspapers," said Miss Holmes.

"Of course it will. Murder in the library. Isn't that a detective story by someone? Good heavens," cried Mr. Latimer, "it is just not possible. Such an inoffensive old woman, too. Who in the world could have any reason to kill her?"

Which only went to prove that Mr. Latimer, like a great many executives, had no idea whatsoever of the life that smouldered beneath the office routine. At that very moment, several people who had excellent reason to kill Mrs. Warren were considering her death with varying degrees of emotion; the person who had just done the killing was shortly to appear in Miss Holmes's office.

The girls huddled round Barbara, who sat in the middle of the room, drinking the cup of tea that Mr. Purley had sent up to her. She had recovered from her faintness, but was utterly exhausted, so that the situation for her, as for Mr. Purley, had somehow lost the edge of reality. But she could not stop talking about it. Again and again she described the dreadful appearance of the dead hand, and each time she mentioned it, the girls squealed and exclaimed.

"I think it was Mr. Rills," said Maureen.

"It might have been Mrs. Bridgwater," said Peggy. "I heard her crying like anything this morning."

"It couldn't have been a woman. No woman would do a thing like that."

"Plenty of women have," said Barbara drearily, adding, "For all you know, it might have been me." Then she put her tea-cup down and began to cry, which, from the point of view of the girls, was the best thing she could have done; their protective instincts were at once aroused and they forgot for the moment their horrid imaginings. They crowded round her, patting her and petting her, telling her not to cry, or to have a good cry and get it over, according to their respective temperaments.

Maureen said presently, "A woman couldn't lift the body and—and do all that sort of thing. Well, I mean——"

Barbara had stopped crying. But across her mind flashed the vision of a beautifully built Valkyrie body, with wide shoulders and powerful, shapely hands. Mrs. Warren, after all, had been a small woman.

"Actually," said Maureen, "it was probably Mr. Allan."

At this point Greta spoke. Up till now she had been unaccountably silent. She had sat there, her dark face sullen and afraid, the great brows meeting, hands tightly folded in her lap. But now she raised her head and said in a husky voice, "It wasn't Mr. Allan."

"He's a horrid man," said Peggy. "Think how rude he was to you. And he swears dreadfully. I'm sure he could do a murder."

Greta said stubbornly, "It wasn't Mr. Allan."

"Why not? How can you know?"

"Because I was with him while Mr. Latimer was shut up in the toilet. At least most of the time. Mr. Purley says she must have been killed then. And she couldn't have been."

Barbara was conscious of an overwhelming relief. The murderer could, of course, have been anyone—Mr. Rills or Mr. Dodds or Mrs. Bridgwater. But in her heart she had had a dreadful suspicion that it was Mark. He had the strength. He had the temperament. He had the motive. And now—— She looked with the utmost affection on Greta, dear, silly little Greta. She said, "What happened with you and Mr. Allan? You never told me, you know."

Greta's face lit up. It was not a happy memory, but it set her in the limelight, it meant she could talk about Mr. Allan, and she still loved him, despite his rudeness, for he was so smashingly handsome, and his voice sent shivers up her spine, even when it spoke so cruelly to her.

"Well," she said, "it was like this, Miss Smith. I knocked and he didn't answer."

"He never does! It's a matter of principle, I think."

"And I had some forms for him—really I had. So I went in. He wasn't there, so I thought I'd wait for him sort of, if you know what I mean. But actually, you see, he was in the little room at the side, where he does his photostats and things. Of course I didn't know that. And suddenly he came back and saw me. I suppose he must have heard me because

I sneezed. I couldn't help it. And he came in——— Oh, Miss Smith, I do think he's smashing, really I do."

Barbara said with a bitter smile, "I bet he smashed you. He doesn't care much for being interrupted. And what happened, then? I suppose he roared his head off at you."

Greta had stood there, pleating her turquoise skirt, looking up at him from beneath the heavy brows, the sensuous face convulsed in shyness and adoration.

He stared at her for a moment. He must have been working at his photostats, for he had removed his coat, and his shirt-sleeves were rolled up to the elbow. His hands and wrists were dripping wet.

Greta was too timid to return the stare. The thick black lashes dropped down, and an embarrassed smile caught at her lips. She thought he looked more smashing than ever, with his sleeves rolled up like that, and the muscular forearms showing; as for his face, it was just like the hero of that historical film, who leapt from the balcony with his sword between his teeth. But she perceived that he was very white and drawn; something in his look sent a brief shudder through her. Perhaps he had a headache; his brows were meeting, and his mouth drawn tight as if his teeth were set.

He said at last—and his voice caught Greta like a physical slap across the face—"What are you doing here? How dare you come in without knocking? Am I allowed no peace and privacy in this damned office, without stupid little half-wits walking in and out as if the place belonged to them? Get out! I'm busy. I don't choose to be disturbed. Get out at once!"

Greta's mouth fell open. The colour flamed into her face. She cried, her voice soaring up, "I did knock, Mr. Allan. You didn't hear me, that's all. And I've got some forms for you. I can't help it if I'm asked to give you some forms, can I? And people shouldn't talk to people like that. My mummy says it's very bad-mannered. Are you feeling ill or something?"

He roared out, "Why the devil should I be feeling ill?"

"Well," said Greta, for she was a reasonable girl, "I thought you must have a pain to be so rude. Or perhaps you're worried about something." She added, "You know, I expect it's your nerves. I expect you've been doing too much. My mummy suffers terribly from her nerves and, when they get the better of her sort of, she gets all excited just like you. Now what you ought to do, Mr. Allan——"

Mr. Allan said in a low, monotonous voice, "For Christ's

sake, get out while you may, for Christ's sake, get out while you may." Then his voice blared in a monumental roar, almost of entreaty, "In the name of——"

Greta was dreadfully shocked. She was a religious little girl, and this appalling blasphemy upset her as the rudeness had not done. She stared at him. She could not ignore the insane rage that blazed from him, a rage that—though she would not have put the words to it—connoted something of desperation and despair. She backed towards the door, and he came after her. She wailed, in a blubber of words, "I think you're m-mad. You ought to be shut up. I'll tell my father. He d-doesn't like people being so awful to me."

Then she fled, for he had suddenly stretched out his hands. There was still a trace of water on them, which trickled between his outstretched fingers to the floor.

"He looked dreadful," said Greta to the girls who, although they had already heard the story, were gazing at her in an awe-struck silence. "Like—like Boris Karloff, or something. I didn't know he was so busy. I didn't know he was in such a temper. To shout at me like that, and say those frightful words, it's the sort of thing one goes to hell for. And when he came at me, I think he was going to hit me, or something." She dabbed at her eyes and blew her nose. "But you see, he couldn't have done the murder, because he was talking to me while there was all that kerfuffle about Mr. Latimer. It was nearly over when I came out. I don't suppose he meant to be so awful, really. But he did shout so, and I was frightened, and he looked kind of horrid."

"I think," said Barbara, her distress swamped in black rage, "that he is the most unspeakable man I have ever met. To speak to you like that. There is no excuse, no excuse at all. I hope he gets the sack. I hope he ends up in prison. To treat you so vilely, just because he's in the devil of a temper, and Mrs. Bridgwater's refused to kiss him."

She saw the girls' faces change, but it was too late. Maureen flushed and swallowed convulsively. Greta's head went down again, her cheeks scarlet. She looked round. Mark Allan was standing in the doorway. He stared at her. His face was quite expressionless. The pause was long enough to make Barbara wish she could sink through the floor.

But he said nothing to her. He turned to Greta, who would not raise her head, but sat there, a little huddled up, her face half-hidden by the mane of dark hair. He said, "I've come to apologise. I was disgustingly rude to you just now. I am very sorry."

He paused again, but she would not raise her head. The scene was like a tableau, with everyone transfixed. He suddenly smiled, the charming smile that so transformed his face. He touched Greta gently on the shoulder. "You must try to forgive me," he said. "It was really unpardonable of me, only you were quite right, I did have a headache, and there was a stack of work to do, and I was just getting down to it, after a quite hopeless morning. Don't cry, there's a good girl. My reputation stinks quite enough without that. Look. I've brought you some chocolates. I thought you might like them."

He put the box down beside her. Greta still neither moved nor spoke, but the tears dripped pathetically on to her skirt. Mark looked down and saw this. Barbara saw him heave a sigh, and make a hopeless gesture with his hands. He said, "I see I am hopelessly in disgrace. Oh, well, I hope you enjoy the chocolates. They are not poisoned."

He went towards the door, in a dead silence. There he stopped and turned round to look at Barbara. He said, amiably enough, "I should like to have a word with you. Could you spare me a moment?"

Barbara said, without grace, "No, I couldn't."

She had the impression that he was trying not to laugh, and then startlingly he winked at her, a flamboyant, vulgar wink, which momentarily contorted the whole side of his face. He said, "It can wait," glanced once more at Greta, who still sat there, with hanging head, and shut the door behind him.

Peggy said, aghast, "He *winked* at you!"

Maureen said, "Do you think he heard?"

"Of course he heard," said Barbara, adding with wild defiance, "I'm glad he did. It's time he had some idea of what decent people think of him." She added, rather wretchedly, "I'm not glad, really. If I'd known he was there—— But it doesn't matter. Everything's so beastly, and one of us is a murderer. We shall all, no doubt, end up at each other's throats."

Greta had at last raised her head. She murmured, half closing her eyes, "Isn't he *smashing?*"

"Oh, Greta," said Barbara in despair. "Oh, Greta——"

"Have a chocolate," said Greta.

Mr. Dodds walked into Miss Holmes's office, and bowed slightly in his old-fashioned, punctilious way when he saw that Mr. Latimer was there.

"Well, Dodds?" said Mr. Latimer.

"I was wondering," said Mr. Dodds, "what I am supposed to do about *Revue de Métaphysique et Moral*. Liverpool University appears to require it urgently. I understand from Miss Holmes that the French Institute cannot supply it, and it has already gone on to the university and bureaux lists without result. It seems to me that the best course is to apply to Paris. The university would accept a microfilm, so perhaps Mr. Allan——"

"Do you want me?" demanded Mark, looking round the door.

"Why, yes," said Mr. Dodds. "I believe we shall need a microfilm from Bib. Nat. If you——"

Miss Holmes interrupted with a restraint that forced the blood into her face, "I do not know if you gentlemen are aware of it, but there has just been a murder committed on these premises. I am sure Mr. Latimer appreciates your zeal for work, but——"

"Surely," said Mark gravely, coming into the room, "the work of the department must go on. Death may come and death may go, but libraries, one presumes, go on for ever."

"Besides," said Mr. Rills's high-pitched voice behind Mark's shoulder, "we are librarians, and therefore the elect of God. To read is human, to catalogue divine."

"I do think——" began Mr. Latimer, eyeing his staff with the utmost disapproval, then looking full at Mr. Rills for the first time, he broke off. There was such an expression on his face that the others turned round to stare likewise, Mr. Dodds with an air of calm interest, Mark with a rather grim smile.

Mr. Rills was plainly overjoyed. Delight and excitement were bubbling forth from him. He made little effort to conceal it, though from time to time he drew his mouth down portentously and tried to scowl. But the next instant the corners of his mouth curved up again, his eyes gleamed; he clasped his slender hands together as if he would force back the laughter that was threatening to escape. The sickly harassed look he had worn this past week was gone. He met the combined stare of his colleagues, and tried immediately to look solemn and sad.

"Don't overdo the mourning, Rills," said Mark Allan dryly. "A simple black band round the arm will suffice. There is no need to wear plumes as well."

At this, Mr. Rills emitted a shrill shriek of laughter, then fled, stifling his mirth, like a child in the classroom. They heard his convulsive giggles as he hurried along the corridor.

"Hysteria," said Miss Holmes firmly. "A most unbalanced young man. If I'd my way I'd throw a glass of water over him." She caught Mark's eye, and added angrily, "Not that you're any better. Or Mr. Dodds, either. Have you no sense of decency? Poor Mrs. Warren is lying in the Russian Union Catalogue—Mr. Allan! Mr. Allan, if you cannot behave yourself, you'd better go away. I've had as much as I can stand. How I'm expected——"

Mr. Latimer said hastily, "Miss Holmes is quite right. This is really not the moment for humour. I am aware, Allan, that you didn't like Mrs. Warren."

"That," said Mark, without a smile, "is an understatement. I detested the old cow, and I thank God she's dead."

Miss Holmes rose, outraged, to her feet. Mr. Latimer said, before she could speak, "I think you'd better go before you say anything more. The police will be here to-morrow, and I cannot feel that remarks of this kind are advisable. I am not, of course, referring to any question of good taste; I am merely suggesting that as a matter of expediency you might do well to hold your tongue. Did you want anything when you came in just now? Mr. Ridley is addressing the staff in a few minutes' time, and I think he is closing the office for to-day, so perhaps your business can wait."

"I heard my name mentioned," said Mark calmly, "so I looked in. I am quite capable of conducting my own business, thank you. I don't require any help." He looked at Miss Holmes, who was trembling with rage and delayed shock. "So we are all to play the hypocrite, are we? We must all love Mrs. Warren from now on, 'the most popular member of the staff', 'never able to replace her'—what damned nonsense."

"She was a first-class worker," said Miss Holmes, nearly in tears.

"The trouble with her," said Mark coolly, "was that perhaps she overworked. One should never overdo things, as many a blackmailer has found to his sorrow. Good-afternoon."

"Blackmailer!" cried Miss Holmes.

"Oh, he's overwrought," said Mr. Latimer, forgetting himself so far as to light a cigarette. "We are all overwrought. It's a most ghastly business, and I suspect that to-morrow, when the Yard men are here, will be even worse. Don't pay any attention to Allan. Oh yes, Dodds. I'm sorry. I'd forgotten about you. What is it?"

"The *Revue de Métaphysique et Moral*," said Mr. Dodds,

with the utmost patience. "It is after all urgent and, though I deeply regret to-day's unfortunate happenings——"

"Unfortunate happenings!" repeated Miss Holmes faintly.

"——I cannot see why all the office work should be held up. People will still continue to read, even though this unhappy lady has passed away, and libraries will still expect us to fulfil their requests. By the way, Mr. Latimer, did you know that Mr. Wilson is now telling everybody that I.L.D.A. is the secret headquarters of the drug racket?"

Mr. Latimer said grimly, "I will go and speak to Mr. Wilson. There is a time and place for all things, but this misguided humour——"

"Oh, I do not think he is being funny," said Mr. Dodds. "I think he really believes he has made an important discovery. This may or may not be so, but in any case, as I pointed out to him, it is unwise to announce it to all and sundry. He has already told Mr. Allan, Mr. Rills, Mrs. Bridgwater, myself, and most of the Reference Room staff. I told him that if one of us were the murderer and indeed connected with this unpleasant racket, it might be very unfortunate for him. He said he could look after himself. I do not believe he can. A pleasant boy, but so very young and so very foolish. I cannot honestly regret the death of Mrs. Warren, who was an unpleasant and mischief-making woman, but I should be sorry to see young Wilson tied to her shroud, for he is an intelligent boy, and has the makings of a reasonably literate librarian. And as most librarians are entirely illiterate——"

"Dodds," said Mr. Latimer wearily, "do you think you could possibly stop talking? As for your *Revue de* What's-it, for heaven's sake let it be till Monday. I'm sure we've all had an appalling day, and the sooner we get off home, the —— Oh, Mrs. Bridgwater. My dear Mrs. Bridgwater, you'd better sit down. Would you like me to get you a glass of water?"

Mr. Dodds looked with disapproval at Mrs. Bridgwater, who had crept in, and who now fell into a chair, her hands listlessly folded in her lap. Her hair was half down. She had plainly been crying for some time, and done nothing to erase the signs. Her blouse was coming out of her skirt. The ash that Barbara had noticed was streaked everywhere. There was a long ladder in her stocking. He bowed again and left; she did not even notice his departure.

She said in a dull, choked voice, "Please, I must go home. I feel dreadful. I can't do the money. I'm sorry, but I just can't. Oh, God," said Mrs. Bridgwater, the sobs rising chokingly in her throat. "Oh, God, I can't stand it, I can't stand it."

Mr. Latimer and Miss Holmes both jumped up, but, weeping frantically, she waved a blind hand at them. "No! Leave me alone. For God's sake, leave me alone. I can't stand any more, I tell you." And with this, she stumbled to her feet and ran from the room.

Mr. Latimer and Miss Holmes looked at each other. He passed a hand across his forehead. "After all," he said, "she's a very highly-strung woman. It's to be expected that she should be upset."

"As I," said Miss Holmes, "am unfortunately not in the least highly strung, I am expected, no doubt, to do her pay packets. Oh, well. I'll send one of the girls along for them." She lifted the receiver. "General office, please. Is that you, Greta? Go along to Mrs. Bridgwater's room, will you, and bring down the money. What? You silly girl! All right. Maureen can go with you." Then she sighed. "There's going to be a lot more of this. Greta won't go alone. I suppose she imagines the murderer is lurking behind the door for her." She shivered suddenly. "Mr. Latimer. Who do you think did it?"

"I haven't the faintest idea," said Mr. Latimer.

Mrs. Bridgwater had stopped crying, and was tidying and rearranging herself. She powdered her face very carefully and, after painting on her lipstick, rubbed a little of it into her cheeks. She did not normally use rouge, for she had the thick, magnolia skin that does not need it, but she could not go home with this appalling pallor. She brushed her skirt meticulously, tucked in her blouse, looked at the ladder in her stocking, and went suddenly white again, so that she had to sit down and light another cigarette. When she had recovered herself, she unfastened the bun of flaxen hair and fumbled in her bag for her comb.

"Shall I take you to the Tube, Mona?" said Mark's voice at the door. He was watching her with a look of desperation that might once have moved her very much. But she only glanced at him out of the corner of her eyes, and went on combing her hair. She said in a brisk, bright voice, "Oh no, thank you. I shall be quite all right."

"I should like to," said Mark, coming fully into the room and shutting the door behind him.

Mrs. Bridgwater remembered what had passed between

her and Henry. She remembered other things, too, but the memory of Mark and the times when she had thought of nothing but Mark, were fiercely blotted from her mind. "No," she said, and her eyes dilated a little, her mouth set in a thin line.

He came a little nearer. There was an incredulous anger in his eyes. "Why not?" he said. "If you are so afraid of scandal, you must surely see that there is nothing very remarkable in my escorting you to the station. It is done every day. And you have had a shock."

"I have had——?"

"Well, murder is, shall we say, a little—a little startling. So why may I not escort you? It will be reckoned as a simple act of courtesy."

"Mr. Allan——" she began, her voice as hard as her eyes, and her eyes as hard as stones.

"Good God!" he said. She might advisably have noticed his tone and expression, but she was deliberately looking past him.

But her voice did falter a little. "Mark," she said, "this has got to stop. I—I didn't tell you, but I had the most fearful row with Henry last night. He accused me of being unfaithful—*me!* He just wouldn't believe I was innocent."

To this Mark said nothing. Perhaps for the first time he saw how little he had known his obsession. But he remained quite silent.

"He threatened to divorce me. I had to swear I'd never see you again. I couldn't be divorced. I couldn't face the neighbours," said Mrs. Bridgwater, and, as she spoke, her fingers were neatly fastening up her hair. "And of course my two darling little boys—— It's no good, Mark. This had to end some time, and it might as well be now. We'll always be good friends, I'm sure. But I mean, it can't go on, can it? There's no future in it for either of us, and, anyway, you—— I mean, well, you can't really love me all that much, or you'd be the first to see that it's really got to finish. Mark, please, you must be sensible."

"So you return to 'Dunroamin'," said Mark. The pulse was throbbing in his forehead.

" 'Dunroamin'? What are you talking about? I don't call my house such an absurd name. You are a silly boy. Well, I must go now. It's been such an awful day, and my nerves are quite shattered."

She stood up, Brunhilde to the life, blonde, statuesque, her beautiful face curving in a smile of the brightest gentility, the magnificent body very upright, hands folded across her black handbag. She said in a high, gay voice, "Bye-bye, Mark. See you tomorrow." The smile grew a little fixed. "The police will be there, won't they? Oh, well. We have clear consciences, after all—— *Mark!*——"

The Valkyrie turned into a spitting harridan. She writhed and struggled in Mark's encompassing arms, dropping her handbag as she did so. She screeched out, in the accent of her childhood, "Let me go at once, you dirty beast! I said it was the end, didn't I? Let me go, you filthy swine."

He had pinioned her arms to her sides. He began to kiss her, while she moved her head frenziedly from side to side, trying to avoid him. She was hysterical with rage. She howled at him, "I tried to let you off lightly. I didn't want to hurt you. Let me *go*. But now you can have it, I'm just about fed up with you, and your tantrums and your dirty pawings about. Keep your hands to yourself, can't you? You bore me. You bore me to death, you make me sick, sick, I tell you. You always have done. Now will you let me go, *Mister* Allan?"

He released her so suddenly that she nearly fell down. There was a streak of lipstick across his mouth. But she recovered her balance, and raising her hand, dealt him a resounding slap across both cheeks. "There," she said, her breast heaving. "There. That's what I think of you."

He did not move. He only stared. His light eyes had grown wide and opaque. As she looked at him, her face began to pucker up. A look of unadulterated fear came upon her, and she half raised her hand again, not to deliver a blow, but as if to ward one off. Then with a gasp, she snatched up her handbag and fled.

He listened to her running down the stairs. He raised his head, and his hands, too; the fingers were clenching and unclenching. There was such wild anger in him that it seemed as if his head would burst.

At last he went back to his own room.

The staff of I.L.D.A. assembled in the Committee Room at half-past one. Mr. Ridley stood on the platform, facing them. He looked ghastly. He seemed to have aged by a dozen years. Nothing in his academic life had prepared him for so violent and sordid a disaster. He was a classical scholar; he had spent his existence among books. But now Mrs. Warren's body lay upstairs in the Russian Union Catalogue room, and he was becoming a trembling old man, sick, disgusted, defeated.

They all fixed their eyes on him. The girls crept together, with Barbara in their midst. Only Mrs. Bridgwater was not there, and Miss Holmes, now sitting in her room, doggedly working out the P.A.Y.E. for the thirty members of I.L.D.A. staff. The men stood at the back. Mr. Rills still gave the impression of some monumental exultation. Mark Allan looked as if he were in a white temper; there was a mark across one cheek, which he touched from time to time. Mr. Dodds sat there, gazing at the ground. Young Mr. Wilson, who appeared to be growing his beard again, was watching with fascinated interest. Only Mr. Latimer sat in the front; he glanced briefly at Mr. Ridley, then away again.

"I need not tell you," began Mr. Ridley in a firmer tone than might have been expected of him, "how profoundly shocked I am—we all are—by this terrible tragedy. Not only have we lost a most valued member of the staff, but the circumstances in which she has—died, are unbelievable and appalling."

He paused, and the pause was filled by convulsive sobbing from Greta, who had detested Mrs. Warren as much as any, but whose simple heart was wrung by the stark tragedy of Mr. Ridley's expression. The other girls began to cry in sympathy; only Barbara remained dry-eyed, filled with horror and fear.

Mr. Ridley continued, "I am sure, however, that Mrs. Warren would have been the first to understand that work in I.L.D.A. must go on."

Barbara at this moment was suddenly filled with an almost irrepressible urge to see how Mark was taking this. But she would not turn round, and she dug her nails into the palms of her hands to prevent herself from doing so.

"I am proposing," went on Mr. Ridley, "to close the office for to-day. With the best will in the world, I do not think that any of us could possibly concentrate on work. In a few moments, then, you will all go home. But I fear you must all come in to-morrow, and it may be necessary for you to stay the entire day. Detective-Sergeant Robins from Scotland Yard will be down to put a few questions to us." He smiled faintly. "I am sure there is no reason for you to be afraid. But you will understand that inquiries have to be made, and I should like to feel that all of you will co-operate to the best of his or her ability. I understand the—the inquest will be held on Thursday, but naturally, only a few members of the staff will have to attend, and the rest of us will go on working, however grieved and shocked we may be. There are just two more things. I should like to have your assurance that you will not gossip about to-day's dreadful occurrence. I am sure you will not. I have always congratulated myself on having a most loyal and dependable staff. And finally, I am sure you would like me to say, in the name of us all, how grieved and sorry we are at the death of a dear friend."

('I will not look round,' thought Barbara, 'I will *not*.') "You will perhaps all wish to contribute to a wreath, but this Miss Holmes has kindly agreed to see to, and the matter will be more fully discussed later."

Mrs. Warren's body was at this moment being carried down the back stairs on a stretcher, to her lodging in the mortuary. Mr. Latimer had arranged that this should be done during the meeting. He alone knew what was happening, and he moved his shoulders uncomfortably.

Mr. Ridley, sick at heart, could think of nothing more to say. He made his staff a little bow, and said, "That is all. Thank you. I shall expect you here to-morrow."

"Very nicely put," said Mr. Dodds, "if unfortunately ironic. I wish Mr. Latimer could be persuaded to give some decision with regard to the *Revue de Métaphysique et Moral*. It is preposterous to keep Liverpool University waiting in this manner. What do you think, Allan?"

"I have given up thinking altogether," said Mark.

"What a bloody lot of tommy-rot," said Mr. Rills. "A dear friend! God's truth! It's the best news we've had for years."

"I think," said Mr. Dodds, regarding him thoughtfully, "that, if I were you, young man, I should curb my natural exuberance until the inquiries are over. What you say may be frank and natural, but the police may find it open to misconstruction."

Mr. Rills gave him a sullen, rather frightened look and fell silent.

Mr. Wilson, who looked a little ridiculous, for the beard was at the sprouting stage and had not yet achieved its full messianic beauty, cried out enthusiastically, "What did I tell you? The poor old girl knew too much. After all, what better place could there be for receiving drugs? We get parcels from all over the world. I know I'm right. But I shan't tell the police till I'm certain." He grinned disarmingly at Mr.

Dodds. "The Wilson Detective Agency, that's me, sir." He remembered and composed his features. "Poor old lady. It was a rotten way to die."

Mark Allan said, "And how, my dear Sherlock, do you imagine the drugs are concealed? After all, we look through the books before we send them out, you know."

"I didn't say it was *books*," said Mr. Wilson, then, "I'm not going to say another word."

"I wish I could believe that was true," said Mr. Dodds.

Barbara came wearily down the stairs. She could not bear to use the lift. As she came to the ground floor hallway, she saw that Mark Allan was leaning against the window-sill. He turned his head and gave her an ironic little half-smile.

"May I solicit you, Barbara?" he said.

She cried out almost hysterically, "You're going to be angry with me, and I can't stand it."

"No," he said. "Why should I be angry with you? I was going to ask you if you'd come and have a drink with me."

She hesitated. It struck her that she wanted a drink more than anything else in the world. She said, "All right. I would like to, very much. But you mustn't be rude to me or shout at me, because if you do, I shall burst into tears and shame you before everyone. I have had more than I can stand."

"That I can believe," he said. "Oddly enough, I've had rather more than I can stand, too. In any case, I am surely not as bad as all that. But I promise to be civil. Shall we go?"

When they had settled themselves at the small round table, she said, "I was very rude to you. I do apologise. I expect Greta can be pretty trying. And it was nice of you to give her the chocolates. I think—oh, it doesn't matter. I couldn't bear to quarrel with anyone. It's all been so unbelievably beastly."

"Did you know," said Mark abruptly, "that Mona has thrown me over in the grand manner, and returned to Henry and respectability. She smacked my face. As you can probably see. I may or may not have deserved it, but none the less it is the first time such a thing has happened to me."

Barbara stared at him, horrified. The marks on his cheeks were quite plain.

"Yes," he said, "I shall not forget or forgive in a hurry. However, as your friend, Charles Fox, said on his death-bed, 'It don't signify.' Once Henry has calmed down again, she will find herself another young man, and so *ad infinitum*.

But I think she will choose someone of a rather more manageable disposition. Do you find her beautiful?"

"She's magnificent. Like some Norse goddess."

"Yes," he said. "Yes. A fine fool I've been, haven't I, to fall for flaxen hair, and a body like the Venus de Milo, complete with arms? Have another drink."

"No, thank you." She looked up at him unhappily. "Perhaps you'd rather I didn't say this, but I'm truly sorry. And to have said what I did—— Anyone would be bad-tempered after that. I know you never forgive, but you must make an exception in this case."

His eyes suddenly focused full on her. "Oh, I forgive you," he said. "Why not? I like you. You are honest. It's a quality that I am beginning to appreciate. Would you like me to take you home?"

"Oh, don't bother, please. I feel quite all right, now I've had a drink."

"I suppose your young man wouldn't like it?"

"Charles? Oh, he wouldn't mind. Only I'm so tired, and I feel I might cry again, so I'd better be on my own. I don't suppose the murderer will walk beside me."

"No," he agreed, "I don't suppose he will. In any case, I don't imagine murderers kill indiscriminately. It is, after all, only a matter of expediency."

"Murder can never be necessary!"

"Do you think so? I hope you will never have cause to change your mind. And so to-morrow we shall be interrogated. It will be like old times. Only I don't suppose the English police employ the methods of the Gestapo. I hope not, at least. Are you contributing to the wreath?"

The colour crept into her white cheeks. "I—I suppose so. I know it's dreadfully hypocritical. But what can I do? You see," she added in faint defiance, "I am very conventional."

"I can see that," he said. "You're a nice girl, after all. You look so angry! Why not? There must be some nice girls in the world. But I see I had better go before we quarrel again. If we are still on speaking terms to-morrow, after shopping each other to the best of our ability, I should like to take you out to lunch. Will you risk it?"

"Thank you. Yes. I—I suppose you are not contributing a penny?"

"I?" He began to laugh. "My dear, I'll contribute a quid, if need be, and with the greatest pleasure in the world. Nothing could satisfy me more. In fact, I shall make a point of heading the subscription list."

Charles said that evening, "My poor darling. You must have had a shocking time. You must have been desperate for a drink."

"No," said Barbara, "I just wanted to get home."

NEXT morning, the staff of I.L.D.A., including the murderer, was once again assembled in the Committee Room.

Sergeant Robins, who was a kindly man, with sons and a daughter of his own, saw the girls first, collectively. He did not think there was much they could tell him, and he did not believe they could have conceivably committed the murder. His idea was to put them out of their misery; he found instead that they were wildly excited and only too anxious to tell him what they knew.

It was Greta who succeeded in being the star. She mentioned vaguely that she had been in Mr. Allan's room round about eleven o'clock. The sergeant thought she would have left the matter at that, but the others did not permit this, and he was given a full account of Mr. Allan, white with temper, using the most shocking words, and then coming down afterwards to console his victim with a box of chocolates. "His hands and wrists were dripping wet," said Greta, turning her large dark eyes on the sergeant, "simply dripping." She added simply, "I hope he didn't catch cold."

There were a few other things. Mrs. Bridgwater had been heard crying. Mrs. Warren was an old bag. And then Greta, from whom this remark inevitably came, clapped her hand over her mouth, and cried, "I say, I shouldn't have said that, should I?" And poor Miss Smith, who found the body, "She's ever so nice," said Greta, "and I think it was a shame——" But Mr. Allan was ever so kind, and had picked her up in his arms. At this point she broke out giggling, and the sergeant, eyeing her in a faint irritation, began to wonder who this Mr. Allan was, who seemed to act so strangely, and who had such an evident effect on the female staff.

Mr. Latimer enlightened him, in a long conversation held before the interviewing started. "Allan," he said, "is a brilliant fellow in his own way, but very neurotic, very neurotic. He had a bad time during the war, you know, and it's made his temper uncertain." He enlarged a little on the others, under the sergeant's persuasion. "Mr. Rills," he said, "works in our Reference Room, and young Mr. Wilson—a nice boy— is studying to be a librarian, and works with him. Mrs. Bridgwater is our Finance Officer, a most competent woman in many ways."

The sergeant had not forgotten the detail about her crying. "In many ways?" he repeated.

"Well," said Mr. Latimer, "she's a woman, after all. But remarkably good at figures. I believe she writes, too. Mr. Dodds, who has been with us for a long time, deals with periodicals. Something of an eccentric, but we value him the more for that. Miss Holmes——" He gave a résumé of the staff, adding, "Oh, and little Miss Smith. Works in the Location Department. Writes novels, but preserves a deadly secrecy about them. Romantic stuff, I imagine. A nice girl. I am only sorry she should have made the dreadful discovery."

"I should like you to tell me," said Sergeant Robins, "anything out of the ordinary which has happened lately. Just anything which does not quite fit into the routine. It may seem trivial to you, but it might after all have some bearing on this matter."

Mr. Latimer hesitated. The sergeant sighed. Somewhere within that hesitation would lie, perhaps, an all-important fact, and he would be prepared to swear that that would be the one fact that Mr. Latimer would choose to keep to himself. Mr. Latimer was, indeed, doing a certain amount of sorting out. He could not help but know that there was something going on between Allan and Mrs. Bridgwater, but he was sure this was irrelevant, and he disliked scandal.

"Actually," he said at last, "there is one thing. I don't suppose it has the faintest bearing, but you might as well know it. We have some seven thousand books on these premises, and some of them are very valuable. It is obviously impossible to keep much check on them, but we have just found out that a number of them have been disappearing at regular intervals. I suppose we might never have discovered it, but Mr. Ridley —our Chief Librarian—was checking a collection left to us some time ago. (We are donated private collections from time to time.) He found that a number of first editions were gone, including a most rare edition of Elizabethan plays. Well, of course, after that, we were compelled to make a thorough investigation. I do not yet know how much is missing, but I am afraid a great deal is."

"And have any members of your staff arrived since these thefts started, sir?"

"It's hard to say," replied Mr. Latimer, "but, as far as we can gather, this has been going on for some eighteen months. All the present staff would have been there then, with the exception of some of the junior typists, and young Jack Wilson, who came six months ago. I suppose," he added with a weary smile, "we are all suspects. It is very unpleasant. The person responsible must have made quite a lot of money on it; one assumes that he or she sold the books. You see, the stacks are open to all the staff, and there is nothing in the world to stop someone going down and carrying away a parcel of books. After all, all of us here carry books around with us at some time or another, it's part of our job. Mr. Ridley is very distressed. The only consolation is that the thefts seem to have stopped."

"When did they stop, sir?"

"Oh, I can't say, exactly. The last book we noticed as missing—an early edition of *Mandeville's Travels*—would be about—let me see now—ten days ago. Of course, as I said, it's quite impossible to check. One cannot count seven thousand volumes every week. We only noticed this because we had a request for that particular edition. And it is, of course, within the bounds of possibility that it has been genuinely borrowed by a member of the staff, who omitted to write out the proper form for it. That, I'm afraid, is something we are all guilty of. But you cannot believe Mrs. Warren was murdered for that. And I'm certain she never stole anything in her life. A most conscientious and honest person. It's dreadful to think she should have died so tragically."

During this conversation, Barbara was sitting next to the girls, who were all discussing their interview. She still felt exhausted. Charles, who had, for once, not pursued the matter of a story for his paper, had said, later in the evening, "Would you not like me to stay?" He added calmly, "It will be quite all right, you know. Only I don't think you ought to be by yourself."

"Of course it will be all right," replied Barbara, a little hysterically, "but my neighbours won't think it all right at all. You'd better go, darling. I don't really want anyone here. I'm so tired. I shall fall asleep the moment I get into bed."

"Well, I'll call for you to-morrow," he said, and with that he left her.

But she did not sleep. With the dark the horrors came, too. She saw again that dead hand creeping out of the sack, to slide with a little thud to the floor. And when at last, in the small hours of the morning, sleep came of a kind, it brought with it an odd tangle of memories, such as Mr. Wilson's beard, Mrs. Warren's laugh, a box of chocolates, and Mrs. Bridgwater's cut hand. She awoke, thankful for the day, sick, shivering; drank hot coffee, and took a taxi to the office, because her legs would hardly bear her.

She saw that the girls were enjoying it all very much. She wished she could enjoy it, too. And then she remembered suddenly and inappropriately that Charles was calling for her, and that Mark was taking her out to lunch. They would presumably meet on I.L.D.A.'s doorstep. But she could not take this very seriously. Charles, thank God, was not the dramatic kind, and possibly they could all go out together, if they could fight their way through the people gathered outside.

The Press was there in full force. At least, she assumed it was the Press; a dozen of them were arguing quite vainly with the policemen on duty at the door. There was also a small crowd of sightseers, mostly women with their children, who pointed out to each other the room where the murder had been committed; Mrs. Warren, it appeared, had been killed on every floor.

She must, of course, have been killed on the fourth floor, so conveniently near the packing-room. No one could carry the body upstairs at eleven in the morning. The fourth floor was inhabited by Mr. Dodds, Mr. Purley and Mrs. Bridgwater, and, of course, Mark Allan. She disliked her own thoughts. She looked round her again. Mrs. Bridgwater and Mark Allan had not yet arrived. Mr. Latimer, she saw, looked very grim, and Miss Holmes seemed to be lost in a world of departmental depression; she was probably brooding on inadequate temporaries. Mr. Rills, standing at the back, slouched against the wall, seemed to have lost his good spirits. He looked very unhappy, and seemed unable to keep still; he fidgeted constantly from one foot to the other, chewing at his lower lip, his hands drumming against his thighs. Mr. Wilson, on the other hand, looked as if this were the gala day of his life. He was reading his newspaper, the manly pipe that he affected clenched between his jaws. The beard was still rather foolish and inadequate. He seemed delighted with the headlines, which Barbara had already seen at breakfast, for it was Charles's paper. She had not been delighted, and what had shocked and sickened her was the portrait of a much younger Mrs. Warren smiling up at her—(inset, Mrs. Emma Warren.) She had never known her name was Emma. How could they have got the photo at such short notice? There was the familiar look of smiling glee on her; one could almost hear the bubble of giggling laughter.

"It's all most frightfully interesting," said Mr. Wilson to Barbara; he was sitting just behind her. "She must have been quite a clever woman, you know. Actually, for a typist, she was very well read." Then he blushed. "I say, I'm so sorry. I didn't mean to hurt your feelings."

"Do you do crossword puzzles, Wilson?" demanded Mr. Dodds, who had just appeared on Barbara's right-hand side.

"No, sir," said Mr. Wilson, instinctively responding to the tone as he had done to his headmaster's, when he was at school, not so long ago.

"Then do one now," said Mr. Dodds firmly, "and when you get back to the Reference Room, look up the definition of suicide in the Oxford dictionary. And brood on it." He looked at Barbara, who began to laugh.

"Don't be cross with him," she said, smiling at Mr. Wilson, to reassure him.

"Well, well," said Mr. Dodds, "to think that I shall now be questioned by the C.I.D. I should have liked to have been interrogated by a detective inspector, but I believe we have to make do with a mere sergeant. Tell me, how is your book going? Has your hero spitted any more of his enemies? And have you decided on the lady's name? I trust you are inserting one of those disguised scenes of sadism; my wife is never satisfied unless the hero beats the heroine at least once. And yet I am sure she would never forgive me if I did it. I may say, I have never tried."

"You, yourself, have confessed to a passion for maniacs," said Barbara crossly, for she took this as a slur upon her sex.

"Ah," said Mr. Dodds, "for all you know, I may shortly be led away with gyves upon my wrists. You look tired. I hope this means you have been writing late. I take a great interest in your literary career, you know."

"Mr. Dodds!" said Barbara, "I don't know what you think of me, but I do have some human feelings, after all. If you imagine that after what has happened, I could go home and write nonsense——"

"Your hero could be accused of murder," said Mr. Dodds insinuatingly.

She glared at him; her mouth began to tremble, despite herself.

"—Which, of course, he didn't do. But he might think he had done it. In a duel, perhaps. You should always use up your material. It is the supreme advantage of the writer that he can profit by his folly, humiliation or unhappy love. In any case," added Mr. Dodds, "you specialise in soldiers of fortune, do you not?—and I think in the circumstances you should enlarge on his character. He will be bad-tempered, of course, with his sword always half out, over-emotional, over-susceptible to all matters of the senses. A dangerous man, with no scruples. No scruples at all, Miss Smith. None, none, none. How well I see him——" His eyes were no longer on Barbara. She turned her head to follow the direction of his gaze.

Mark Allan had just come in. He stood for a moment by the door. Barbara saw his face with a sudden, dispassionate clarity. It was magnificently handsome, and then she became aware again of that strange vitality and magnetism, found her colour rising and grew, for some reason that she did not understand, most dreadfully afraid. She met Mr. Dodds's eyes; he surveyed her steadily, then almost imperceptibly shook his head.

She would not look any more. She would not think of him. She would think of Mr. Andrews, an ill-tempered man, over-emotional, and with no scruples at all. But what nonsense it all was. All decent people had scruples.

Then she saw that Mrs. Bridgwater had arrived.

She looked quite composed, though the light blue eyes fluttered, and there was a colour in her cheeks that was not natural. She was, however, her well-groomed self, with skirt brushed, a fresh blouse, unladdered stockings. She gave Barbara a gay little wave, then, after a moment's hesitation, sat beside Mr. Wilson, who started, then flushed with pleasure.

She said in a gentle, deprecatory voice, "You don't mind if I sit here, do you?"

Mr. Wilson, blushing to his very eyes, said that he did not. He wondered if Mrs. Bridgwater would like a cigarette.

She turned her gaze full on him. "I should love one," she said. "How thoughtful you are. I think the quality I admire most in men is chivalry. I think it should be taught from earliest childhood. I have two little boys of my own, you know."

(They were twelve and fourteen, but, from the way she

spoke, Mr. Wilson at once visualised them as chubby things in rompers.)

"I do try to make them considerate. I hope you don't mind my saying this, Jack—I may call you Jack, mayn't I? How sweet of you—but I've always noticed how charming your manners are. I do notice these things, you know. And charm and good breeding——"

"Guns poised for action, Mona?" said Mark, coming across the room. He sat down calmly on her other side.

Barbara's heart constricted with jealousy. He might have sat near her. Then she saw the look on him; his face was alive with devilment, the luminous eyes snapping with cruel amusement. She saw also that Mrs. Bridgwater's look of understanding sweetness had been replaced by something less seductive; beneath the rouge an angry red was creeping into her cheeks.

"I see, my dear," said Mark in a voice that carried, "that you have resumed your scalp-hunting. The Dyaks, so I understand, used to hunt for heads until the kindly anthropologist persuaded them it would be better to hunt for wild swine. You seem to have reversed the process. But of course you are naturally superior to the rest of human kind. Most of us, when we have had a bad egg for breakfast, do not care to try another, for at least some time. But you are obviously of a stronger nature, and you at once select for yourself a fresh egg, soft and lightly boiled. I hope it agrees with you better than the first one did."

Mrs. Bridgwater had little armour against this kind of thing, and she was furious that Mr. Wilson should be the audience. She began to lose her temper. She said in a voice grown sharp and refined, "Will you please go and sit somewhere else?"

"Why?" said Mark, making no attempt to move. "I enjoy sitting beside you, Mona. I like watching you in action. Just go on as if I were not here. Mr. Wilson is waiting, I'm sure. In a moment, Wilson, she will tell you how charming and understanding you are—if she has not already done so— bestow on you a smile fit to melt your marrow, smoke all your cigarettes, agree after maidenly hesitation to accept a drink from you, then, when she has spent all your salary, she will say that really you're a naughty boy to be so extravagant, pat your hand—this is only the first stage, mind you, so don't lose heart—and not see you again till next Friday."

'Really,' thought Barbara, who heard all this, as did every-

one else, 'no one in any age could call him a gentleman.'
She turned away, pretending she was not listening, but as the
conversation was being carried on directly behind her, she
naturally heard every word.

Mrs. Bridgwater was scarlet with fury. She said in a trembling voice, "Will you please go away? If you stay here a
moment longer——"

"And what will you do?" said Mark, lounging back against
his chair, a cigarette dangling from the corner of his mouth,
his mocking eyes fixed on her. "Do you know, Wilson, she
slapped my face yesterday? You had perhaps no idea that
such things took place in a library. But they do, I assure
you. I believe she wants to do it again. But I shouldn't
really, Mona, if I were you."

Poor Mr. Wilson had never in his nineteen years come up
against a parallel situation, and his beard was not far enough
advanced to hide his acute embarrassment. He thought,
'They are being so *vulgar*.' It distressed him very much, but
there was no denying that anger did not improve Mrs. Bridgwater's appearance. He was a little alarmed and, even as he
dived in to her rescue, he moved away; their arms had been
touching.

"I expect," he said, in his uneasy, youthful voice, "that
Mrs. Bridgwater was dreadfully upset." He flushed as he met
Mr. Allan's gaze. He was one of the few who were on
reasonably good terms with him, for he was prone to hero-
worship, but he did not care much for taking on such an
opponent. However, he had committed himself now, and he
added, "I'm sure we are all in a state. And of course for a
woman, it's much harder."

"Don't you believe it, Wilson," said Mark. "Women are
as tough as nails."

"Perhaps the women you know are," said Mr. Wilson
defiantly, "but after all, Mrs. Bridgwater is an artist."

"You're very sweet, Jack," said the lady, and, forgetting
Mark's words, patted his hand, at which Mr. Wilson, who
had not forgotten, started and looked alarmed.

Mark said idly, watching this pantomime, "If I were your
father, sir, I'd send you abroad. To India or somewhere remote so that you'd come back either dead or immune to the
attacks of suburban pussy-bitches."

Mrs. Bridgwater rose to her feet. "I am not staying
here——"

"To be insulted?" said Mark, smiling at her.

She moved away. Even in her anger she moved with

beauty, and both Mr. Wilson and Mark watched her, the one in great unhappiness, the other with a momentary gleam of pure anger.

"I think you're fearfully rude," said Mr. Wilson, "and, anyway, I'm not going to India. I don't like wogs, for one thing."

"You don't like *what?*"

"Well, natives, then. I like Kipling, you see," said Mr. Wilson, and, as he was now on firmer ground, spoke with great enthusiasm. "I think he's greatly underrated. Like Newbolt. I think they're fine, and I can't understand why people pretend to prefer these modern johnnies; I bet they couldn't produce anything half so good." Out of the corner of his eye he still watched Mona Bridgwater. He went on speaking with great rapidity, hardly aware of what he was saying. "I mean to say—that thing, you know, 'The colonel's jammed and the gatling's dead, The sand of the desert is sodden red'—marvellous." He added sadly, "I don't think I've got it quite right."

"Really, Wilson," said Mr. Rills, who had been listening to this with an acid smile, "such language. What will mamma say?"

Mr. Wilson flushed crimson again. He did not quite follow this, but he knew it was something indecent, and he was a gentle boy who never used bad language.

"Shut up, Rills," said Mark unexpectedly. "Why don't you take up moth-hunting? You spend your life jabbing pins through people."

"Oh, I don't mind," said Mr. Wilson, restored by this unforeseen alliance. "I expect he's nothing better to do. One needs to occupy one's mind."

"If you have a mind to occupy," said Mr. Rills, looking at Mark as if he wished the pin were a javelin, and that in his hand.

"Now I," said Mr. Wilson, watching Mrs. Bridgwater sit down beside Barbara, "am always busy. This drug thing— you know, I'm really on to something."

Various people turned to stare at him. But Mr. Wilson, flattered by Mark's rallying to his defence, and a little above himself with one thing and another, went on excitedly, "Mind you, I'm not telling you anything. But I'm sure I.L.D.A. is one of their depositories, or whatever you call it, and I believe—I believe I know how it's done. I'm not sure, of course. But I've given a lot of thought to it. Poor Mrs. Warren must have found something out."

"Don't you think," said Mr. Dodds, in a voice as dry as the autumn leaves, "that you might take warning by her example? Perhaps Mrs. Warren did find something out. We'll grant you your premise, if you wish. But you should ask yourself further where she is now. A mortuary is a fine and private place. I shouldn't go there, if I were you. As a destination, it is something of a dead end."

"Oh, nonsense!" cried Mr. Wilson. "I can look after myself, can't I? I'm a man, after all. No one's putting me in a sack. You can't believe that if I find out about such a disgusting racket, I wouldn't do my duty——"

"Nobody minds your doing your duty," said Mr. Dodds, "if only you wouldn't talk about it so much."

"It's a horrid business," continued Mr. Wilson, very excited. "Why, it's worse than—than murder. People who take drugs go mad. There was a play on the wireless about it. I think dope-pedlars should be flogged. Not," he added, "that I believe in corporal punishment."

Mark Allan, who was watching him, began to laugh. He clapped the boy on the shoulder. The light, bright eyes stared derisively into the young, flushed face. "All right, Jack," he said, "all right. When you discover this infamous racketeer, you shall have the flogging of him, and not believe in corporal punishment while you administer it. What clues have you now? We will serve as your Dr. Watsons."

Mr. Wilson opened his mouth to speak, when Mr. Dodds, with one of his exasperating irrelevancies, said, "I wish I could feel that some work is going to be done next week. When I mention the word, such glances are cast at me as to make me feel that I have committed the worst breach of taste imaginable. I did, however, have the effrontery to glance at my post this morning, and I see that *Métaphysique et Moral* has still not been supplied."

"Ah, to hell with metaphysics and morals," said Mark. "I have sent out for your damned microfilm, sir. I wrote to Paris last night, just before we went home. Are you satisfied now?"

"Despite your bad manners, Allan," said Mr. Dodds gravely, "I have always found you a most conscientious worker."

Mark smiled and bowed to him.

"Big Brother is about to speak," said Mr. Rills.

Mr. Ridley, who deserved such an appellation less than most, had risen to his feet. He looked as if he had not slept at all. He said, "Thank you all for coming. We have with us Detective-Sergeant Robins and Police-Detective-Constable Hall, from Scotland Yard. Mr. Latimer has kindly agreed to loan his office for the interviews. I am sure you will give Sergeant Robins all the help in your power."

Barbara saw suddenly that Mr. Rills looked as if he were on the verge of collapse. She saw, too, that Mark's eyes were fixed on Mr. Rills's face, which had grown a greenish-white. She was so intent on this, and wondering if she should offer Mr. Rills a cigarette or a glass of water that Mr. Ridley's next words made her jump and go pale herself.

"I think, Miss Smith," said Mr. Ridley, "that the sergeant would like to see you now." He gave her a slow, encouraging, though unhappy, smile. "The girls will tell you that it is not a very terrifying experience. The Yard has no great name for brutality."

There was a faint laugh at this, but Barbara, rising to her feet, found panic flooding over her. The feeling was familiar; after an instant's reflection, she realised that this was how she had felt when she had taken her final *viva* at Oxford.

"Your hero," said Mr. Dodds, "would march in, hand on hilt. And after all, the penal code was much fiercer then."

Mark had switched his eyes to her. He was whistling between his teeth some rhythmic phrase that went, 'Pom-pom-pom-pom.' She saw his amusement and grew angry. She walked out, her head held high.

They had been kind to her. Only they were all so old, and they all looked as if they'd taken Firsts. You could not imagine them as undergraduates, careering down the High, being progged, or taking young women on the river. "Well, now, Miss Smith. Sit down. Let me see——" A rustle of papers. "Ye-es——" A long pause. "Tell me, Miss Smith, what would you say was the main influence——"

"Good-morning, Miss Smith," said the sergeant, seeing a small, pale young woman with large eyes and untidy dark hair. "Sit down, won't you?"

A faint laugh surged up in Barbara's throat. Would he ask her about the Lake poets whom she did not like, or the Metaphysicals, whom she practically knew by heart? Then she looked fully at Sergeant Robins, and was comforted. He was very ordinary, dressed in a plain grey suit; he looked kind and not at all formidable. She thought he would be a good husband and father, keep a wire-haired fox-terrier, and play darts at the local. The young police constable—what was his name? Hall—watched her in a pleasantly impersonal manner and, when she turned her eyes on him, smiled.

Sergeant Robins said, "You are the young lady who found the body, aren't you?"

"Yes."

"It must have been a nasty shock for you."

"Yes." He must have seen her tremble, for he said kindly, "You must try not to brood on it. Try to look on it as something you've read in a detective story. Do you read detective stories?"

"Yes."

"So do I. Very absorbing. Now. Would you tell me just what happened?"

Barbara passed her tongue over her lips. "I was coming down in the lift—for lunch——"

"From what floor, miss?"

"The third. We work there. It's the Location Department."

"And Mrs. Warren worked with you?"

"Yes."

"So you were going down to lunch? And Mr.—Mr. Purley, I believe, was in the lift with you?"

"Yes." She told him how she had tripped against the sack. "I'm afraid I don't quite know what happened after that. I—I fainted. It was very silly of me, but it was the hand, you see——"

"The hand?"

She explained, and somehow in the telling, found that the horror was slipping away. "And Mr.—Mr. Allan carried me into my room."

"Mr. Purley stopped the lift, then?"

"I suppose so. I don't know."

"And Mr. Allan. He deals with your microfilms, doesn't he?"

"Yes."

"He must have been on the third floor, then."

"I don't know. I'd fainted, you see."

"The sack must have been very insecurely tied," said Sergeant Robins reflectively. "If it hadn't fallen open, miss, what would have happened to it?"

"It would have stayed in the basement for the week-end. The books are deposited on Tuesdays and Fridays. We are doing a stock-taking and getting rid of duplicate volumes. The books would have been dispersed among the public libraries, I think."

He asked her a few questions about her work, then he

said, "You were on the fourth floor at eleven o'clock, weren't you, looking for Mrs. Warren? Where did you look?"

"I called in on everybody. Mr. Dodds, Mrs. Bridgwater and Mr. Allan."

"Mrs. Bridgwater," said the sergeant. "She's the lady who does the accounts? I understand she was very upset?"

"I don't—I don't know."

"When you came into her office, Miss Smith, how did you find her? Was she upset about anything then?"

"No. She seemed just as usual." But her flush betrayed her; she had never been able to lie with conviction.

He said, with mild surprise, "One of your young ladies heard her crying."

"Well—she—she's highly strung, you know."

"You mean, she often cries in the office?"

"No! Well, I really don't know. I don't have much to do with her. We are very departmentalised."

"Did she tell you why she was crying? Had she hurt herself in any way, do you think?"

"Well, it might have been her hand. Oh, I don't know," said Barbara, confused and unhappy, for the sergeant's questions, though delivered so quietly, followed one another without a pause.

"What was the matter with her hand?"

"She'd cut it. Opening a tin of tongue for her husband's breakfast."

"My wife," said the sergeant, "never gives me tongue for breakfast. I believe there has been some kind of understanding between Mrs. Bridgwater and Mr. Allan?"

Barbara said angrily, "I know nothing about it. It's not my affair."

"Unfortunately in a murder," said Sergeant Robins, "everything becomes everybody's affair." But he did not pursue the subject. He only said, "You went in to see Mr. Allan, didn't you?"

"I did." Her voice had grown stiff, and the sergeant shot one brief look at his colleague.

"And how did you find him?"

"Just as usual. I asked him if he had seen Mrs. Warren, and he said he hadn't."

"In no way upset?"

"No."

"I understand he had been very rude to one of your girls?"

Barbara saw at this point what she might have seen before—that I.L.D.A. must now be as exposed to the public gaze as if the front partition of the building had been blown away. She said coldly, "He is a hot-tempered man, and he overworks. I don't expect he meant to be rude."

"And Mr. Dodds? Nothing noticeable about him?"

"Nothing whatsoever," said Barbara in great relief, happily unaware how changed her tone had become.

"Tell me," said the sergeant. "Mrs. Warren—was she a nice lady? Did you like her?"

Barbara said after a pause, "She was a perfectly horrid woman, and I didn't like her at all. But that doesn't mean I murdered her. I wouldn't murder anyone. But I don't think anybody liked her very much."

"And why was that, miss?"

"She was so inquisitive, always meddling in other people's business, and criticising. She knew everything that was going on."

"She would know all about Mr. Allan and Mrs. Bridgwater then?"

"I don't think there was anything to know," said Barbara as composedly as she could.

"Did she give you the impression that she had discovered anything of particular importance on the day of her death?"

Barbara considered. "Well, she was always discovering something, you know. She did seem rather excited. Happy and—and laughing to herself. We didn't think much of it."

"We?"

"The girls and I. I suppose we just thought she was a bit more unpleasant than usual."

He asked her a few more questions, as to the nature of Mrs. Warren's work, and so on. He did not, to her relief, mention Mark Allan again. But as she was leaving, he said suddenly, "You write novels, don't you, Miss Smith?"

Barbara, at the door, swerved round on him, then laughed. "Do you know that too?" she said. "Yes, Sergeant, I write novels. Romantic, historical ones with heroes you'd want to run in. Soldiers of fortune——" She broke off. She flushed scarlet.

The sergeant, watching her, said agreeably, "Most interesting, I'm sure. You must let me read one."

When she had gone, he said, "I don't suppose there's anything in it. Nice young lady. Doesn't know how to lie, does she? But one can't completely ignore it. I must say, I'm very interested in Mr. Allan. I think we'll see him next. We'll keep Mrs. Bridgwater waiting a little."

The young police constable said in a voice of faint surprise, "I think the young lady's rather struck on Mr. Allan."

"I think the young lady's head over heels in love with Mr. Allan," said the sergeant. "And if he is as I'm beginning to think he is, I hope she's got a young man to shake some sense into her. He doesn't sound the sort of person I'd care to have my daughter running round with."

Mark Allan sauntered in, hands in pockets. He did not look co-operative. He glanced them over as if they were to be interrogated, not he. He saw a stout, grave little man, with neck bulging over his collar, mopping at his face with a vast handkerchief. An ordinary little man.

He whistled softly, 'Pom-pom-pom-*pom*——'

The others had looked ordinary, too, only of course the uniform was impressive.

They had huddled together in attics, cellars, trenches, barns, crouching with their ears to the radio—'Pom-pom-pom-*pom;* pom-pom-pom-*pom*'—tuned in so low that they could scarcely hear it themselves. Sometimes they would twiddle on other stations. They would listen for a moment. Gairmany calling, Gairmany calling. You're defeated. Finished. Your homes are ruined. Your families dead. A thousand bombs will fall on you—— Ah! Turn that—off!—Pom-pom-pom-*pom!*

"You're English, aren't you?"

"Je ne comprends pas."

"You're English, aren't you?"

"Je ne comprends pas."

"Come on, now. We know you're English."

"Je ne comprends pas."

At last it would be in French. *"Who are you?"*

A shrug.

"Who are your friends?"

"I do not know."

"Where are your headquarters?"

"I do not know."

"How many of you are there?"

"I do not know."

They took him away. He came back, presently, with blackened eyes, broken teeth, one useless arm, scarcely able to stand. Then it started again. *"You're English. Who are you? Who are your friends?"*

I do not understand. I do not know.

Pom-pom-pom-*pom*——

Still he'd got even with the b——s. The trouble with those home-made things was that you just didn't know when they'd go off. But the risk had to be taken. *On s'en fout, quoi!* The result had been a little startling. Even the *copains* had been surprised. . . .

"Mr. Allan, sir, isn't it?"

"I do not——" He jerked himself back to the present. "I am. Mark Allan."

"Captain Allan, I believe?"

"No! Certainly not." He shot the sergeant a look of sudden, blazing fury. "I am not a member of the regular army. It is not customary to use one's war-time rank as a straphanger."

The sergeant seemed unperturbed. "Sorry, sir. I had heard of your war record."

"Ah," said Mark, "I suppose you are implying that like thousands of others I have graduated in murder. I assure you that such graduation in civilian life is, like a university degree, which incidentally I also have, a thing best forgotten."

The sergeant said mildly, "I wonder if I might check over a few points with you. We are assuming that the lady was murdered while Mr. Latimer was locked in the toilet. I understand there was something of a commotion."

"When a deputy librarian is locked in the lavatory—I beg your pardon, Sergeant—toilet," said Mark, making the word sound so peculiarly improper that the young constable glanced swiftly at his superior, "a certain commotion is bound to be caused. It didn't interest me. I had my work to do."

"Quite, sir. What were you working at?"

"I was doing my photostats. Any objection?"

"And I believe the young lady came to see you? Miss—Miss Greta——" He checked the name on his papers. "You were very angry with her, I understand."

Mark said bleakly, "I don't like being interrupted. In any case, the girl's a damned fool, and I've no time for fools. I am not aware that I was particularly angry, but if she says so, I must have been."

The sergeant said, "You must have been aware of it, sir, because you brought her down a box of chocolates afterwards."

"So I did."

"To console her?"

"There could hardly be any other motive. I'd no wish to seduce her or poison her, if that's what you're implying."

The sergeant ignored this. He showed no signs of losing his temper. He said, "During this commotion, were you alone on the floor? Apart from the visit of Miss Greta, I mean?"

"I haven't the faintest idea," said Mark shortly. "I've already told you I was working. When I'm working, I don't come out into the corridor to see if anyone else is there. I don't leave my door open, either. But if you want to know if I spoke to Mrs. Warren, why the devil don't you ask me? Anyway, I'll tell you. I did. I can't tell you the time. I don't check these things on a stop-watch. But I saw her all right, and not long before what you call the commotion. The old bitch came into my office and tried a spot of blackmail. I didn't murder her, but it's the purest miracle I didn't. A more poisonous old she-devil never walked this earth, and thank God someone's had the sense to shove her off it, for in the end I probably would have done it myself."

"Blackmail?" repeated the sergeant.

"That is the word."

"What was she blackmailing you on, sir?"

"That's my business."

The sergeant said, after a pause, "Was Mrs. Bridgwater in her room during the disturbance?"

"I do not know," said Mark, looking full at him, the light eyes wide and expressionless.

"It would be of some help," said the sergeant in a slightly different tone, "if you could be more co-operative."

"I am not here to help you. I've already told you, I'm glad she's dead. I do not know who killed her, but, if I did, I'd shake him by the hand."

"Did Mrs. Bridgwater know about Mr. Latimer?"

"You'd better ask Mrs. Bridgwater." His eyes turned to the young constable, and he smiled. *"You* had better ask her."

"And what do you mean by that, sir?"

"Ask Mrs. Bridgwater!"

"Was Mr. Rills on the fourth floor?"

"He was. He acted as messenger."

"So you did come out of your room, sir?"

Mark did not answer for a second. They saw him straighten a little. He was a very tall man, and he dwarfed the sergeant by several inches. He said at last, with that odd smile of his which so transformed his face, "At least you don't use a truncheon. I did not come out while I was working. But after the late Mrs. Warren left me—and she left pretty quickly, I can assure you—I did emerge to make quite sure she was gone. Rills came running up the stairs, a couple of minutes later, I suppose. I don't know where Mrs. Warren went, or if she met Rills. There are two lifts in this building. She may have taken one of them. I neither know nor care. You'd better ask Rills."

"At no time, then, did you notice anyone going into the packing-room, during Mr. Purley's absence downstairs?"

"I was in my room, doing photostats."

"Miss Smith came in to see you later, I believe?"

"As you have just interviewed Miss Smith, I find that question entirely irrelevant."

"We have to check everything, sir," said the sergeant. "Do you know of anyone, apart from yourself, who had a grudge against Mrs. Warren?"

"Apart from the whole library, no. Incidentally, you must speak to our Mr. Wilson. He is full of the most interesting theories."

"We will certainly speak to Mr. Wilson. Thank you, sir. I think that will be all for now." He added, "I dare say the ladies and gentlemen would like to have their lunch. Perhaps you wouldn't mind staying on, afterwards. Thank you. Good-morning."

He turned to Police-Constable Hall. "A most interesting gentleman," he said. "I wonder why every office has its private wolf and its private informer? I am beginning to think we may be taking on a great deal more than we bargained for."

It was half-past twelve. The staff of I.L.D.A. dispersed for lunch.

VI. ERRORS OF OBSERVATION 519.6

DURING this Saturday afternoon—it was hot and sultry, with an occasional distant mutter of thunder—half the staff of I.L.D.A. began to quarrel with the other half, and Barbara, for the first time in her life, quarrelled with Charles.

He was waiting for her, outside the Library. There was no sign of Mark, and this irritated and piqued Barbara very much, so that when Charles asked her if the ordeal had been very bad, she snapped at him.

"You could hardly expect it to be pleasant," she said. "We are not all newspaper men." Then she apologised immediately, for there was really no excuse for such rudeness.

But her temper was still smouldering as they walked towards the pub, especially as it was the same pub where she had sat with Mark. An ominous lump rose in her throat at this memory, and then for the first time she saw with clarity the path that she was treading. A great astonishment and remorse seized her so that she found she could not eat her lunch at all; she sat there, pushing the food around with her fork, and wishing the *tête-à-tête* were over.

She stared at Charles. There was nothing she could say. Dear Charles, I still like you very much, but I have fallen in love with the kind of person you could never equal in a thousand years. Dear Charles, in my heart I am fonder of you than of him, but I am not sick when you are not there, and even sicker when you are, though you are peaceful and good and kind and companionable, and he is none of these things; with him it is like living permanently with a thunderstorm.

She said at last, "Would you please give me a cigarette?"

The thunder crackled in the distance; the heat lightning shuddered about them.

"You haven't eaten your lunch," said Charles.

"It's too hot to eat."

"Why don't you tell me all that happened?" he said. "You know it always makes you feel better."

Suddenly she blazed at him; her emotion was pushing her remorselessly out of control. She cried, "So you want me to tell you all about it, so that it can appear in your beastly paper to-morrow?" Then, "Oh, Charles, I don't mean to be so abominable, I don't, I don't—— But it's all been so disgusting, and I can't bear to think of it, and I can't think of anything else."

He said calmly, "You think you've fallen in love with this fellow Allan, I suppose."

She stared at him, yet the sequence of events had been so unreal that not even this could really surprise her. She said at last, as another person had said a long time ago, "I do not know."

"I don't know, either," said Charles, in the most detestable voice of reason, "but I know you think you have."

"How can you know? I've hardly mentioned him."

"Perhaps that's why. You've mentioned everybody else. But you never told me you had a drink with him."

"You've been spying. Charles, really——"

"No," he said very sadly, "I've not been spying. But you see, I did call for you on Friday. Only I came a few minutes late. I saw you walking off with him. You don't imagine I followed you, surely? I went home. I didn't want to interrupt you. I should have thought nothing more of it, only—only when I said I was sorry not to have been there, you didn't even mention it."

Barbara said, after a pause, "So you tried to trap me. I don't find that pretty. But I'm sorry I didn't tell you. I—I think perhaps we'd better not be engaged any longer." And she began to tug at her ring, which in the way of all rings obdurately refused to budge; the tugging looked preposterous, so she had to stop.

"As punishment," said Charles in a strained voice, "this seems a little harsh. But if that's how you wish it." He looked down at her hands. The fingers of the right hand were still touching the ring. He cried out so loudly that the other lunchers turned to stare, "Oh, to hell with the bloody ring! Take it off with soap, and flog it. Buy yourself some eighteenth-century books with it, or a sword, if you prefer it, to lay between us. But for God's sake, don't be so silly. I don't grudge you the ring. I don't grudge you anything. But I'll say this, for it no longer matters what I say: he's not the right person for you. Perhaps I'm not, either, though you've made do with me well enough, for the past two years. But he's not right. There's something very wrong with him."

He was going to say a great deal more, but he perceived that she was on the verge of tears, and somehow he could not bear her to cry in front of him and everybody. So he broke off short, then, gathering up his pile of books and papers, went to the bar counter without another word, and paid his bill.

Barbara, watching him go, unable to say anything, unable even to say she was sorry, which she was to a degree that threatened to disintegrate her, thought irrelevantly that Mark, in such a situation, would almost certainly have left the bill with her—which would, of course, have served her right.

At this point, the ring, which she was still fiddling with, slipped off her finger.

By two o'clock the staff of I.L.D.A. was reassembled for the second act. Tempers were rising high. Only Mark—normally the most ill-tempered member—and Mr. Wilson were in good humour. Even Mr. Dodds was irritable and when Mr. Wilson, in buoyant good spirits and making a great deal of noise, started talking again about his secret discovery, said fiercely, "For goodness' sake, boy, hold your tongue."

"All right," said Mr. Wilson, aggrieved, "I'm sorry if I bore you, sir. Perhaps," he added more happily, "I may bore you less, later on. In fact, I jolly well think I'll give you the surprise of your life. The more I think of it—— The funny thing is that it's so easy. I suppose the Yard johnnies are always looking for something involved and sinister. And this—— But I won't talk about it any more." And he looked so radiant, so much I would an if I could, that Mr. Dodds longed to box his ears, and said so, adding, "I'd like to lock you up in your room for a week, on bread and water. That'd quieten you."

Mr. Wilson, resenting this insulting emphasis on his youth, was about to reply with spirit, when Mark Allan said, "You know, Jack—I may call you Jack, mayn't I?——"

"I'll knock your block off in a minute," growled Mr. Wilson, blushing a fiery red.

Mark suddenly grinned at him. "By all means. But seriously, I think Dodds is perfectly right. He's a damned prosy old bore—you'll forgive me, sir——"

"I have always admired your candour, Allan," said Mr. Dodds.

"—But what he says is sensible. If you really have found

out something—and I do not for one moment think you
have——"

"You'll see," muttered Mr. Wilson.

"All right. I'll see. But if you have, for God's sake keep
quiet about it. Anybody would think you were playing a
little game. Murderers can only be hanged once. Are you
crying out for the rôle of second corpse? I should have
thought you'd prefer to live out your full three score years
and ten. Let the matter alone. It's not your province. Besides,
if I have to be perpetually stumping up for wreaths, I shall
soon be ruined."

"Funny, aren't you?" said Mr. Wilson, looking rather less
than his nineteen years. Then he said very solemnly, "I
know you all laugh at me, but if this racket's what I think it
is, it's something pretty beastly, and it's my duty to help to
expose it. It's no good your looking like that, Allan. One
must play the game. It's like that poem about 'his captain's
hand on his shoulder smote'."

Mark said grimly, "Be careful that it smites your shoulder.
It might conceivably smite you in a more lethal place." He
surveyed for a moment Mr. Wilson's flushed and rebellious
countenance. "But obviously I'm wasting my time. Play the
game and play the fool, and be damned to you. I am not,
thank God, the guardian of little boys."

Mr. Wilson felt at this point that he was not being appreciated. Anyone would think he was still at school, the way
they were all talking. Deflated, he turned towards Mrs.
Bridgwater, but she was sitting in the far corner, and did not
even raise her head to smile at him.

"I am afraid, Wilson," said Mark Allan, "that the lady has
other things to think about. Perhaps she's thinking about her
husband." He said this in a clear voice, and Mrs. Bridgwater
must have heard him, for she coloured up. But she still did
not raise her head, and Mr. Wilson sat down, some distance
away, chewing on his pipe for consolation.

Mr. Rills, first on the afternoon list, rose with a jaunty
air. He lit a cigarette carefully before he strolled out of the
room. It was shockingly difficult to steady his hands. He
stared contemptuously about him; he suspected they were all
watching him.

Mark Allan said, "What's the matter, Rills? You don't
look as happy as you did yesterday." But then that was
Mark Allan's way of talking; Mr. Rills hated him with a
bitter intensity, and, behind the curtain of his mind, asso-

ciated him with the bullies who had made life hell for him at his public school.

He did not answer, but he thought, 'He'll be sorry for this. I'm neither blind nor deaf, and I'm going to tell this detective bloke a few things that'll surprise him.' The thought momentarily buoyed him up, but, as he crossed the corridor to Mr. Latimer's room, his steps began to lag. In his nostrils was the smell of school, that combination of paint and chalk and sweat and boy that even now could sicken him. Before his eyes the cream distemper of I.L.D.A.'s walls was turning into buff and green. They had all been waiting. Watching. Eyes peering at him from doorways. The whisper hissing round him, "I say, did you know? Rills is going to be sacked . . .'

How terrified he had been, stark, staring, screaming terrified. He knew there was no chance. There never had been. Life had always been unfair. His parents had sent him to this abominable school; they said it would make a man of him. It had made of young Rills a coward and a liar. He had had the life and breath bullied out of him. He was slight and delicate, with a dangerous tongue, a slight lisp, and a horrid facility for tears. It was only when he was sixteen or so that he had at last gained for himself a certain place in the school hierarchy, gathering around him a few kindred spirits who had æsthetic tastes above the boors and bullies who cared for nothing but physical prowess. He had become editor of the magazine, a leading light in the dramatic group. What a fool he had been to get himself in such a mess. But one never thought. One borrowed the money. One was going to pay it back. The funds of the group were so seldom used. It was just his usual damnable luck that the theatre outing had been arranged. There was no way out. The sum was too large to raise, and oh, God, he could never tell his father, never . . .

Outside Mr. Latimer's door stood Mr. Rills, A.L.A., and huddling within him was young Rills, aged seventeen, sweating with terror, his bowels turning to water. The door, when he pushed it open, seemed as heavy as lead. He heard their remarks, quickly silenced. His hearing had always been acute. "Not a desirable boy in any way. A bad influence." And then it had all been quiet, and so very, very final. In the circumstances they felt it best that he should leave. There would be no public expulsion. His parents had been informed. 'That is all, Rills, thank you. You may go.'

He had smiled at them. It was a smile he had cultivated; he bestowed it on the bully who kicked him, the prefect who beat him, the snubbing companion—'We don't want to set next to *Rills,* do we?'—the sarcastic house-master. He had thanked them in an airy, jaunty manner. And then he had locked himself in the lavatory and cried, because he was afraid of what the boys would say, of what his father would say, of what the world would say.

"Good-afternoon, sir," said the sergeant. "Won't you sit down?" Then, "Now, sir. What can you tell us about this business?" And his eyes registered a slight young man, with a long, narrow, pale face, immaculately dressed, with tie and shirt toning in. A very, very frightened young man.

Mr. Rills said carefully, "Well, Sergeant, I believe I could tell you a few things of interest, but——" He drew out a silver cigarette-case. "Do you smoke?"

"No, thank you, sir."

"What exactly do you want to know?" asked Mr. Rills, peering at him over the match flame. The room, thank God, had steadied a little.

"Anything you can tell us, sir," replied the sergeant, registering further that this young gentleman was the kind to spill all the dirt obtainable, probably not popular with his colleagues and plainly anxious to talk about them. "Can you give me any information on Mrs. Warren?"

Mr. Rills considered the matter. "A lady with a mission, Sergeant. A mission to organise the world. I think she wished to know more about us than we did ourselves." He added, after a well-timed pause, "I cannot pretend that I really liked her." He gave a little laugh. "I expect you want to arrest me now, don't you?"

Sergeant Robins said stolidly, "No, sir. We are not making an arrest at the moment. Were you on bad terms with her?"

"Oh no," said Mr. Rills, "I am not on bad terms with anyone, really. Live and let live has always been my motto. We were always perfectly amiable to each other. But I am sensitive to atmosphere, Sergeant, and, frankly, I found her aura an evil one. I could never have made a friend of her. Indeed, candidly, Sergeant—you don't mind my speaking candidly, do you?——"

"Of course not, sir," said Sergeant Robins; he had never been so be-sergeanted in his life, but his face expressed nothing but a grave interest. Only Police-Constable Hall, who was morbidly fascinated by the colour scheme of shirt and tie, fidgeted rather uneasily in his seat.

"Well," said Mr. Rills, leaning back and blowing a smoke-ring—he was beginning almost to enjoy himself—"candidly, then, I am not surprised she was murdered. She knew all about Mr. Allan and Mrs. Bridgwater, for instance—our local romance, by the way. It must have been very embarrassing for them. Of course, an office is a difficult place to carry on an affair in."

He glanced sideways at the sergeant, who showed no emotion. He went on, "Of course they weren't awfully discreet. I don't work on their floor, but time after time when I went up, I would run into little scenes here and there. Mrs. Warren must have enjoyed herself no end. I'm not sure—I'm not committing myself, mind you, but I'm not sure if she didn't try a spot of blackmail. You see, she went to evening classes, and one of her classes was taken by Mrs. Bridgwater's husband. I'm not saying there's anything in this, mind you, but it seems to me a matter you might wish to pursue a little farther."

He paused again, but Sergeant Robins saw no point in making any comment; the young gentleman was plainly well away.

Mr. Rills continued, "Personally, I shouldn't care to blackmail Mr. Allan. He's a *fearfully* bad-tempered man. And so violent. Why, I remember we once had a man here working in the packing-room, and he went into Mr. Allan's office one day and started tidying his desk, and the language—my dear Sergeant, you never heard such words. We are very respectable here. Unless, of course, you don't approve of free love. Personally, I think people should do what they like. But Allan actually kicked the fellow out, but *literally*, Sergeant, literally. One does so abhor violence. However, I don't suppose he'd be so violent with a woman, though of course he did hit her once."

"He *hit* her?"

"Oh yes. Didn't he tell you? It was only in fun, of course, but I don't think she liked it very much. I was a bit shocked, actually," said Mr. Rills. "After all, she was over sixty. And Allan's such a big fellow. But I'm old-fashioned, I expect. Oh, and there's another thing, I don't really know if I ought to tell you."

The sergeant's eyes flickered, but he only waited in silence.

"It's something I overheard," said Mr. Rills. "I wasn't meant to overhear it. But my hearing has always been very acute. Perhaps I really shouldn't. What do you think?"

"If you feel it's important, sir, you had better tell us."

Mr. Rills looked a little embarrassed. He knew well enough that it is difficult to call eavesdropping by any other name.

But then he remembered the many things he had suffered at Mark's hands, and the contempt with which Mrs. Bridgwater had always treated him, and he said quickly, the lisp more pronounced than usual, "It was at lunch last Wed—no, last Thursday. The day before she was murdered. We were all in the canteen. And there are arm-chairs there, Sergeant, and after lunch we all sit about and smoke, and so on. Mr. Allan and Mrs. Bridgwater were concentrating more on the so on, if you take my meaning—holding hands and gazing into each other's eyes, and all that sort of thing. I saw she seemed very upset, but I didn't think anything of it. And then—this really startled me—he said in quite a loud voice—now, let me get this right—he said, 'Mona'—that's her first name, you know, so appropriate—'Mona, take something flat with a sharp edge, a file would do, and hit her across the back of the neck, just here.'" He touched a point at the base of his skull. "Then he said, 'She'll never tell Henry anything again.' Henry's the husband, you know. And then—then Mrs. Bridgwater said, 'Don't speak so loudly,' and after that I didn't hear anything more." He added, "Of course, I don't suppose it means anything. But it's interesting, don't you think?"

"Very interesting, sir," said the sergeant. He looked squarely at Mr. Rills. "There's another thing I would like to ask you. I understand from Mr. Latimer that a certain number of books have been disappearing from the Library. I'm not a reading man myself, but I understand that some of them were extremely valuable, and could have been sold for large sums of money. I am wondering if the lady knew anything about this. Could you give me any information, sir?"

Mr. Rills, now chalk-white, had risen to his feet. All his self-composure had vanished. He said harshly, "I know nothing about it. Nothing at all. I cannot see that this has anything to do with the murder."

"I never said it had anything to do with the murder, sir," said the sergeant. "I only wondered if Mrs. Warren, who seems to have found out so much to her disadvantage, was also using this as a means of blackmail."

The smell of chalk and paint and sweat and boy overwhelmed Mr. Rills. He sat down again suddenly and burst into tears.

When at last he had gone, dragging his shame and humiliation with him, the sergeant and the constable looked at each other. Sergeant Robins rubbed his forehead and sighed. "Not what I call a very nice type of gentleman," he said.

"But I doubt if he'd have the guts to do a murder. The old lady certainly seems to have been sticking her neck out. I think we'll have to see Mr. Allan again. It's funny how everything seems to point to him. I wonder what the next one's going to be like."

Mr. Rills, his voice now under control, said, "You're next, Wilson."

"Good-oh," said Mr. Wilson, and beamed with excited happiness.

Mark, who had been watching Mr. Rills's face, stepped up to him. Mr. Rills was only five foot three, and Mark, standing so close, seemed like a mountain. He had already had a great deal more than he could stand; every nerve in his body was quivering, and he could see nothing ahead but disgrace and more and more humiliation. Perhaps they would send him to prison. Perhaps they'd even pin the murder on him and hang him. He raised his anguished eyes to Mark's, and saw nothing there but a bleak menace.

"I expect," said Mark, "that you've been enjoying yourself."

The unhappy Mr. Rills, who had certainly been doing nothing of the kind, tried to back, but he was pinned against the wall. He said, almost in a whimper, "Leave me alone. Do you hear? Leave me alone. I won't be bullied like this, I tell you, I won't."

"What have you been saying, Rills?" said Mark.

"Nothing! What—what do you think I've been saying?"

"I think," said Mark evenly, "you've probably been shopping us all to the best of your ability. Have you?"

"No!" wailed Mr. Rills, now utterly back at school, lost most dreadfully in that jungle of savagery.

"I hope that's true, for your own sake," said Mark. "However, I've no doubt I shall know in due course." He moved back a little. "You don't seem to have had an easy passage. You're looking upset. Has the sergeant proved a little more shrewd than you bargained for?"

Mr. Rills would have given everything he possessed to hit out against that arrogant face, staring down into his. But of course he could not, and there was room to move now, so, his face working, he shoved past Mark, who made no effort to detain him, and fled to his own room. And there he sat down, with nothing but despair and humiliation to keep him company, and at last he rested his head on his arms, so still that he might have been asleep.

Young Mr. Wilson stepped in for his interview, with the feeling of the brilliant detective confronting the well-meaning but incompetent bunglers of the Yard. He knew in his heart that this was quite ridiculous, but it was also fun, so he chewed firmly on the stem of his pipe, and wished that his beard had grown properly so that his youthful, rounded face were a little more concealed.

He greeted them casually, and sat there, head a little bowed, a meaning smile playing about his lips, as the sergeant asked him various questions.

"I understand, sir," said the sergeant at last, "that you have some theories on this matter. We should be very interested to hear them. Sometimes the bystander sees things that we don't, and," he added with some psychological acumen, "you might have noticed the one thing that's needed to make the whole problem fit into pattern."

Mr. Wilson was sorely tempted. The sergeant was looking at him in a most flattering way. It was just like the detective stories. He opened his mouth, then suddenly shyness came upon him. For the first time it struck him that it was a daft sort of idea. After all, in real life, people surely didn't—— They would laugh at him. The brilliant young detective switched into a shy young man of nineteen who had, numerous times in his life, been hauled on to the carpet for a too lively exercise of his imagination. He had always had brilliant ideas; occasionally they had worked, and often they had not. He had nearly failed his cataloguing examination because of a wild plunge into fantasy that Mr. Dewey would never have approved of. He looked sideways at the sergeant—decent sort of bloke, probably wouldn't laugh to his face—but he could imagine how they would snigger when he had gone. He ran his finger under his collar, blushed in that confoundedly awkward manner he had never been able to cure, and mumbled, "Oh, I don't know. I don't suppose there's anything in it."

"We might be the best judges of that, sir," said the sergeant encouragingly.

"Well," said Mr. Wilson with sudden candour, "you see, I sometimes get hunches, if you know what I mean, and they seem fearfully good at the time, but they don't always work, and really, if you don't mind, I'd rather see how things turn out. Naturally, I'll let you know if I find out anything really important. I hope," said Mr. Wilson, recovering himself a little, "that I know my duty as a citizen. I should never dream of withholding information from the police."

The sergeant frowned, not so much in annoyance as with a vague feeling of presentiment. He said, "Could you not perhaps give us some idea, sir?"

"No, no," said Mr. Wilson, "I'd rather wait. I expect it's all nonsense, anyway. The others all think so."

"You've mentioned it to your colleagues, then?"

"Well, not really. I suppose I did let on that I might be on to something. No details. Nothing like that." Mr. Wilson raised his bearded face and bestowed a disarming and charming smile on the sergeant. "I've got rather a big mouth, I know. They're always telling me so. But I'll keep really mum on this. Because if it's what I think it is——"

"Yes, sir?"

"Nothing, nothing," said the great detective. "Just a theory, you know. Scarcely that, really. Well, Sergeant, if there's nothing more I can do for you——"

The sergeant said gravely, "Look, Mr. Wilson, I don't know what you have in mind, of course. As you say, there may be nothing in it. But I'd like you to remember, sir, that there's been a person murdered and, from all accounts for sticking her nose into what didn't concern her, and there is a murderer loose here and, if he thinks he's likely to be found out, he won't hesitate to kill again. After all, let's face it, what has he—or she—to lose? You say you've mentioned this to your colleagues. Could you tell me which ones?"

"Oh," said Mr. Wilson, a little angry because he felt he was being put in his place, "Mr. Dodds, and Rills and Allan and Mrs. Bridgwater and Mr. Latimer and—and that little Smith girl—you can't think any of them did it. I mean, they're nearly all librarians."

"There is no professional distinction in murder," said the sergeant with a sigh. "I sometimes think that if we only had the blunt instrument to hand at the one black moment that descends on all of us, we'd all be murderers at one time or another. Fortunately, we don't. Well, sir, if you won't, you won't, and that's all there is to it. But frankly, I'm disappointed in you."

Mr. Wilson looked sulky and excessively young.

"I had hoped you could give us a pointer. I can only ask you to be careful, sir."

"I'm not a complete ass," said Mr. Wilson, rather straying from his rôle of detective.

The sergeant made no comment on this, only said, "I suggest that you at least try to keep quiet about your investigations. And when you have something concrete, please come at once to me. Will you do that?"

"Naturally," said Mr. Wilson stiffly, "I hope I know my duty as a——"

"Thank you," said the sergeant, "I don't think I need keep you any longer. Will you please ask Mrs. Bridgwater to come in?"

They heard Mr. Wilson whistling cheerfully as he walked down the corridor.

"Young idiot!" said the sergeant angrily to Police-Constable Hall. "Damned young fool! I don't suppose for one moment he's on to anything, but if he is—— Told everyone about it, of course. Sometimes I wish we could use a spot of third degree. He'll now be telling them all that he's had a little confidential chat with me, and that'll tickle the murderer no end."

"Oh, we had a nice little talk," announced Mr. Wilson. Mark Allan was still there; Mr. Dodds was talking to Mr. Latimer, and Mrs. Bridgwater, her hands tightly folded, was sitting there, gazing into space. "He asked me what I thought about it. I said I would prefer not to discuss it until I could really support my theory, but I gave him one or two little hints, you know. He was interested—oh yes—positively begged me for details. But, No, I said. No, no. Not until I'm certain. The moment I have my facts, I said, I'll lay them before you. 'I think,' I said, 'you'll be surprised.' Nice fellow. Hardworking, though not, perhaps, very inspired. However, I think we should work together very well." Then he added, "Oh, by the way—— Mrs. Bridgwater. They want to see you." He said reassuringly, "They are very nice. And not particularly quick in the uptake, I think." He blushed, amidst the startled silence. "I didn't mean—— Well, anyway, they would like to see you. Just routine, you know."

Mark Allan swerved round to look directly at Mrs. Bridgwater, who avoided his gaze, turning her head away. She said graciously to Mr. Wilson, "Thank you for telling me. Fortunately," and here she gave a little smile, her eyes slanting at an unnatural angle in an effort not to meet Mark's, "I have a clear conscience, so, you see, I just don't mind. I expect it's different for some people."

Mark said, "You will find them interesting. And—interested. And not quite so slow in the uptake as Wilson seems to think. It is surprising the way office gossip seems to percolate.

Especially as our friend, Rills, seems to have undertaken the rôle of percolator."

"Well," she said, "as it doesn't concern me, it hardly matters, does it?"

"Would you like me to escort you?" began Mr. Wilson, but she thanked him prettily, and said she would prefer to go on her own.

She was thankful to get away from Mark. His bitter hostility took her breath away, like a biting wind. She could not believe that he, who had once so overwhelmed her with his love, who had beat upon her with his desire, should now hate and despise her. She did not consider the slaps she had administered. She had always, throughout her life, ignored the things that were most conveniently forgotten. But, as her conscience was by no means clear, she had to stand in the corridor for a moment to regain her control. Fear and anger shook her. Like many women, whose beauty depends on their calm and statuesque bearing, she was not at her best when emotionally disturbed. There was a dull red in her cheeks, and the pale eyes, never her best feature, grew small and sunken in her head. She beat her fingers on her handbag. She lit a cigarette, and her temper flamed and flickered with the match. As if it wasn't bad enough to know what she did, and be interviewed by the police. To be so spoken to in public. Of course he just wasn't a gentleman. He never had been. Even when they had been friendly, he had often used the coarsest expressions, and his way of making love was anything but refined. She shook her head to rid herself of the memory when that love had blown upon her like a sea wind, when his hands had charmed her blood, when the very sound of his voice had made her gasp and tremble like a young, lovelorn girl.

She sailed into Mr. Latimer's office. The sergeant saw a large, blonde, handsome woman who glanced at him idly, then concentrated her oddly pale blue eyes on Police-Constable Hall, who started perceptibly beneath their impact. The sergeant frowned at him. He was a small man, and he found this large fairness a trifle daunting.

He asked her to sit down. Mrs. Bridgwater turned on him the smile she reserved for the lower classes, the smile which had made the grocer, during the war, give her an extra quarter of butter, which made bus conductors let her on, even when there were five standing. It had no effect on Sergeant Robins whatsoever, except to make him concentrate his attention more fully; he saw then that her hands gripped her bag until the tips were white, and that she sat with her knees close together, as if to stop them from trembling.

His eyes slid down to her hands. He saw that one of them bore a strip of pink plaster along the base of the little finger. He said abruptly, "What have you done to your hands, Mrs. Bridgwater?"

She started. She had not been prepared for this. But she recovered herself quickly. She said in her clear, sweet voice, her accent very correct, "Oh, *that?* So silly—I was opening a tin. Of baked beans. For my husband's breakfast, you know. He does so like them. I daren't eat anything like that, because it's fattening, so I just have tea without milk."

The sergeant interrupted her without ceremony. "What can you tell me about Mrs. Warren?"

"Poor, poor woman," said Mrs. Bridgwater. "Such a shocking thing to happen. Have you any clue as to who did it?"

"My clues depend on my information, madam. What information can you give us?"

"Oh, we all liked her," said Mrs. Bridgwater reflectively. "A nice old lady. Very hard-working. Of course she did disagree with one or two members of the staff—Mr. Allan, for instance—but I'm afraid that was his fault rather than hers—he's such a touchy man, you know. Still, if one murdered everyone one disagreed with, Inspector——"

"Sergeant, madam. Did you like her?"

"But of course! I like everyone. I am very easy-going."

'I bet you are,' thought the sergeant vulgarly. "I understand," he said, "that you quarrelled with her last Thursday morning in the ladies' cloak-room. Can you tell me what the quarrel was about?"

"Who told you that?" cried Mrs. Bridgwater. At that moment she did not look easy-going at all.

"We get our information from various sources. You did quarrel, I believe?"

"We had a little argument, yes. I suppose it was mostly my fault," admitted Mrs. Bridgwater with a shy, girlish air that did not match her flickering eyes and restless hands. "It was over something quite silly. Do you really want me to tell you?"

"If you please, madam."

"It was because of my smoking. You see, I smoke a great deal, it's my nerves, and really we're not supposed to do it. Because of the books, you know. I admit I was in the wrong, but one doesn't like being told off, and I was rather tired, so I suppose I just flared up. Of course we both laughed at ourselves later, and were good friends again. It is a great relief to me. It would have been frightful to have ended on bad terms. Of course I am very sen——"

Sergeant Robins, who had been turning over his notes, said, without looking up, "I understand you were crying in your office on Friday morning. May I ask if this was on account of your disagreement with Mr. Allan, or did the disagreement occur later? You slapped his face, I believe."

The young constable was so startled by the look that appeared on Mrs. Bridgwater's face that he forgot his manners and stared. Her eyes were as hard as pebbles, the mouth drew down, and she had drawn back her head, snake-like, as if about to strike.

She said in a voice from which all the warmth and charm had fled, "I cannot see what business this is of yours. I didn't know the police rummaged in the gutter for their information. I refuse to answer."

"You are within your rights to do so," he admitted, "but I think it would be better if you did."

She said again, obstinately, "I refuse. It's nothing to do with the murder." She hesitated. Then she forced a smile to her lips, and her voice grew softer. "I'm sorry. I shouldn't lose my temper. Only my nerves, you know—— Look, Inspector——"

"Sergeant, madam."

"Oh dear, I do seem to be getting everything wrong, don't I?" It should have been a pretty confusion, but it was not pretty, only desperate. "Look. If I tell you something in confidence—I swear it's nothing to do with the murder——"

"In an enquiry of this kind, nothing can be regarded as confidential. It's entirely up to you. But I think it would be better for you to tell me."

She said, with the air of one taking a great decision, "Then I will. You look marvellously trustworthy. You see, Mr. Allan—oh dear, how embarrassing this is—well, he's fallen in love with me. I suppose it was a teeny bit my fault. But you know how it is. One is flattered. Though I'm a very happily married woman, Inspector, actually."

The sergeant opened his mouth and closed it again.

"I know it was very weak of me. Only one never *thinks*, does one? Actually, he was quite besotted. If I'd realised—— I do see now I'm terribly to blame. And on Friday evening he came to my room—I suppose he was upset, too—but he started making the most incredible violent love to me. Well,

I mean, what could I do? I have my reputation to think of, after all. So I slapped his face, and truly, I think he deserved it. I'd never given him the least encouragement, after all. I suppose he told you I had?"

"No, madam. He never mentioned it at all."

"Oh!" She was very disconcerted. "Who told you, then?"

He did not reply, only said, "Is it true, Mrs. Bridgwater, that Mr. Allan told you how to kill Mrs. Warren, and then said, 'She'll never tell Henry anything again.' "

She went so white that they both thought she would faint. But she did not. She said almost in a scream, "That's a complete lie."

"You are quite sure?"

"Of—of course. What an outrageous thing to say. *Who*——"

He said unexpectedly, "Do you know anything about the making of photostats?"

"No! How should I? It's not my job. But I insist on knowing who——"

"Well, I think that's all, thank you, Mrs. Bridgwater. I may want to see you again later. I shall be in and out of this office during the next few weeks. Would you ask Mr. Allan to come in again, please?"

He said, when she had gone, "I wish she would stop calling me 'Inspector'. Upon my word, I'm almost sorry for Mr. Allan. Scared to death, isn't she? I think a few inquiries should be made about her home life. I think our Mr. Rills was telling the truth. And I want investigations made into Mr. Allan's army career. Make an appointment for me, will you, with his bank manager. What *are* photostats and microfilms, by the way?"

Mrs. Bridgwater, coming out of the cloak-room and about to make her way downstairs, met Mark Allan in the corridor. She looked at him. She thought, 'He can't *really* hate me.' She said hesitantly, "I left a message for you. They want to see you again. Mark——"

"Well?"

She could not pretend, even to herself, that there was anything lover-like in that monosyllable. But she hated to be defeated. She said, in her softest voice, "Mark—I—I'm sorry. I know I—I haven't behaved very well to you."

"Haven't you?" he said. The bitter contempt and anger in his eyes hit her like a blow.

She was afraid. She began, "Well, I've apologised, haven't I? I don't want to be on bad terms with you."

He interrupted her with a brief laugh. "You're afraid I'll inform on you, aren't you? There's no need, I assure you, my dear. All the informing is being done for us. By the time this is through, there'll be nothing left of your virtue to dazzle Henry with."

She looked aghast and, it amused him to see, furious. "You don't mean to say they'll bring Henry into this?"

"Of course. What in God's name do you expect?" He leant against the wall, insolently surveying her. She would gladly, if she had dared, have boxed his ears again. But she did not dare. He went on, "You're not such a fool as all that, Mona. You and I have one of the best motives in the world for putting the old girl out of the way. But I don't know why I bother to tell you that. You can't really imagine that I don't understand why I was pushed so quickly. But it's too late, you know. You might as well have hung on to me for a little longer. It wouldn't have made the slightest difference. As it is, it merely gives the impression that you've been in the damnedest hurry to throw out your liabilities. You're beginning to see that, too, aren't you, my girl? That's why it's, 'Mark, I don't want to be on bad terms with you.' But we are on bad terms, and we're staying so, for good and all. Do you think," he said, raising his voice, regardless of the fact that most of the I.L.D.A. staff were scattered about the building, "that I'm the sort of person to put up with such treatment? To have my ears boxed for trying to kiss you, to *kiss* you, when the time was that you came creeping into my office for no other purpose, when you let me do anything I liked with you, apart from going to bed with you, naturally, for that wouldn't have been quite nice, and the neighbours wouldn't have approved. Don't worry. There'll be no more kisses, or anything else. I wouldn't kiss you now if you offered me a hundred pounds and a free ticket to Tahiti." Then he laughed again. "Though I might, at that. Especially for the free ticket. You bloody, suburban, vicious, edge-of-the-bed little slut. I should have raped you and be done with it."

She was beginning to cry. She sobbed, "Someone will hear you. How can you be so cruel?"

"Oh——!" He used a word that shocked her gentility to the core. "You talk like a cheap film. You and your artistic soul. You're nothing but a cheap, third-rate little trollop, without the guts to fulfil your obligations. So far and no farther, that's your motto, isn't it, and I never mattered a damn, anyway. Oh, I'll not inform on you. Not because I give a brass farthing for you, but because I'd be doing myself at the same time. Snivel away. It doesn't improve your looks. But there is one thing I'd like to ask you."

She cried out hysterically, between her sobs, "Let me pass. Let me pass. I w-want to go home."

"Just a minute. Why were you in such a state yesterday? Oh, never mind the sensitive stuff. You know and I know that you're as sensitive as Nelson's Column. But you were in a state, weren't you? Why? I want to know. And I will know." He blocked her way, regarding her with such an expression that she cowered, the panic surging up in her throat, fit to choke her.

"Perhaps you saw something?" he said, his voice very low, his light, bright eyes fixed on her. "Or heard something? Tell me, Mona. I should like to know."

She screamed out, "I saw nothing. Nothing! Mark, don't look at me like that. I—I wouldn't lie to you."

His expression had grown hard, intent, considering. He said at last, "Perhaps it's as well you saw nothing. After all, there is a murderer loose, Mona. It might prove quite awkward for you if you had seen something you shouldn't. You are quite sure?"

"Yes! Yes!"

He still considered her. Then he shrugged his shoulders. "Oh, well," he said. "It don't signify. Go home to your husband. If he's any sense, he'll beat you. I would." Then he added, "By the way, I'd leave young Wilson alone, if I were you. He's too young. He wouldn't make a meal for you. I know your aim is to make me look ridiculous, but I don't think I wish to be made as ridiculous as all that. You will leave him alone, won't you? Won't you?"

"Yes," whispered Mrs. Bridgwater, the tears flowing down her cheeks. Then she said suddenly in a low, vicious voice, "Someone heard you telling me how to kill her. The sergeant knows. I expect that's what he wants to see you about."

"And how did you explain that away?"

"I—I said it was a lie."

"Oh, I don't think that was very intelligent of you. I'll go and see him." He half turned then, focusing his gaze on her again, said softly, "You really saw nothing? You're sure?"

She screwed her eyes up. She could not answer. He waited, then without another word, stood aside to let her pass. She scuttled past him, her dignity all forgotten, her only desire to put as much distance between them as possible.

He watched her running, with a bitter smile. He listened to the high heels tapping as she bolted down the stairs.

Then he said aloud, "I wonder what the devil she did see."

MARK, on his way down, stopped at Mr. Rills's room on the second floor. He pushed the door open and stepped inside. But Mr. Rills had gone home. Mark came up to his desk and idly examined the papers there. There was nothing of importance, except a small pile of application forms, one of Barbara's university lists, returned from Liverpool University, with the word 'Closed' scrawled across it in red ink, and Willings Press Guide. He opened the drawers. In the second one was a sheet of paper scribbled over. He picked it up. It seemed to be a series of accounts. Twenty pounds. Three pounds, five. Four pounds, eleven and six. There was a long column. The sum total was a large one. Mark did not think this was on the credit side, especially as Mr. Rills had run his pencil through the addition so viciously that the paper was torn.

Then he went down to Mr. Latimer's office.

"I wanted to ask you two things, sir," said the sergeant. "One of them concerns your work." He glanced up at Mark when he said this. He said afterwards to Police-Constable Hall, "Did you notice the odd way he stands when you question him? With his hands hanging at his sides, his eyes fixed on the wall behind your head. You'd think someone was jabbing a bayonet in the small of his back." He said to Mark, bluntly, "I understand you gave instructions to Mrs. Bridgwater on how to kill Mrs. Warren?"

"I did."

"Why did you do that, sir?"

"I suppose," returned Mark, casually enough, "that it must be because she was a pernicious woman who deserved to be killed."

"Is this to do with the blackmail you referred to before, sir?"

"Rills has been enjoying himself. One can hardly blame him. Yes."

115

"You know that Mrs. Warren was killed in the way you described?"

"Yes. It's a useful technique. You don't even need a weapon. You can use the side of your hand—so." He demonstrated. "No blood. Not much mess. The effect is the same as that of a judicial hanging. But Mrs. Bridgwater didn't kill her. Neither, incidentally, did I. As for Rills, he might have done, but I doubt if he'd have the strength or the guts. He's the kind who'd shove half a pound of arsenic into your coffee, and have a fit of hysterics afterwards. And he'd never be able to stand up to any cross-examination."

'But you would,' thought the sergeant. However, as this view of Mr. Rills coincided with his own, he only said, "Thank you, sir. Did it not seem to you a dangerous piece of information to pass on, even in joke?"

"It wasn't in joke. My sense of humour doesn't lead me to such excesses. I have said I didn't kill her, but I haven't said I wasn't going to, if need be."

"The lady, I understand, was proposing to pass certain information on to Mrs. Bridgwater's husband?"

There was a slight pause. The sergeant, who was trained to notice such things, saw that Mark's attitude had suddenly relaxed, that his hands had slid comfortably into his pockets.

"She was. If she had not already done so. You had better ask Mrs. Bridgwater."

"Thank you for answering so frankly," said the sergeant. "And now——"

"You've no need to thank me. After everybody's frankness to-day, it seems that I have little alternative. Only if Mr. Rills is found with a broken neck you can certainly blame me."

"It's not Mr. Rills I'm worried about, sir," said the sergeant, with a great appearance of candour. "It's Mr. Wilson."

"That young fool. Has he been telling you his precious theories?"

"I'd feel happier if he had. He appears to have been telling everyone else."

Mark shrugged. "He's only a kid. And a damned stupid one, though less objectionable than most. He's been reading Sherlock Holmes. Not for one moment do I imagine he's on to anything. Well? Have you finished with me?"

The sergeant suddenly smiled at him. "Well, sir, technically, yes. But I really wished to ask you a favour. You deal with the microfilms and photostats, don't you?"

"I do." The faintest stiffening of the shoulders—the sergeant was not sure. There was at least no change of expression.

He said, almost diffidently, "I should be most grateful if you would explain your work to me."

"I can't imagine why it should interest you," said Mark; a hint of temper flickered in his voice.

"Possibly not, sir. But I like to know about things. It's part of my job, as you might say. One never knows when facts will come in useful."

"Do I have to explain the Dewey cataloguing system to you, then, and his benighted form of spelling? You will find us all classified. 'Disposal of the Ded'—614.6. 'Influence of Sex'—615.55. You will note how close they are to each other."

"Most interesting, sir. I see I must have a look at Mr. Dewey."

"You're welcome, Sergeant!"

"But those microfilms—what are they, exactly?" His eyes glanced casually at Mark's face. There was nothing there to read at all. And that intrigued the sergeant, who would have expected to find irritation, amusement, boredom. But the face, with its hard, cleanly-chiselled features, was blank; the light eyes, meeting his, were cool and undecipherable.

Mark said, "If you will come up to my office, I will show you."

The sergeant walked upstairs after him. He looked down at Mark's desk, a small, insignificant man, several inches below his instructor who faced him, and held out to him what looked like a large photographic spool.

Mark said, his voice a little remote, "We send out for a great many rare books, and for a large number of foreign periodicals. The reader cannot always get them direct. If the reading matter is long, it may come in microfilm form. You may look at this, if you like. It is an article by a gentleman called Massei, from the *Bollettino dell' Istituta di Diritto Romano*. It was published in 1941—a date, incidentally, which makes me homesick, but which has probably no interest for you. It is required by Glasgow University, and comes to us from the Biblioteca Nazionale Centrale, Rome. It goes off Monday."

"You get a great many of these, sir?"

"Yes."

"From all parts of the world?"

"Yes. They weigh very little. I do not think they could be used for killing anyone."

"Quite, sir. And photostats?"

"Those I do myself. If you like," said Mark quite amiably, "I'll do one for you now. It'll save me time on Monday. You shall come into my dark room. You can regard it if you wish as Bluebeard's secret cache. There are no bodies in it at the moment, but of course this is the weekend." Then, his hand out to push at the side door, he laughed. "I'm cast for the rôle of first murderer, am I not? You are quite right, after all. I am more qualified than most. I know how. I have no illusions as to the sanctity of human life. And I have long been used to looking after myself in circumstances which could make pity ridiculous, mercy obscene, and sentimentality suicide. Now——"

The room was like a pantry, with a sink at one end and a long table, on which lay three trays. At the other end was an object like a box with a pneumatic cushion covering it.

"A reader," said Mark, his voice a derisive imitation of a university lecturer, "requires a photostat of the frontispiece of this book. It represents, as you will see, a nineteenth-century admiral in full regalia. We take the book so, carefully flatten down the page. We then take a piece of what is called, if you want the technical term, reflex contact document paper—the shiny side is the business end—and lay it upon the admiral's face, so. Then we place this box upon the paper, so. We press the switch, and the cushion, as you see, lights up. We count one and two and three and four and five. Switch it off. Now. You see these three trays. The first holds the developer, the second ordinary water, the third the fixer. We'll put the gentleman in to develop. Look, here he comes. It's the negative, of course. Makes him look a little devilish, don't you think? But then we do him again to get the positive. First, however, we wash the developer off him, and place him in the fixer. Then we lay him on blotting paper to dry, and repeat the process for the positive." He did this in silence, until finally a perfect reproduction of the admiral lay before the sergeant's eyes.

"Very clever," said the sergeant. His eyes slid to Mark's powerful, long-fingered hands. He looked round the little room. Mark, watching him with a faint smile, said idly, "I sometimes fancy that detection must be like the children's game. Are you cold, Sergeant, or warm, or perhaps very warm?"

"It is very warm, sir," replied the sergeant, as if he had not understood. "Must be near the eighties. Quite upsetting when one's not used to it."

Mark watched him go. Then, as if this were an ordinary working day, he sat down at his desk, and picked up the microfilm sent by Rome Bib. Naz.

From the high tide of murder I.L.D.A. sank back into the shallows of routine. On Monday no one talked of anything but the murder, on Tuesday the subject was dying down, and on Wednesday Greta went up to the fourth floor without thinking of asking for an escort.

On Thursday, the inquest was held. Interest revived, but as only Barbara, Mr. Latimer, Miss Holmes, Purley and Mark Allan attended, it was brief. It was not quite the ordeal that Barbara had expected, though it was very hot in the courtroom, and for one moment she thought she might faint. The sickness rose in her throat again as she listened to the doctor saying that the findings were compatible with a blow delivered high up on the back of the neck, that hæmorrhage was obvious in the erector spinal muscles just below the skull, and that great force must have been necessary to cause death. But this passed. The verdict was, Murder by person or persons unknown.

The staff did not officially attend Mrs. Warren's funeral. Mr. Latimer, however, went as in duty bound. There was a magnificent wreath. The list of subscriptions lay in Miss Holmes's office. Barbara, glancing at it, saw that Mark had contributed five shillings, this being five times as much as anybody else. When she saw this, she blushed scarlet, though there was nobody to see her. A few minutes later she met him in the corridor. She would have passed him without a word, but he caught hold of her wrist.

"And what is the matter with you?" he said, most impertinently, she thought, for he had not even spoken to her these past few days. "Are you not speaking to your old friends? Perhaps you, too, look upon me as a murderer? Or is it simply your reputation you are afraid of? Still, your reputation would not be harmed by saying good-morning to me, nor am I likely to kill you for doing so."

Barbara did not struggle, but she wished he would release her wrist. The magnetism within him was flowing through her veins so that she felt helpless, engulfed, with alien, disrupting thoughts scudding through her mind, and a desire scorching her that frightened and shocked her. She managed to say, however, "I see you contributed most generously to the wreath."

"Why," he said, "don't you think it was enough? I will go

immediately and lay a bunch of roses on her grave, if you say so. No one shall call me ungenerous. Death is, after all, something of an occasion. Specially in this case."

"You're really outrageous, aren't you! I don't think you can have any proper feelings."

"I have a great many improper ones. Why don't you come to my office and talk to me?"

"I have better things to do with my time," said Barbara, then looking at him, flushed and laughed. "I'm sorry. That was very childish. But please let me go. Someone will come and——" She suddenly turned her head away. "I'm not Mrs. Bridgwater. You accuse her of making a hobby of young men. Are you sure you don't make a hobby of young women?"

"Oh," he said, moving his hand down so that it clasped hers—his fingers were cool and strong—"One makes a hobby of everything. Sometimes, though, one finds a rare specimen. We'll go out one day, you and I. Shall we? Decently and properly as people should. What shall we do? Have dinner in the Corner House, with the band playing selections from the 'Merry Widow', or would that be too evocative of our dead friend? And then go to a flick, and hold hands? No. We'll walk. I'll show you parts of London that will give you a hundred ideas for your novel. I know my London rather well. We'll go back two hundred years and walk the Embankment; the sweet Thames shall run softly till I end my song, and tell you of all the women who have loved me, and how at least half of them committed suicide. Did you never think, by the way, of that great scene in the L.C.C., when they selected their quotation? I wonder who thought of it. Some little clerk, perhaps, who couldn't afford the wireless, and so was reduced to reading. Poor devil. And so he goes down to posterity. Sometimes one feels the Thames must gather momentum with every fresh misuse of the quotation. You have a pleasant hand to hold. I must hold it oftener. A rebellious, long-suffering hand, yet not so rebellious as Kensington Gore demands."

"Why," said Barbara faintly, "do librarians talk so much?"

"Possibly because they cannot read. When are you coming out with me? To-morrow? The day after? The day after that? It is the middle of August. There are a hundred and twenty odd days left to us. Name one. It shall be all as you please. A barge, perhaps, with the 'Water Music' to accompany us. We'll go east, to the wharves and docks; we'll leave the genteel west behind us."

She did not answer immediately, but pulled gently at her

hand, which he released without a word. Then she said, "I—I am rather busy. Perhaps one day next week?"

He said nothing.

"Well—Thursday, if you like."

He bowed his head. His smile, she suspected, was a little derisive. He must have been perfectly aware of his power. But it did not seem to matter, only she was a little afraid, and without being able to put the slightest reason to it. She shot him a swift glance, then turned to go.

"Thursday, then," he said, adding, "If, of course, we are all alive on Thursday."

"What do you mean? Do you think—— You can't think there'll be another murder."

"Ah, why not? The victim served up in a pie, perhaps. Examine your canteen lunch. Before we're through, we may litter the Library with catalogued corpses, and then the murderer shall be buried to his ears in books, and die famished in the stacks, crying at the last:

> 'If one good deed in all my life I did,
> I do repent it to my very soul.'

I must," said Mark in his normal voice—his face, she saw, was lit by some strange, inner excitement—"do some photostats. Which reminds me, the sergeant is still with us. I have seen him here three times already this week. Well. It shall be Thursday. Unless by then you have considered the matter, and decided it would be wisest not to associate with me. But it will still be Thursday, even then. Till then, I'll not molest you. Though it seems that if I did, no one would notice, except perhaps yourself. We all seem to be locked up in our private worlds, with our own special devils to torment us. The old lady did better by her dying than she could have dared to hope."

And this, as Barbara perceived, was true. There was little talk of Mrs. Warren, but her squat and stubborn ghost was always with them. Mr. Rills, with white, angry face, no longer uttered barbed quips at everyone's expense. He spent as much time as he could in his room—after a long interview with Mr. Ridley, from which he emerged as if the flesh had been stripped from him. He spoke to no one, and fairly ran at the sight of Mark Allan, who, it was true, watched him in a reflective and rather ugly way. Indeed, Mark, who, as Barbara was compelled to notice, had something of the school bully in him, was careful to meet Mr. Rills as often as he could, and to bestow on him that slow, derisive smile which made the wretched young man glance frantically about him to make sure there was somebody within call. Barbara did not like Mr. Rills, but she could not help but feel sorry for him. Besides, Mark in this bullying mood displeased her; it seemed that he derived a cruel satisfaction from the young man's palpable fear.

Mrs. Bridgwater, too, was strangely silent. She had given up coming to the canteen so that Barbara seldom met her, but she had to notice—and this surprised her—that Mrs. Bridgwater would scarcely speak to Mr. Wilson, who was very hurt by this, and at last dared to question her directly.

"I say," he said, going very red. "Have I done anything wrong? I mean, you seem sort of angry with me."

"Why should I be?" said Mrs. Bridgwater coldly.

"Well, I don't know. I—I just wondered. I mean, I know I talk too much, and I thought perhaps I'd let off my big mouth and upset you. I'm awfully sorry if I have."

"I don't know what you're talking about, I'm sure," returned Mrs. Bridgwater, then looking at his unhappy face, softened a little. Really she couldn't be so rude to the poor lad. "Jack, dear——" she began, then, out of the corner of her eye, saw Mark Allan approaching. Her voice grew hard and abrupt. "I really haven't time to stand here, gossiping all day. You may have no work to do, but I have." And with that, she left him, to stand there, embarrassed, a little angry and utterly bewildered.

"Women!" said Mr. Wilson to Mark Allan.

Mark stared contemplatively after Mrs. Bridgwater. He said, "You're too young to go whoring after married middle-aged females. Good God, she's nearly old enough to be your mother."

Mr. Wilson, stung beyond caution, retorted, "I expect you only say that because she threw you over."

Mark's eyebrows, at this, shot up so alarmingly that he went scarlet, and began to stutter, "B-by the way, I th-think I've really g-got on to something at last."

"You're referring, I presume, to Mrs. Bridgwater. Well, get off her."

"No! Of course not. Oh really, Allan, you're always laughing at me. No, I'm being serious. Surely you read your newspapers?"

"Ah, the drug racket. Well? How's it done? You had better tell me so that I have an occupation for my old age."

Mr. Wilson had little sense of caution, but at this moment

he suddenly remembered the sergeant's words. He looked up at Mark. Allan was a decent fellow, really, though not many people had a good word for him. From time to time he borrowed ten bob off him at the end of the week, and there had been the occasion when he had confided some minor crisis to him and received perfectly sound advice, without the moral seasoning that so many would have considered essential.

"Well?" said Mark again. "Any secret messages sent with the photostats? Are little bags of cocaine inserted beneath library labels? Are postage stamps insidiously tainted? Come on, boy, play the game, and tell your captain all about it, and then we'll run the racket together, the wide boys of I.L.D.A., librarians in crime."

Mr. Wilson's eyelashes went secretively down. This was sufficiently odd in itself, and Mark's considering eyes lost their laughter, and fixed themselves intently on the young man. "Are you taking a course in discretion, Jack?" he said. "Or is it simply that you don't trust me?"

"Look," said Mr. Wilson, speaking very quickly, and looking unhappy, "you're always ragging me, and I know you think I'm an ass, but honestly, cross my heart, I think I'm on to something. I mean, it's just a fluke, of course, and I did start this for fun, and I don't really imagine I'm a detective or any rot like that, only—you know the way it is. People laugh at you, and you just go on in a kind of spirit of dash-it-all. You must know what I mean."

"Yes," said Mark, "I know what you mean."

"And so—well, I went on. And suddenly I had a sort of hunch, and it was too silly for words, only——" Mr. Wilson's voice faltered. "I think perhaps it wasn't so silly after all. Of course, I'm still not sure, and it does seem rather far-fetched."

"Don't you think you could tell me about it?"

"No, sir," said Mr. Wilson, unconsciously reverting to his schooldays. "You see, I think it might be dangerous, and I wouldn't like to involve anyone else."

"Do you think," said Mark abruptly, "you could ignore the captain's hand for one minute, let the gatling jam and the colonel rot, and so on, and tell me what all this is about? I am neither so elderly nor so foolish as you seem to imagine. And I'm not laughing at you, damn your eyes, so stop staring at me as if I were all the avenging headmasters rolled into one. I have never ignored the fact that this might be serious. I think it is serious. And I should be sorry to see you killed. You'd better drop this, you know. Forget about it."

"I can't," said Mr. Wilson, almost in despair.

"Do you want to be a corpse?"

"No."

"Well then? What the hell does it matter to you if a bunch of crazy neurotics need dope to keep them going, and a kindly gentleman offers to provide them with it, cash down?"

"It's a matter of principle," said Mr. Wilson.

"Oh, Christ!"

"I do have principles, you know."

"Others don't!"

"All the more reason for me to have them. Anyway," said Mr. Wilson, looking shamefacedly at Mark, "I expect you have them, too. I mean, there must be things you feel you can't do, or things you feel you must do. And—I know I'm putting things very badly—but in a real emergency you just have to act, never mind if you like it or not, or whether"—he blinked as he said this—"you're scared stiff."

"What you forget," said Mark, "is that the murderer may feel the same way. He mayn't want to murder you, but, if he's in danger of being found out, he probably will."

Mr. Wilson said nothing. It is not comfortable at nineteen years to face the immediate prospect of violent death. There was a coldness spreading inside him which no captain's hand could have dispelled.

Mark said suddenly, in a harsh voice, "During the war, I was hiding in a barn with half a dozen others. There was a baby amongst us. The Germans were only a hundred yards away. If they'd known where we were, it would have been the end, not only of us, but of a great many more. And the baby started to cry."

Mr. Wilson stared at him.

"We wrung its neck," said Mark, looking straight at him. He gazed into the boy's shocked, appalled face, and made a dreadful descriptive gesture with his powerful hands.

Mr. Wilson whispered, "You couldn't. A *baby*. It's not true——"

"Of course it is. You know very well it is. It was a question of one baby, or twenty, thirty, forty men. The Boches had their own ways of getting information, you know."

Mr. Wilson instinctively backed. "It wasn't *you*——"

"I said 'we', didn't I? Perhaps it was me. I won't tell you that. It doesn't matter, anyway. I'm telling you this to show you how strong is the instinct for self-preservation. If it's a question of the murderer's life or yours, why, God help you, Jack, and I shouldn't depend too much on divine intervention."

Mr. Wilson said nothing, but, as Mark came nearer him, backed even more.

"You've got your final exam, next month, haven't you? Well, why don't you work for it? Leave detection to Sergeant Robins. It's his business. It's not yours. Hold your tongue and forget about this confounded business."

Mr. Wilson stammered, looking very sick, "It's not possible. A *baby*——"

"Oh, damn the baby! You're scarcely weaned yourself." Mark suddenly raised his voice. "All right. All right. Go ahead. Play the great detective. Ferret out everything, nose into everything, dig up all the dirt and scatter it around. But dig yourself a nice grave, too, while you're about it. For by God, you're going to need it. And may your principles comfort you for all eternity."

Mr. Wilson, when he was alone, took out the little notebook he carried in his pocket, together with a handful of newspaper cuttings, and began comparing a long list of dates. For the principles which sounded such frightful rot when one talked about them were very real things to him, for he believed in God, and the ultimate defeat of evil, and a great many other old-fashioned and blush-making things that one hardly dared mention.

Miss Holmes's private world at that time was one ridden by temporaries. Everything was going just as badly as she had prophesied. Temporaries came, and temporaries went, and each one was more trying than the last, and the work produced shocking beyond belief. The first one was a visiting Australian who, after half an hour, told the girls that she just could not understand how they stuck it, they must be simply bored to death. Then, after complaining of the noise, the draughts, and the lighting, she announced that she would tell off Mr. Dodds for his appalling handwriting, and that, if Mr. Allan scrawled any more of his rude notes on the forms, she'd give him a piece of her mind he'd remember to the end of his days.

She was a woman of forty, with an aggrieved air and a hacksaw voice. Mr. Allan did scrawl another of his rude notes and she did give him a piece of her mind, upon which he gave her in return such a piece of his that she immediately left, saying that she had never been so spoken to

in her life. This was probably true, but it did not help Miss
Holmes, who had again to ring the agency.

The next, who stayed three days, was a young and languid
girl who drawled out to the fascinated Location Department
that she was really an actress, and would shortly be on in
the West End. She was decorative but she coudd not type;
all her work had to be done again, and at last she, too, left,
taking with her a large amount of office stationery, and
promising the girl they should all come to her first night.

The third was mad, talked to herself, and pulled pieces off
her mittens. The girls were appalled and awed; no one could
help listening to the eternal monologue, and the day's out-
put was such that Miss Holmes was forced to ring the agency
yet again.

She said inevitably to Mr. Latimer, "How I am expected to
run this department, I do not know. The work is just piling
up. I think I shall resign."

Mr. Latimer, who knew she would do nothing of the sort,
sighed, restrained his temper, and said, "It's not easy for any
of us. If this goes on much longer, we shall have all our staff
leaving. What with Mr. Rills——"

"Disgusting young man," said Miss Holmes. "He should
have been fired a long time ago."

"I believe Mr. Ridley has decided to keep him on, provided
he returns the money. He is, after all, a good worker, and
clever at his job. I think he's learnt his lesson. He's very
young, after all. But of course it isn't easy. And he seems
to have been spreading so much scandal, and he's at daggers drawn with Mr. Allan, and scared stiff of him into the
bargain."

"I have always thought," said Miss Holmes, "that Mr. Allan
did the murder. If you'd heard what he said to that wretched
Australian woman. I can't repeat it, because it wasn't decent."

"I can imagine it," said Mr. Latimer dryly. "From all accounts she deserved it. And really, Miss Holmes, if you don't
mind my saying so, you mustn't go about accusing people of
murder. It's actionable."

"I don't go about accusing anyone of anything," returned
Miss Holmes, "but I'm entitled to my own thoughts as much
as everybody else, and I think he's the murderer, and that's
all there is to it. What's the matter with the little Wilson boy
these days? He creeps about, almost without a word. Has
he some trouble at home? He looks positively frightened."
For she had a soft spot in her heart for Mr. Wilson who
was always polite and friendly to her.

"I expect it's his exam. It must be getting near."

"Or Mrs. Bridgwater, perhaps. I'd the impression she'd got her hooks into him. Though she's quieter, too. That's a relief, I must say. From time to time," said Miss Holmes, pinning two forms together with vicious accuracy, "I get extraordinarily tired of the artistic temperament which seems to allow people to ignore all their responsibilities and generally make a nuisance of themselves."

"How is the newest temporary?" inquired Mr. Latimer hastily.

Miss Holmes gave him a weary and ironic smile. "Oh, we'll never get rid of her. She adores the place. It's a pity she can't type as well as she talks. She never stops. The girls call her Dizzy Dot."

Miss Dorothea—"you must call me Dot, dear, everyone does"—Langdon turned out such howlers on her forms that even Greta was shocked. She talked incessantly in a loud, high voice, but was so friendly and good-natured that no one had the heart to reproach her. Barbara, who was tired and irritable, found her exasperating, especially as her nature was an officious one, and she took upon herself the duties of the entire Library. However, the resulting confusion was partly forgiven her for the memorable episode known as the silencing of Mr. Allan.

It occurred on her second day. Barbara was standing by the lift on the fourth floor at lunch-time. Mark came out of his room to stand beside her and, without a word, slid his hand round hers. At that moment an agitated cry of, "Wait for me, oh do wait for me," came from behind them, and Miss Langdon, her head bound up in a yellow scarf, leapt heavily into the lift.

Mark shut the gates; this seemed to unleash Miss Langdon's tongue. She turned her bright, smiling face on Mark, though his look was such as to freeze more timid smiles at source. She cried, "How nice of you to wait for me. Fact is, I'm meeting Eric, the boy-friend, you know, and I don't want to be late, because we had a terrible row last night, and we're getting married in October, and now I'm not sure if we're getting married or not, because, you see, we've both such strong personalities, and it's so difficult, isn't it, if you don't know which is going to dominate which——"

They reached the third floor.

"He's really a clever boy, but, you see," continued Miss Langdon, stamping on Mark's foot in her excitement, and knocking Barbara's handbag to the floor. "—Oh, so sorry. Is that my fault? Clumsy, aren't I? Well, as I was saying, he's full of temperament, he's an M.P., you see, at least he's going to be an M.P., at the moment he works with the Gas Company and——"

They reached the second floor.

"—of course his career worries him, but then so does mine, I play the piano, you look musical, Mr.—Mr. Allan, isn't it?—one can always tell, there's an artistic look in the eyes—the moment I saw you, I said, 'There's an artist.' And what with my piano and his politics—— He's coming to dinner, tonight, and I thought I'd get him wine, do you know anything about wine?——"

They reached the first floor.

"—Only it mustn't cost much, because I haven't any money, and it's so difficult, one has certain standards one must live up to, and if I'm going to be an M.P.'s wife—— You must tell me about your music, Mr. Allan. What do you play? I play the piano, love Chopin, don't you? Can't bear all this typing, of course, but what's a girl to do, one has to keep oneself. I expect it's the same for you, Mr. Allan, isn't it? You must come and meet the boy-friend some time, I expect you'd have a lot in common—— Oh, here we are. Bye-bye!"

Miss Langdon waved gaily at Mark, tossed a second-class smile to Barbara, and scampered off.

Barbara had almost forgotten how to laugh. Indeed, the episode for her had a certain bitter humour, for to stand so near Mark and not be able even to speak to him was a torment. But the hysteria caused by Miss Langdon's speech and the look on Mark's face were too much for her. She leant against the wall and laughed helplessly, so that for a moment she could not speak a word.

Mark folded his arms across his chest, and looked at her as if he hated her. He inquired, "Well? Have you finished?"

"You must admit," she said, "it's your defeat. Ah, Mr. Allan, you must play the piano to me sometime—*Mark*!"

For Mark, his face black and haggard with rage, had abruptly turned his back on her, and walked away. Barbara stared after him, her laughter turned to a monstrous lump in the throat and an ominous pricking in the eyes. She called out his name again, but he would not turn. She did not see him for the rest of the day. And after that she hated Miss Langdon with the utmost intensity.

But Miss Langdon's ebullient personality helped greatly to restore the Location Department to its normal state. By the time she had decided, on her own initiative, to send a form to an organisation that never loaned to outsiders; had, for no known reason, scrawled 'cancelled" across one of Mr. Dodds's periodicals; and finally translated a French title into grossly inaccurate English, she had almost erased the memory of Mrs. Warren and the fact that her murderer was presumably still in the building.

Indeed, the Location Department was now very much as it had been. Greta sent out for a book typed as 'Immoral England', and Maureen transcribed a medical treatise on the 'Renewal of the Body' as the 'Removal of the Body'. Love affairs were spoken of, domestic difficulties discussed, and Mrs. Warren's body lay in a London churchyard, forgotten by everyone, except for Sergeant Warren and a few of her relations.

And Barbara was typing sections of her book again. She had fallen into this; it had swung into an obsession. When Mr. Dodds walked into her room, she instinctively put a hand over her typewriter, as she had done in the old days.

"Oh, don't mind me," said Mr. Dodds, "I'm delighted to see you working again. How is the soldier of fortune?"

Barbara hesitated, and flushed. She was tortured with the ambivalent complex of the writer—the desire to talk about her work, and the terror of laying herself open to ridicule. But after all, Mr. Dodds knew so much already, and the only person she would have discussed her novel with had apparently left her for good, for she had not had a word from him since their quarrel. And now that she had also quarrelled with Mark, she thought a great deal more of Charles, and was filled from time to time with a nagging sense of dismay.

But he did not write, he did not call, he did not ring. And Mark stalked by her like some savage, avenging Elizabethan ghost; it looked as if he would never forgive her for that one brief impulse of laughter, and the gulf between them was as deep and wide as the sea, so that she seemed to be standing on a cold, barren shore, her hands, unheeded, held out miserably to him.

She looked up at Mr. Dodds, who was pottering about in his usual manner. She said, "The soldier of fortune is going magnificently. I think it's the best thing I've ever done. He's so real. He's not good, he's not a hero, but he lives, and I can write about him as if I'd known him all my life. And yet, how odd it is. It is, after all, a fantasy world."

"Yes," said Mr. Dodds, "a fantasy world."

"And usually that world cracks at a touch of reality. But

now it's as if *that* is the real world, and this, where I live, pure fantasy. Do you think, perhaps, I am mad? Will I hear voices? Will it become a kind of Berkeley Square, so that I step back into my imagination? I don't want that to happen. It frightens me. And yet my—my soldier of fortune is the realest person I know."

He did not answer immediately, which was unusual in Mr. Dodds, who, as Mr. Rills had once remarked, never gave a plain answer, but always made an oration. Then he said, briefly enough, "So you've forgotten about the murder?"

"No. How could I? But one can't think of it all the time."

"I do."

"But why? It's done with. And—what's the use of pretending?—we none of us liked her. She's gone, and somehow there doesn't even seem to be a gap."

And as she said this, a section of her mind whispered, 'What are you saying? This cannot be you talking.'

"There is a gap," said Mr. Dodds. "Oh, not because of Mrs. Warren. She was just a silly woman, though I suppose she had the right to live as much as anyone else. But there is a gap, and that gap lies in a certain person's mind. You cannot kill, Barbara, and get away with it. To take another human being's life is so final, so irrevocable, such *hubris*, if you like, that it must in the normal course of events change you. And the person who did the killing is still with us. Is your soldier of fortune a murderer?"

"Not really," said Barbara, flushing again. "He is suspected."

"But he didn't do it?"

"No. I couldn't have that."

"And quite right, too," said Mr. Dodds, nodding his head. "I entirely approve. Well, Barbara, stay in your fantasy world. There are other worlds you could enter with more danger. Where are you up to now? Are you perhaps writing a love scene?"

"Yes. Yes. The—the heroine has fallen in love with him. It is writing itself." Then she cried, in a sudden panic of honesty, "Oh, Mr. Dodds——"

He looked at her.

"I have the feeling that—that I'm getting into rather a horrid sort of mess. And yet I can't stop. Nothing like this has ever happened to me before. Do you know who the murderer is?"

"I have always known," replied Mr. Dodds, "but, unlike young Wilson, who fills me with the utmost alarm and

despondency, I do not propose to talk about it. I have no
proof. I can do nothing. I can only say what I've said before—and it doesn't matter if I'm repeating myself, because
nobody listens to me in any case—that there is a gap in the
murderer's mind, and what lies there is not pleasant and can
do no good. You are already in your Berkeley Square, you
know. You have been there for a long time. One day you
will be forced out. Be careful, my dear. To kill needs
ruthlessness, egotism. A killer is always dangerous. I hope
your Mr. What's-his-name can draw a sword to guard you.
And in the meantime, I still want to know what has happened to my microfilm of *Revue de Métaphysique et Moral.*
Soldiers of fortune are all very well, and murder, no doubt,
is all about us. I wonder if I could incapacitate young Wilson
just a little, break his leg, or something, enough to keep him
at home for the next couple of weeks——"

"Mr. Dodds!"

"But of course, no one co-operates with me in my work
and, with things as they are, I feel that the smallest trifle
could blow us sky-high. Go on with your novel, young
woman. I'd feel happier if you were writing it all the time."

"Mr. Andrews looked down at her," wrote Barbara. " 'We
will go out together, one day,' he said, 'just you and I.
Decently and properly as people should. It shall be all as you
please. A barge, perhaps, with the "Water Music" to accompany us'——"

She stopped typing. The arid grass rippled in the wind; the
smell of the sea was in her nostrils. To be blown sky-high,
on s'en fout, quoi, pom-pom-pom-*pom*—— A gap to crawl
into, a gap in a person's mind, oh, God, to be there, to be
there, *jusqu'à la fin du monde,* with arms to hold, and a
mouth to kiss, and at the end a hempen rope swinging in the
breeze——

She gave a gasp and a sob, jerked herself up. She sat
there, staring out of the window; the windows of the Reference Room, which faced her, danced and flickered before her
eyes.

VIII. PYROTECNICS, EXPLOSIVS, MATCHES, ETC. 662

THE great row over *Revue de Métaphysique et Moral* burst late on the Monday; Miss Dorothea Langdon acted to some extent as the fuse.

She was now firmly established in I.L.D.A. She continued to mind everyone's business, and meddle in everyone's affairs; she persistently told the world about her fiancé, her marriage problems, her piano playing and her temperament. She came into Mr. Latimer's private office to tell him how much she loved her job. She stopped Mr. Ridley on his way to lunch, to ask his opinion of the sweater she was knitting for Eric. And she developed a mild passion for Mark Allan. "Oh, it doesn't mean," she assured the girls, "that I'm unfaithful to the boy-friend, or anything like that, but really, he is the most devastatingly *rude* man I've ever met. I do so love rudeness, don't you? And I feel he's dreadfully frustrated in some way or other, so I might be able to help him. Perhaps he's sex-starved. So embittering for a man. Do you know anything about his private life?"

She asked this question in her high, clear voice, during morning tea-break in the canteen. Barbara was beside her, and Mrs. Bridgwater not far way. The girls broke into a shocked giggling, and Barbara nearly dropped her cup and saucer in the effort to control herself. Miss Langdon, unperturbed, continued, "I am determined to find out what is wrong. Of course, it isn't just good-neighbourliness, I must confess. He's so fearfully attractive, isn't he, with that lean, dark face, and so tall, too? I love tall men. Don't you girls know anything about him?"

"He's smashing," said Greta, whose own passion had somewhat died down through lack of fuel, but who still professed romantic feelings, and who regarded Mark as if he were some unattainable film star.

"Isn't he?" cried Miss Langdon. "Oh, isn't he? But I want

to know what is wrong. I will, too. I'm very persistent, you know."

Then Mr. Rills, at the other end of the room, raised his head and said, "Ask him."

"Oh no——" began Barbara, but Miss Langdon only burst into a great laugh and cried on the crest of her laughter, "Do you know, I really think I will."

Barbara fell silent. Her distress was not really due to Miss Langdon. Since the episode in the lift, Mark had obdurately refused to speak to her. This morning, he had met her in the corridor. He turned on her a bleak, forbidding countenance, and made as if to pass her. But she caught hold of his arm; her misery was now such that she was scarcely aware of what she was doing.

She said desperately, "What's the matter?"

"Nothing," he said, and jerked his arm away.

She said, before she could stop herself, "Oh, darling, this is quite ridiculous——" Then she flushed scarlet, and here he did pause, to say curtly, "I don't like being made a fool of. I can't stop your laughing at me, if you're bad-mannered enough to do so, but at least I do not choose to invite that particular form of bad manners again."

The tears sprang to her eyes, and she stood there, not knowing what to do or say. But she was sure that he had noticed the tears, and this helped her to recover herself. She managed to say, "Very well. I can only say I'm sorry. I'll try to remember not to laugh again. Only—only I haven't laughed much, lately, what with the murder and one thing and another, and I suppose it was a relief to be able to laugh at all, so I overindulged myself. It won't occur again. If I ever do feel like laughing, I'll think of the murder. I might even —even join Mr. Wilson, and play Watson to his Holmes. Please forgive me for having bothered you."

She walked on very slowly. She hoped against hope that he would come after her to comfort her. But he did not, though she had the impression that he looked at her very intently. Her vision, however, was blurred, and she preferred not to raise her eyes to his.

This occurred at ten in the morning. It had not started her day happily. Miss Langdon's remarks at eleven did not help, and she went back to the dogged typing of her university list. There was a bitter cold inside her that the August sun could not touch. She made two quite ridiculous mistakes, and finally tore the third stencil, so that she had to start it all over again. And at this she wept convulsively,

beating her fists on the desk, not troubling to dry the tears
that rained down. And after that she worked for a while with
fierce concentration.

Miss Langdon did not ask Mark what was frustrating him.
Perhaps even she quailed before such audacity. But she was
determined to help him, and soon the opportunity came,
though Barbara, typing in her own room, did not hear of
this until later when the day had come to its catastrophic
end.

At two-thirty, Mr. Rills, dealing with his afternoon post,
opened up a microfilm which had just arrived from the
Bibliothéque Nationale. This was a mistake on his part, and
he was furious and appalled at having committed it. All microfilms went automatically through to Mark Allan, and Mark
Allan, who, as Mr. Rills knew only too well, was angered
by so many things, lost his temper to a degree beyond
civilisation if anyone dared to interfere in his work. Mr.
Rills dropped the microfilm on his desk as if it were a red-
hot coal, said, "My God!" in varying tones of horror, and
wondered what the devil he could do now. His relationship
with Mr. Allan was already so impossible that he would on
no account see his enemy alone. He had, after all, spoken a
great deal to the sergeant; Mark knew this well enough, and
Mr. Rills, overcome by conscience and fear, was reduced to
a state of sick panic.

He looked wretchedly at the microfilm. It consisted of an
article from a periodical called *Revue de Métaphysique et
Moral*, required, according to the international demand note,
by Liverpool University. Mr. Rills sat there, chewing at his
lower lip, and the longer he sat there, the more terrified he
became. He had never had courage of any high degree; such
as he had now failed him utterly. He could visualise the
scene. He would be shouted at, sworn at, insulted. He would
not put it past Allan to use physical violence. Mr. Rills had
endured a great deal these past few days, including the unpleasant interview with Mr. Ridley, and an even more unpleasant one with his bank manager. He said aloud, "Oh,
God, what am I to do?", looked at the microfilm again, and
for a second had the wild thought of throwing it into the
waste-paper basket. But this he did not dare, for the post-
room would have entered up the package, and if Allan discovered that Mr. Rills had actually been throwing his precious
microfilms away——

Mr. Rills said, "Oh, God!" again, and decided that, whatever happened, he would not go into Allan's office. Oh, in

theory, it was easy enough—"I say, Allan, the post-room sent this to me by mistake, and I'm afraid I opened it. Sorry, old boy——" No. Oh no. Then suddenly he thought, 'If I send it direct to Liverpool, the odds are he'll never know. He'll get the receipt, of course, but it'll be one in many, and after a few days it should be easy enough to distribute the blame somewhere else.' A brilliant idea, born of abject fear, came to Mr. Rills. If he could persuade one of the Location Department girls to send the parcel, it would then be Miss Holmes who would get the full blast of Allan's wrath.

He straightened his tie, and combed back his hair, then put the microfilm in his pocket.

As he opened the general office door, he could hear that appalling young woman holding forth as usual. Despite his anguish, a faint, unhappy laugh spluttered from him. He'd give his ears to be there when she asked Allan if he were sex-starved.

"And, my dears," she was saying, "he actually said he was sorry. I've never known him to apologise before. I mean, he's awfully casual as a general thing. Not rude like your marvellous Mr. Allan, of course, but just casual, if you know what I mean. And I said to him, 'Eric,' I said—— Hallo, Mr. Rills."

She turned a beaming and friendly smile upon him. "And to what," she said, "do we owe the honour?"

Mr. Rills gave her a look of utter distaste. He hated her from her kindly, round face, surmounted by hair done in a horse's tail, to her long, thick-ankled legs; he hated her voice, her smile, and her whole manner. He turned his back on her. He said—one might as well do this properly—"Any of you girls seen Mr. Allan?"

"I wish we had," said Miss Langdon.

He tried to ignore her. He said, "He's not in his room. And this microfilm must go to Liverpool University by the afternoon post. It's extremely urgent. I wonder if one of you girls would pack it up and send it for me?"

They did not respond as he had hoped. They looked at each other doubtfully. They did not dislike Mr. Rills, whom indeed they scarcely knew, for he never came near them, but they had a hearty respect for Mr. Allan, and it seemed to them that this might cause trouble.

"I don't think we ought to," began Greta.

"You'll have to ask Miss Holmes," said Maureen.

"She's not in her room," said Mr. Rills swiftly, "and really, this is terribly urgent."

"Ask Miss Smith, then," said Peggy.

Mr. Rills had no intention whatsoever of asking Miss Smith. His sharp eyes had perceived long ago that there was something between Allan and Miss Smith, and to bring her into this would be undesirable, to say the least of it. He opened his mouth, but, before he could say anything, Miss Langdon had cried out, "I'll send it off for him, bless him. The poor fellow's obviously overworked, and I'd love to save him this, even if it's only a tiny thing. Give it to me, Mr. Rills, whatever it is, and I'll send it off at once."

Mr. Rills was startled by this unexpected ally, but took the microfilm from his pocket and handed it to her.

"What a quaint thing," remarked Miss Langdon. "What does it do?"

"The fate of the nation may depend on it," said Mr. Rills. "Yours is a great responsibility, Miss Langdon. I feel Mr. Allan will be deeply grateful to you. But don't mention it to him, will you? Temperamentally he dislikes being in anyone's debt. I am sure, however, you will notice his silent appreciation."

"But, Dot, you can't——" began Greta, when Mr. Rills had left the room.

"I jolly well can," said Miss Langdon, busily pulling out paper and string from her drawer. "I've always wanted to help Mr. Allan. And every little counts, you know."

(Which, as a great many people were to discover, was perfectly true.)

It was only when the parcel had gone down to catch the three-thirty post that Maureen exclaimed, "But Liverpool University is closed——"

"Never mind, dear," said Miss Langdon. "The deed is done. One assumes Liverpool University will eventually open again. Mr. Allan wants it to go, and go it shall. Besides, it's five and twenty to four. Did I tell you that Eric brought me a bunch of roses yesterday——?"

Mark Allan, working in his room, looked at Mrs. Bridgwater in the dispassionate and contemptuous way she had come to dread. She was a sentimental woman. She had chosen to forget the bitter words that had been spoken between them. She could only remember how much in love with her he had been not so long ago. 'How fickle men are,' she thought. 'They use us and are finished with us.' Surely there was some chance of their coming together again, and then she could share with him the fear that was now her constant companion. And he was so very handsome, and exciting, too, and after all one didn't just fall out of love.

She said with difficulty, for he was regarding her as if he hated her, "Mark, I had to come in and see you. I do so hate quarrelling with you like this."

"Do you?" he said.

"Of course I do. Look, let's be friends again. After all," she said, turning upon him the pale blue eyes that had once provoked such passion in his own, "there's no reason why we shouldn't. Just because of a silly little tiff—I mean——" She stopped. So unmistakable was the cold hostility in the face confronting hers that the words she was speaking suddenly scalded her throat. She was quite at a loss. She had never been in such a situation. It had always been the men who had pleaded, and she who had laughed and said, 'Silly boy, you mustn't be naughty, you know,' and so on. But she must break this down; her fear had grown into an intolerable burden, and Mark was surely the only person who could help her. She forced her shaking voice down to a lower register and instinctively altered her stance, so that the curve of her breast and the magnificent line of her throat were shown to best advantage. "Mark," she said again, "it wasn't my fault. I am married, not very happily, but after all, I do owe Henry something. And he has been so difficult. Of course, it's all right now, really, but I'm so unhappy, Mark, so unhappy——"

"Are you?" said Mark, and reached out his hand for a sheaf of forms.

She said, "I thought you loved me. I suppose it was just the usual thing. Men are all the same." Then the fear cramped her stomach again, so that she was compelled to screw up her eyes. She looked at him, the unresponsive face bent over his work. He must help her, he must, otherwise she would go mad. She cried out, "If I—if we——"

"If we what?" he said, and the look he gave her was so ugly that she backed, nearly falling over a chair as she did so. What she had been about to say was something she had never said in her life before, and to say it in cold blood to someone who seemed as if he would prefer to cut her throat, was more than she could endure. She said in a small, flat voice, "Nothing." But she still stood there, her hands hanging down, and then in desperation she cried out again, "I need your advice. You once said you would do anything for me, you said you would even kill for me. Won't you help me, please, Mark? Please. I'm so unhappy and I'm in such a mess. And you're strong and brave, and you always know the way out of things. Mayn't I stay here a little and tell you about it?"

The answer he gave her was not in words. He said nothing. But he smiled at her, then raised his hand and touched his cheek.

"Oh!" cried Mrs. Bridgwater. "Oh, it's so unfair, so unfair." Then she turned and ran from the room, for she could not face that look any longer; it stripped her beauty and power from her so that she felt ugly, ridiculous, obscene.

She sat in her own room for a long time. She said aloud, over and over again, "Oh, God, what shall I do?"

Mark stared after her then, as the door was shutting behind her, half rose to his feet. There was a frowning, reflective expression on his face. But then he shrugged his shoulders and sat down again, concentrating on the work before him.

At half-past three he came out into the corridor, and there, at the top of the stairs, met one of the young women from the post-room. She gave him an apprehensive look and said, "I'm so sorry about the microfilm, Mr. Allan."

"What microfilm? What are you talking about?"

The girl said unhappily, "Well, you see, I'm new here, and I didn't know. I didn't mean to send it down to Mr. Rills, but I thought it was his department. Did he bring it up to you? I'll go and get it if he didn't——"

There was a pause. 'Mr. Allan shouts,' they had told her, 'but you mustn't mind, and he usually apologises afterwards.' She was very young, and she watched him in growing panic. His face had grown oddly blank. He said at last, quietly enough, "When did you take it down to Mr. Rills?"

"After lunch, Mr. Allan. Would you like me to ask him for it?"

He smiled at her. "Oh no," he said. "I'll go myself." He added pleasantly, "It's not your fault. You'll learn the work in due time."

"I don't know why," she said to her colleagues a few minutes later, "you say he shouts. He couldn't have been more charming. I think he's ever so handsome. Just like a film star."

This was at three-thirty-three.

At three-thirty-five Mark Allan pushed open Mr. Rills's door. Mr. Rills, who had been congratulating himself on his clever management of an awkward situation, looked up to see Nemesis blocking the doorway, and went chalk-white. Mark

shut the door behind him with a slam. His face was a devil's
mask of rage. "Where," he said in a roar that engulfed Mr.
Rills in its volume, "is my microfilm? Where is it? Where is
it? What the hell do you mean by hanging on to it, you
bloody, sneaking, meddling, perverted little——"

The young woman from the post-room, one floor below,
said, "What on earth is all that row?" She opened the door a
little. "It sounds as if someone's gone mad."

"It sounds to me," replied her friend, "like that charming
Mr. Allan. Good gracious! One would think there was a
murd——"

She broke off. The two girls stared at each other.

Miss Holmes was dictating a letter to Maureen. "With regard," she said, "to your request for T. Telford—T-e-l-
f-o-r-d—— T. Telford's 'Survey and report of the proposed
extension of the Grand Union Canal', published in 1804, I
regret to inform you—— Oh, really, this is too much. How
I'm expected to do any work when there's such a row going
on? What's happening in the name of goodness? That'll be
Mr. Allan, of course. It's a pity no one slapped him when he
was younger. But this is impossible. Maureen, stop giggling.
It's not funny when grown-ups behave like children. Get me
Mr. Latimer—— No. No. Get me Mr. Dodds on the phone.
And hurry. I never heard anything like it in my life." She
suddenly went pale. "Do get a move on, child. It sounds——
Oh. Mr. Dodds. Mr. Dodds——"

Mr. Dodds, looking elderly, donnish, and in his own way,
rather formidable, stepped into Mr. Rills's office. There did
not seem to be the massacre he had expected, but Mr. Rills
looked like death and seemed near tears; he was flattened
against the wall of his room while Mark, with fury flaming
round him lika a corona, was standing over him, his chest
heaving up and down, his face so drawn with temper that he
no longer looked sane.

"Well, Allan?" said Mr. Dodds, in his dryest voice. "What
is all this? Are we now turned into Bedlam? If that is so,
we had better ask the fine ladies in, and let them pay a fee
of a shilling for doing so, as they did in the old days. We
will certainly provide them with a most remarkable exhibi-
tion."

Mark said between his teeth, "Get out!"

Mr. Dodds carefully shut the door. "I shall do nothing of
the kind," he said. "I'll even pay you a shilling, if you

like. I cannot understand why people go to zoos, for surely there could be nothing more zoological——" He smiled at Mark. "You know," he said, "you'll really have to put up with me, because you can't do anything about it. I'm an old man, I'm delighted to say, and nearly twice your years, so you really can't knock me down. Do tell me what this is all about. Rills, I suggest you sit down. What can have happened to provoke such a storm? The ladies are all terrified out of their wits, and you really cannot blame them, for your voice, sir, must carry as far as Senate House."

Mr. Rills shrieked out, "He's mad! He's mad! He's not safe. He's a murderer. Send for the police, for God's sake, send for the police!"

"Now, now, Rills," said Mr. Dodds soothingly, "we're all mad, nor'-nor'-west, after all. Will neither of you tell me what all this is about?"

Mark Allan moved away. He appeared to have regained his composure, but he was still breathing fast, and from time to time his eyes flickered back to Mr. Rills, with an expression in them that made the young man cry out again, "He's the murderer, I tell you. He'll kill me!"

Mark said, "I suppose it's not so important. But if Rills" —and the knife edge slid back into his voice—"would be kind enough to tell me what has happened to the microfilm, I might be able to do something to remedy the confounded mess he's made with his usual, bloody, interfering incompetence."

"I told him!" wailed Mr. Rills. It seemed as if he could not address Mark direct. "I told him. That young woman, the one who talks——" A sob caught in his throat, for he was most dreadfully frightened; for the last ten minutes it had seemed as if murder had laid its bloody finger upon him. "She's posted it—to Liverpool University. I told her not to, but she would do it."

"You told her not to——" began Mark, his voice rising again.

"It's not my fault!" cried Mr. Rills, as he had cried at the age of five, and consistently from then onwards. "It's not my fault if people bring me parcels, if the department is so in-incompetently run."

"Ah!" said Mark, in a contemptuous rage, making the sound end in a guttural, and he raised his hand and swept it down an inch away from Mr. Rills's face, as if he would hit him. Then he said to Mr. Dodds in a tone of the utmost formality, "I beg your pardon, sir, for having inconvenienced you. I will now transfer my attentions to the young woman who talks. You needn't worry about her. I shall not murder her. I only murder on even dates. As for you——" He turned again to Mr. Rills, who cowered back, looking piteously at Mr. Dodds for help. "I'll deal with you later, and in a way you'll remember. You abominable, lying little toady. You'd hang your own grandmother if you thought you'd get sixpence out of it."

"I say," said a voice at the door. "What on earth is going on? Is somebody ill? I don't want to butt in, you know, but really, you're making the most filthy row."

Mark, swinging round to look at Mr. Wilson's youthful, bewildered face, burst out laughing, and then it seemed as if he could not stop; he laughed and laughed while Mr. Dodds steadily watched him, and Mr. Rills mopped at his face with a quivering hand.

Then he said, still shaking, as if hysteria had seized him, "A clue for you, Jack." His smile was a grimace. "The clue of the lost microfilm."

"What microfilm is this?" inquired Mr. Dodds.

"From a French magazine, sir. *Revue de Métaphysique et Moral*. It has at last arrived from Paris, and now, I gather, has gone to Liverpool University, which happens to be closed. Really," he added, his voice grown soft, "you have been extremely clever, Rills. However, I'll now go and see the young woman who talks. Only this time I'll do the talking."

"Chance'll bother you," muttered Mr. Rills, but dared not say this very loud.

Mr. Wilson, throughout all this, had said nothing. Mark Allan, as he came into the corridor, clapped him on the shoulder, saying, "And how is detection going, Sherlock? Is your case now complete?"

Mr. Wilson did not reply.

"Well? Are you not on the track of the murderer? May we not soon expect an arrest?" His gaze focused on Mr. Wilson's downcast face. His smile vanished. "You should inform the sergeant, Jack, lest the fell sergeant gets ahead of him."

Mr. Wilson still said nothing. He walked slowly away to his own room, and a phantom on a pale horse slid behind him as his shadow.

Mark opened the general office door, swept them all with his gaze, then came towards Miss Langdon, who bestowed on him a flashing smile. "Did you," he said, "post that microfilm to Liverpool University?"

"I did," she replied cheerfully.

"Oh, crumbs!" whispered Greta to Peggy. "I knew we shouldn't——"

"And who gave you permission to do so?"

"Oh, I never ask permission," returned Miss Langdon, meeting his blazing eyes with the utmost calm. "Poor Mr. Rills wanted someone to send it."

"He did, did he?"

"Yes, and the other girls thought they'd better not, so I did it. I knew it would save you trouble, and I always think," said Miss Langdon, patting at a wisp of hair that had fallen across her cheek, "that you look so harassed and overworked, Mr. Allan. I know the signs, you see, because Eric—that's my fiancé—is just the same, and I do so like to help people when I can. You worry a lot, don't you? Do you sleep all right? Eric takes some wonderful tablets——"

Mark said in a low voice that cut across hers, "I should think that anyone engaged to you would take tablets of cyanide. I am not interested in your tablets, nor in your concern for my welfare. I am only interested in the fact that you, who are working here on a purely temporary basis, should have the damned impudence to take upon yourself a matter that concerns me, and me alone. You dare to tell me that you have posted this microfilm off, on your own responsibility, when——"

"I believe in taking responsibility," said Miss Langdon. "I say, your nerves are in a shocking state, aren't they? Why are you making such a fuss about a silly old microfilm, anyway? The way you're carrying on, one would think it was a matter of life and death." She broke into one of her breezy laughs. "I know what it is, Mr. Allan. You can't deceive Dot. You're the murderer, and the microfilm holds the secret, deadly drug with which you poison people. Eric always says I ought to write books, I've such an imagination. Do you know——"

She stopped short. She was not a perceptive young woman, but the expression on Mr. Allan's undeniably handsome face as he moved silently across the room and stood beside her, was such as to make her eyes widen and her smile diminish. She instinctively put a hand to her throat.

"If," said Mark, in a voice as tight as a fiddle-string, "you have such an imagination, Miss Whatever-your-blasted-name-is, I suggest you employ it for your own good, and imagine what happens to young women who take too much upon themselves, and have the impertinence to think they can manage everyone else's affairs for them." He added, "You're fired. You'll go. This instant."

"Oh no, I won't," replied Miss Langdon with spirit, "I don't work for you."

"Christ!" he said. "If you did——"

"I work for Miss Holmes. And I'm sure she won't fire me. My work is perfectly satisfactory. Isn't it, girls?"

Nobody answered her. The room was filled with an appalled silence.

"You talk of managing everybody else's business," she went on, "but I'd like to know what you think you're doing. You should practise what you preach, Mr. Allan. I mean to say, you're good-looking and clever and all that, but it doesn't give you the right to speak to me like that, and I'm certainly not taking my notice from you." Then she said coaxingly, "I say, don't get in such a paddy with me. If I've done something wrong, I'm sorry. There! I can't say fairer than that, can I?"

Mr. Allan, confronted with this description of the temper that was consuming him, could for the first time in his life think of nothing to say. What he would have wished to say, even he could not, in a room of teen-age girls. What he would have wished to do, even he could not do. He swung round, his face white, and left the room. But he could not avoid hearing Miss Langdon's next remark as he closed the door. "I think," she said, "it really must be his sex life. It usually is with men, you know. Eric——"

"Jesus!" whispered Mark, and put his hands to his face. Then, "This won't do, this simply won't do at all." He stood there, very still. He would have never have behaved like this in the old days. It would have been as much as his life was worth. Perhaps it was, still. That confounded little bitch was right. His nerves were in a shocking state. He stood there, forcing composure on himself, pressing his mind down, down, down.

Then he stepped into Barbara's office, across the corridor. She had heard nothing of the row; she was on the other side of the building, and she was now rolling stencils off on the Gestetner. She did not even hear Mark's entry, and when his hands descended on her shoulders, she started, and the stencil she was just inking fell into a dozen creases.

"Good-afternoon, Barbara," he said. "Good-afternoon, darling. For that is what you called me. And I was so churlish that I didn't even answer. Will you please forgive

me? I have just been told that my nerves are in a shocking
state and"—his face twitched into a smile—"the reason is
my sex life. I think this is very true. Won't you help me?
Perhaps we could start the cure now." His arms came round
her as he spoke; he held her against him for a moment,
then kissed her very tenderly. She could feel his heart pounding like a drum; there was a glistening of sweat on the face
pressed against hers. He was shaking from head to foot. She
said in a whisper, "Oh, my darling, my darling, what is the
matter with you, what is wrong?"

"Everything," he said. "Every bloody thing in the whole
wide world. Except you, except you. Let me hold you for
a little. Don't speak. Just stay still."

The sea wind blew strongly, there was anguish, ugly words,
then peace, except for his heart thudding against her breast,
pom-pom-pom-*pom*——

"*Jusqu'à la fin du monde*," she said, then, dazedly, "I
don't know why I said that."

"Do you know that, too?" he said, very low.

"What? No—I——"

> *"Dans un grand lit carré,*
> *Nous dormirons ensemble,*
> *Jusqu'à la fin du monde*——

I used to sing that. Where did you learn that?" But he did
not give her time to answer. He said, in his ordinary voice,
"I'll not be here to-morrow afternoon. I'm having half a
day's leave, thank God. But you and I are going out Thursday."

She drew back a little. "Are we, Mark? Is it safe? After all,
I might—I might laugh at you again."

He gave a deep sigh. "Ah, please do," he said. "Laugh
at me always. I need it so badly. I'm sorry I was so abominable to you. You must try to forgive me. I cannot be at
loggerheads with the universe. If I wring everybody's neck, I
shall be left alone, like the existentialist mouse running round
the earth to eternity, beneath the cold moon. Don't abandon
me. Don't ever abandon me."

"I couldn't," she said, "however abominable you are."

They stood there for a while, his arms clasped round her.
His heart had quietened. The shaking had stopped. She put
her hand up to touch his cheek, then she said, "I've put
stencil ink all over your shirt. I'm so sorry."

He released her. He laughed. "Damn my shirt," he said.

"Where shall we go Thursday? You shall lay down the itinerary, and you may laugh at me every five minutes, if you wish. Where shall we go, Barbara? Anywhere you like. Anywhere, as long as it's far, far away from the damned office, and that damned young woman who makes me feel that if she opens her mouth once more, I shall ram my fist down it."

"Did she really say that about your sex life!"

"She didn't say it to my face. But that is what I heard. She also said a great many other things. For God's sake, let's not talk about her. Do you want me to be sick? There are surely more interesting things to talk about. Myself, for instance. And what a swine I am to make you so unhappy."

She held out her hands in a gesture of submission that came strangely to her. He would have taken hold of them, but she moved away, back to the machine. She said, "I must finish this. Miss Holmes will be angry with me if I don't."

He said gravely, "It is difficult to run your department when neurotic and possibly erotic librarians insist on making love to members of the staff. It makes discipline so difficult. It holds up the work. What a good thing that objectionable Mr. Allan will be out of the way to-morrow."

She refused to answer this. She was trying to uncrease the stencil. She only said, "Where are you going?"

"Oh," he said. "Up north. A matter of business. How do you work this thing? We used to have an apparatus for rolling off a news-sheet, but it was nothing like this."

She began silently to roll off the stencil. She knew he was watching her, not the machine. She finished at last—it was not easy in the circumstances—and just as she put out her hand to peel the stencil off the roller, the door opened and Mr. Rills came in.

Mr. Rills, for the past half-hour, had been talking to Mr. Dodds. Being very ashamed of himself, and perfectly aware that he had not distinguished himself, he was temporarily stripped of histrionics, and listened to Mr. Dodds with a humility that for once was not assumed.

"You know, Rills," said Mr. Dodds, "it really is partly your fault. I am not excusing him; his temper is excessive, and I deplore such a lack of self-control. But the natural human instinct, when it sees something cowering away, is to kick, and Allan, if I may say so, has that instinct over-developed. Still, it's surely tempting providence to call him a murderer to his face. I suppose you also told that to Sergeant Robins?"

"Of course not," cried Mr. Rills, then, furiously, "Well, I didn't *tell* him. I suppose I implied it." He turned wildly on Mr. Dodds. "What do you expect? I'm human, aren't I? He's a damned swine. He's always been a swine, and especially so to me. Because I'm smaller than he is and because I've some artistic sense and don't go around roaring my head off, he treats me as if he were the bully in chief of a public school. I can't stand it, I tell you. I can't stand it, and I don't see why I should. I know he is the murderer."

"Don't you think that is all the more reason for keeping quiet?" said Mr. Dodds. "If you've definite evidence, tell the sergeant, by all means. But if it's just what you modern young people call a hunch, and you've nothing to substantiate it, I think you should keep quiet, and certainly not go calling him a murderer to his face. No one would like it. I wouldn't myself. And Allan is not the most tolerant of men. Why on earth didn't you take the microfilm up to him? I can't really understand what all this fuss is about. It seems a natural and harmless mistake."

"He'd have said I'd taken it on purpose. You don't know him. You don't know how he's behaved to me. If you knew what I've had to put up with——"

Mr. Dodds sighed.

"Some people," said Mr. Rills, passionately warming to his theme, "are naturally sensitive. I can't help it. It's not an advantage. It means you feel everything doubly. But, by God, I'd rather be like that than have a skin made of cast-iron, like Allan."

"I wouldn't say that of him," said Mr. Dodds consideringly, "at all. Rather the reverse, in fact. But surely if you'd gone to him and said, 'This has come to me by mistake, sorry I opened it——' "

"Him and his damned microfilms!" Mr. Rills, encouraged by this talk about himself, was reverting to his normal state of of mind. "He's got a mania about them. He wouldn't have believed me. He'd have kicked me out of the office."

"Oh, come now."

"God!" said Mr. Rills. "How I hate these overgrown schoolboys. A fine and handsome chap that the women swoon over—six foot, isn't he? No doubt you agree with him, sir. No doubt you think that gives him the right to hit people like me, who are not overgrown, and who have been brought up to the idea that physical violence is no argument. Of course, the women fall for him, and that flatters his vanity. First that blonde bombshell of ours, and now that silly little Miss Smith——"

"Quite," said Mr. Dodds, rising to his feet. "I see you are recovered, Rills, and so I'll leave you. I see, too, that it's no good my offering you advice, because you certainly won't take it."

Mr. Rills said unexpectedly, "Thank you for coming in just now. I—I'm a fearful coward, I know."

"Oh, well," said Mr. Dodds, "we're all cowards in some ways. And, if it's any consolation to you, I think your enemy is more afraid than most."

"Is he!" Mr. Rills's face brightened. "What of? I'd love to put the screw on him." He met Mr. Dodds's eye. "You're thinking I wouldn't dare. I suppose I wouldn't. Well, anyway, thank you. I'll fetch some rough paper from the Gestetner room, and then I'll get down to work." His lower lip quivered a little. "You don't think he'll come in again?"

"No," said Mr. Dodds compassionately. "By now, no doubt, he's blown up half the Library, and is probably working hard in his own room. Where's young Wilson got to? I want to see him."

"I suppose he's in his room," said Mr. Rills, and made his way up to the Location Department on the third floor.

But young Mr. Wilson was not in his room, and Mr. Dodds, when he discovered this, stood on the threshold of his office, looking angry and disturbed. On his return to his own room, he rang Mr. Latimer, to ask if the sergeant were in to-day.

"No," said Mr. Latimer. "He'll probably be back on Friday. He is making inquiries, whatever that means. I wish to God this whole business were cleared up. What was that shattering noise I heard just now? It sounded just as if it were in the Library."

"Oh, I don't think so, sir," said Mr. Dodds.

Mr. Rills, when he saw Mark Allan, stopped abruptly in the doorway. Barbara, looking from one to the other, found herself swept unexpectedly by a blast of hysteria. It was almost as if she heard the screams and cries. She could not make out which of them was the focal centre of this strange disturbance. How changed everything was. In the old days, the sending of volume one instead of volume two had been the only catastrophe, but now the atmosphere was charged with every kind of disruptive emotion.

She stared at them both. Mr. Rills had grown white, but then he changed colour easily. Mark, on the other hand, was expressionless and still, yet she felt within her that the hysteria emanated from him.

Mr. Rills was feeling sick. If he had even suspected that Allan was there—— But it was too late to turn back. The humiliation that he had endured flooded him afresh. So he was a coward, was he? His heart, his breathing, his trembling knees, spoke for him, but he ignored them, only raised his head and said in a voice that quavered and sparked, "Oh, I am *so* sorry to have disturbed you."

Barbara, ignoring the implication, said quickly, "It's quite all right, Mr. Rills. I was only showing Mr. Allan how to manage the Gestetner."

"Is that what they call it nowadays?" inquired this new, not-to-be-quelled Mr. Rills. "The modern poets use cruder terms, but I dare say it comes to the same thing in the end. However, I mustn't interfere with the work of Mr. Allan's department, must I, Mr. Allan?"

Mr. Allan said nothing at all.

Mr. Rills did not like this but, still resolved to assert himself, said to Barbara, whose presence, he felt, afforded him some protection, "Mr. Allan hates having his work interfered with, you know, whether it's microfilms or——"

Mark still did not answer, but he stretched out his arm to the Gestetner, removed the stencil from the machine, then, holding it in his hand, its surface glistening with ink, advanced on the now petrified Mr. Rills.

He said, quite pleasantly, "What a tiresome little creature you are, aren't you?" then suddenly raised the stencil on high and laid it full upon Mr. Rills's face.

Barbara cried faintly, "Oh, my God," as Mr. Rills, swearing and shouting in muffled tones, flung himself about the room, tearing wildly at the stencil which came away in fragments, leaving him to look like a nigger minstrel, the whites of his eyes and teeth gleaming in their black surrounding.

She could not endure it. This was the moment to assert herself, to prove herself superior to these two grown men who were behaving in so incredible a manner. She saw that Mark was laughing silently, and indeed the sight of Mr. Rills, with his black face, was so dreadfully comic that she felt the hysteria surging up in her own throat. She tore herself from Mark's grasp—for he had grabbed at her wrist—and ran into the general office.

She cried out, "Oh, please come. There's the most dreadful scene going on. Please! You must do something."

She had left the door open, and Mr. Rills's sobbing shrieks came down the corridor.

"Oh, crikey!" said Greta, then her eyes grew enormous. "It's not another murder?"

"It soon will be," said Barbara, nearly in tears. "Oh, do please come. I don't know what to do with them. I think we're all going mad."

Miss Dorothea Langdon, at this point, rose decisively to her feet. "I'll come, dear," she said. "I can't imagine what's happening, but obviously someone has to stop it, and Eric always says I am good in an emergency."

She walked swiftly and steadily into Barbara's room. Then her mouth fell open. For a second she stood there in aghast silence. Then, completely ignoring Mark, who was leaning against the Gestetner, and still laughing in his silent, suppressed way, she went up to Mr. Rills and took him by the arm. He turned on her a ghastly face. He had been weeping in helpless and mortified rage; the tears had made rivulets in the ink which had now dried on his features. He was very near collapse.

"Come along with me, dear," said Miss Langdon, "and we'll soon have that nasty stuff off your face. Never mind now. Just come with me. No one will see us, and we'll shut ourselves up in the pantry, shall we, and see what soap and water will do?"

"Try the correcting fluid," said Mark, still in the grip of his unseemly mirth.

At this, she dropped Mr. Rills's arm and came up to him. She said, "You ought to be ashamed of yourself. You, a grown man, to treat this poor boy in such a manner. I think it's disgusting. I hope you're sacked for it. I only wish Eric were here, he'd know how to deal with you. I think, personally, if it's any interest to you, that you're the most revolting, disgusting, stupid, ill-mannered beast I've ever met, and that's all I have to say to you." And with that, she turned her back on him and took Mr. Rills's arm again, saying in a coaxing voice, as if she were talking to a small child, "There now, there. Come along with Dot, and she'll have you right as rain in a jiffy. Poor dear, it's a shame, it really is. He ought to be put in prison. This way now. You poor thing, I don't wonder you're upset."

Mark had made no reply to her outburst. He and Barbara listened to the stumbling passage along the corridor. Mr. Rills

was sobbing; it was a shocking sound to listen to. Barbara
walked across to the window and stood there, looking out.

"I gather," said Mark to her shoulders, "that I am now utterly in disgrace."

She said, without turning round, "Please go. I don't ever
want to see you again or speak to you again."

"Do you mean that?"

"Yes." And knew, as she spoke, that she did not mean a
word of it. He had behaved shamefully, with a brutality
that she would not have thought possible, but the thought of
not seeing him again was intolerable. But she would not
look round. There was a silence. Then the door slammed.

She began inevitably to cry. The tears streamed down. She
said aloud, "I can't bear it, I can't bear it." The university
list that had to go off this evening lay on her desk. She did
not even consider it. She was alone now in a cold, hostile
world, where the wind had changed, so that the small, comfortable things of life had been blown away; she was defenceless, terrified, lost——

("You're English, aren't you?"
"Je ne comprends pas——")

She said, *"Je ne comprends pas."* She did not know why
she said it. She was wild with grief and despair; she struck
down at the window-sill with her hand, then whimpered at
the agonising pain. She said again, the sobs catching at her
breath, like a child which has cried itself to the state of
not being able to stop, *"Je ne comprends pas."* Then, gasping,
almost out of her mind with misery, she turned.

Mark was leaning against the door, watching her. His arms
were folded across his chest. There was that look on his face
that she had seen before, cold, considering; it gave a strange
impression of power. The amusement was gone, leaving only
an air of grim reflection, as if it were she who had behaved
unpardonably, as if he were meditating on the best way to
deal with her.

She could only stare at him.

He said, "Well? Is the little fit of temper done with?"

To this there was nothing to say. She found herself blushing and trembling, as if she really were in the wrong. She
was silent.

He said calmly, "Not every man would put up with this
kind of thing, you know. I have noticed before that you indulge in childishness from time to time."

Her eyes opened to their widest. But she still said nothing. Once she had had spirit. But then that was a long time ago.

"However," he said, "I'll overlook it this once. But you'd better not let it happen again. Tantrums, after all, are only permissible in the young, and you, if I may say so, are not so young as all that. But I suppose I must forgive you, though I think you might have the decency to say you're sorry."

She said—it was like some physical compulsion—"I am sorry, Mark."

"I should think so," he said. Then he said, "Come here."

She came. It was shameful to her that she should, but she came. She came close to him and, as his arms came roughly round her, she closed her eyes and then, almost against her will, flung her own arms about him, gripping him frantically, rubbing her face against him, sobbing again. Then she felt the tremors running through him, and knew instantly that it was all an act, that he was magnificently amused, entirely delighted with himself. But she did not care. The current was switched on. She heard him say, "Oh, let's forget about this whole damned business. We're not going to quarrel, you and I."

She said—perhaps it was the last flicker of individuality in her befogged mind—"You really are a swine, Mark."

"A swine?" he repeated. She could hear the vast amusement crackling in his voice. "That's a fine word to use to me, my girl. You're dangerously placed, you know. Do you think it's safe to speak to me like that?"

No. It was not safe. She knew that. But she only said a little bitterly, "I've said I'm sorry. I don't know why. I think all reason has left me. I think you're detestable, and I love you so very much, so very much."

"Ah!" he said. It was a long, deep, satisfied sigh. "You're a good girl. You shall kiss me."

"No," she said, "no——" She struggled away from him. "You must go. You must. I shan't get my list off, and I shall get told off for it, but I must make a pretence of doing some work, and—and I hope you have a good journey to-morrow, and I—I shall see you properly on Thursday, if we don't quarrel irrevocably before then."

"That," he said solemnly, "is after all entirely up to you."

And, with this as *coup de grâce,* he left her.

In the pantry, Mr. Rills, with scrubbed face, a few faint traces of ink still here and there, was, unbelievably, holding Miss Langdon's hand and pouring out his heart to her.

And down on the second floor, Mr. Wilson, who had now returned to his room from the basement stacks, where for the past hour he had been pacing up and down, at last made up his mind.

IX. FISHING, HUNTING, TARGET SHOOTING. 799

THE major row provoked several minor outbursts. Mark Allan was summoned to the office by an unhappy Mr. Ridley, who disliked delivering a moral lecture to anyone, and who eyed the grave-faced culprit confronting him in acute dismay. He had, however, no choice, for Mr. Rills had burst into his office first thing in the morning, accompanied by that extraordinary temporary from the location Department who stood at his side throughout the interview, calling him—unbelievably—'dear', and exhorting him to tell the whole story.

Mr. Ridley was shocked to the depths of his civilised soul, and sickened, too. It seemed to him a bestial atrocity; it was unfathomable that people could act in such a way.

"But why," he said to Mark Allan, "did you do such a thing? How could you? What possessed you? I don't understand how anyone—— I really am not sure if, in the circumstances——"

He paused. Mark was extremely competent at his work, and it was so difficult to find reliable staff. Perhaps it was, after all, a kind of brain-storm. He said as sternly as he could, "If anything remotely like this occurs again, Allan, I shall be compelled to ask you to look for another post. You will, of course, apologise to Mr. Rills."

"Naturally, sir," said Mark. He was looking at some point on the wall, above Mr. Ridley's head; it was a mannerism of his that Sergeant Robins had already noticed.

"And to Miss Smith. It must have been a terrible shock for her."

"I will certainly apologise to Miss Smith," said Mark. His eyes shifted briefly to Mr. Ridley's perturbed, bewildered face, then up to the wall again.

"In fact," said Mr. Ridley, almost despairingly, "you seem in one brief afternoon to have achieved what must be a

153

record, even for you—the feat of upsetting in one way or another every single department in the Library."

"If," said Mark, "you like to assemble the staff, I will make a public apology to them all."

Mr. Ridley at last succeeded in meeting his gaze. He could not miss the barely concealed mockery. He said in a voice that had gone flat and dull, "Mr. Allan. This is not for me an amusing situation, though I perceive that it amuses you. May I remind you that we have had a murder here, and that since that time almost everything that I have tried to build up seems to be crumbling to pieces? And a piece of pure hooliganism like this—— I don't know if I should let you stay here." He stared unhappily at Mark as he said this. "What do you think yourself?"

"It is up to you, sir," said Mark. "I can only promise you that this will never be repeated."

Mr. Ridley said, almost hopefully, "Perhaps you have not been feeling well lately. I have thought once or twice that you were looking over-tired."

"Yes," said Mark, "that is possibly true. I am tired."

"Well, you're taking the afternoon off, aren't you? Go a little earlier, if you like, and see your doctor. I think," said Mr. Ridley, "that we are all getting over-wrought. I only hope that Sergeant Robins can soon clear the matter up."

"Does he think he's near the solution, sir?"

"I don't know. I had the impression—— But I don't know. After all," said Mr. Ridley, "I, like you, am one of the suspects."

Miss Holmes, when she heard the shocking story, flew into one of her worst moods, and embarked on what her staff called a purge. She scolded everyone. She scolded Barbara for not finishing her list, for permitting Mr. Allan to disturb her. "I'll give him a piece of my mind," she said, and was furious, when she went up to do so, to find he had already left. She scolded Miss Langdon for meddling in what was none of her concern, threatened to dismiss her, but desisted on receiving an urgent request from Mr. Ridley. Miss Langdon was now, naturally, something of a heroine, and the girls, who had once laughed at her, regarded her with admiring respect.

Sergeant Robins was informed of the business by Mr. Latimer on the phone. "I don't believe," said Mr. Latimer, "that it has the slightest bearing on the murder, but you asked me to let you know if anything out of the ordinary occurred. And this, God knows, is not the kind of thing that usually happens. Of course, you must take into consideration that Mr. Allan and Mr. Rills have always been at daggers drawn, and naturally at a moment when we are all under such a strain——"

The sergeant repeated this conversation to Police-Constable Hall, who said, "It all seems to fit in, sir."

"I think," said the sergeant, "that by the end of the week we should have all the evidence necessary—— I understand the gentleman is taking the afternoon off. I want him to be followed."

Mr. Wilson waited until twelve o'clock noon. For once in his life he did not mention his purpose to a soul. He did not wish to talk about it. He avoided them all. Mr. Allan, of course, was gone home. Mr. Rills was out at lunch. Mr. Dodds was having an argument about handwriting with a member of the Reference Room staff. And Mrs. Bridgwater was also at lunch; she was the last person he wished to see. Mr. Wilson, filled with the oddest premonitions, had now screwed up his courage to the point where nothing must be allowed to deflect him.

He crept into the room. There for a second a fear that was older than the hills of the ancient world gripped him so that he stood for a while, his young face white and drawn. It was almost as if he sensed that the bleak shadow was standing not far behind him.

But it was noon, and the sun was high in the sky, and he was young and strong, and the ancient hills were far away. Mr. Wilson set his shoulders and quoted to himself the lines that everyone laughed at, yet which held for him a comfort and an exhortation. "Be a man, my son," he said, then stepped swiftly forward and snatched from the desk the thing he had come to examine.

And the shadow waited with a grim patience.

Mr. Wilson came back into the corridor, whistling to himself an air from one of the Gilbert and Sullivan operas. He did not really feel like whistling, but it helped to keep his courage up. He put the object in his pocket—it was small—and, glancing swiftly over his shoulder, stepped into the lift. He was not going to be fool enough to examine it here. He was not such an ass as they all thought him. No sacks for Jack Wilson. If silly old women had to open their big mouths, well, it was very sad and all that, but they were asking for trouble. But then *she* had not really known what she was up against. He knew. It was not easy for him to know, for he had a heart from which the pity spilled like overflowing milk, but he knew now that a person could be ruthless and reckless and bad. It was a knowledge that had kept him awake for many nights. But the person would not find out until it was too late. He had, after all, taken precautions, chosen his moment well. He took the lift down to the basement and came out among the stacks.

The shadow walked swiftly and silently down the stairs, noting the lift's progress.

Mr. Wilson stood there, alone, in the stacks. He believed he was alone. The stacks were always an eerie place. Around and about him stretched long, long corridors of books, each corridor with its individual light. The place smelt cold, even in the summer heat; the dry, musty odour of dust and paper and board and calf clung to the unventilated air. Mr. Wilson's feet echoed cavernously on the stone flags, which were uneven and sloped here and there so that, if one were not careful, one tumbled into the bookshelves.

He switched on a light. He stood now where Barbara often stood, hemmed in by the *Gentleman's Magazine* and the *Annual Register*. The eighteenth-century volumes, in their crumbling calf binding, scattered brown dust on him as he brushed past them. He did not notice this. The past held no interest for him. It had been a great bone of contention at school. ("Wilson, what were the dates of the main events in the reign of Elizabeth?" "But, sir, it was all such a long time ago.") And yet now he had a horrid feeling that he was being watched by some ghostly thing that was in essence dead. For the first time he permitted himself to voice the suspicion that he had not been very wise. He had wanted solitude, but solitude could be dangerous. Perhaps it would have been better to have shut himself up in the lavatory. But he was here, and he had never been a coward, and after all no one had seen him, and he had come down alone in the lift.

Spotlit by the electric bulb above him, he turned his eyes towards the long, unlit corridors that stretched to right and left of him. He had a wild desire to run their length, and switch on light after light. His breath was coming fast. Despite the cold, the sweat was pricking his forehead. He glanced over his shoulder. There was no one there. No one. In the bright, unshaded light, his shadow tailed into the darkness where the other shadow stood, motionless, watching, waiting.

Mr. Wilson took a deep breath, set his lips, then, digging his hand into his pocket, pulled out the object he wished to examine. His hands were shaking and slippery with sweat. He glared at them, as if by doing so he could still them. "Nerves, Jack!" he said aloud, "nerves!" as he had done at school, whether it was an exam, a football match or a thrashing. And then the object slid through his fingers and clattered on to the stone floor, where, being as it was, it rolled down the sloping surface, to lie hidden beneath the stacks.

"Oh, dash it all!" cried Mr. Wilson, and bent down to look for it. A primitive awareness of danger stirred his entrails, as if the shadow, now behind him, blew cold upon him. He half jerked round, but it was too late. The shadow's hand swept down. His head smashed into a roaring flame, and then he fell fathoms deep into the old, his shoulder knocking against the shelves as he did so.

The shadow now moved fully into the light. Glancing briefly at the boy as he lay there, it knelt down to search for the missing object. But this was not to be found, and the shadow had obvious reasons for not wishing to stay too long. It collected, therefore, a couple of volumes from the shelves and turned calmly back towards the lift, only pausing to touch Mr. Wilson's eyes and mouth and to switch off the light.

Mr. Wilson was dead. He lay there in the curled-up position he had once held in his mother's womb, only his head was flung back at a grotesque angle, and his young, defenceless, bearded face, with protruding tongue, stared, unblinking, into the eternal dark.

The murderer had not been lucky with Mrs. Warren, but had unusual good fortune with Mr. Wilson. The young man, being a student librarian, had always alternated his time between the Reference Room, Mr. Dodds's department and Mr. Allan's. Everyone, therefore, assumed he was somewhere else; people said vaguely, "Where on earth's young Jack Wilson got to?" but nobody found his absence surprising. The staff of I.L.D.A. left, therefore, without the faintest idea that another murder had been committed, and Mr. Wilson's body might have remained undiscovered until the next day had not Mr. Purley, before finally locking up, gone downstairs to make sure that no one was left behind. It had once happened that an over-earnest student, reading among the stacks, had been locked in all night, with the electricity switched off at the main. Mr. Purley never forgot this. Grumbling, he went downstairs, switching on the lights, so that Mr. Wilson's body lay in plain view.

Barbara left I.L.D.A. at five-thirty. She had not enjoyed her day. There had been a great deal of work to do to make up for yesterday, and she, like everyone else in the department, had received a long lecture from Miss Holmes on her utter inadequacy. It seemed that everyone was making the most foolish mistakes. Miss Langdon had sent a form to Boots, when the location was clearly marked as 'Barts'. Peggy had written up to the Massachusetts Institute of Technology, when it should have been the Manchester Institute of Technology. "There may not," said Miss Holmes in bitter irony, "be much distinction in your mind, but there is, after all, a certain geographical distance between them." And Greta had asked the British Cotton Industry Research Association (B.C.I.R.A.) for a manual on 'the art of dying'. Miss Holmes, on reading this, was about to embark on a further tirade, but then, perhaps, it struck her that the mistake was a rather sinister one, so she passed over it hastily and returned to the attack on Barbara.

"A disgraceful stencil," she said. "What's happened to you, Miss Smith? There are at least six mistakes in the first page alone. If it had been typed after—afterwards, I could understand it, but you must have done it in the morning. I don't know what Mr. Latimer will say, I'm sure."

Mr. Latimer, who had other things to worry about, did not, of course, even glance at the list, but Miss Holmes always liked to assume that he kept an eagle eye on all the work that was done. She wound up inevitably with, "How I am expected to run this department, I do not know," then walked from the room to fabricate a quarrel with Mr. Dodds on the subject of his handwriting, and to argue with Mrs. Bridgwater about the new cheap carbons which, far from being economical, lasted only a tenth of the time of the ones they had used before.

'Perhaps,' thought Barbara, looking wistfully at her watch, 'it is as well that Mark is not here, for he would be certain to involve himself in a further and even more disastrous row.'

She decided to get a meal out. In the older and happier days, Charles would have called for her. A desperate longing came upon her, as one longs for the familiar appurtenances of home. But she had, after all, chosen her road, and she would walk it to the end, though what lay beyond filled her with

either—they only thank him for having helped them and their families, and they enclose snapshots of various kinds. You'd get the impression he was a universal benefactor. As for phone calls, he's not on the phone, and presumably makes his calls from I.L.D.A. or outside boxes. He's not in touch with his family. There's a sister. One of our men got on to her. She says she hasn't heard from him for years. It sounds as if she didn't want to. But now, about today———"

Barbara, beside him on the trolley, said to him again, after he had taken two tickets for Canning Town, "Darling, tell me what has happened. You seem possessed. Have you had wonderful news? Have you trampled down your enemies and risen triumphant above them?"

"Did you," said he, "have the temerity to address me as darling in public? No jury of matrons could do otherwise than condemn you. Where are the snows of Earl's Court? This is scandalous, shameless."

"Do you mind?"

"Oh, I—I left Earl's Court some time ago. My father was a clergyman—oh yes, he was, you know—but I fear I can no longer be termed a communicant. You may call me darling, if you wish. I find it forward, but not unpleasing. You may say it again. Well? I was once a schoolmaster. I exact obedience from my pupils. Well, Smith? We are all waiting."

And this, indeed, was true, for he had not troubled to lower his voice, and the conductor and passengers were listening with the greatest interest.

The conductor said suddenly, "Give her a kiss. She'll call you anything then."

Mark turned to smile at him. Barbara, a conventional girl, found herself seized and kissed soundly. Such a thing, in full view of an audience, had never happened to her in her life. The passengers began to clap. But as nothing now could matter at all, she made no protest, only turned to lie against his shoulder, as his arm came round her.

An old man, getting off at the next stop, winked at them. "You look happy. I like to see people happy. Don't see much of it these days."

"I am happy, sir," said Mark, "and I'll tell you why. Because I'm successful, because I get what I want, because my good fortune stays with me. I was always the lucky boy. They prophesied my damnation, but they went to hell, not I. And now—now I'm luckier than ever. Do you know, when I came back to London this evening, I swore I'd kiss this girl before the night was out, and now I've kissed her, and the night is scarcely begun."

"And the best of luck to you!" said the old man.

"You've pulled off some big business deal," said Barbara.

"You might call it that," he said, his strange eyes widening. "Oh, you might call it that. If you don't want me to behave in a way that will land me in the courts, you'd better move away from me. I'm not to be trifled with this evening, or indeed at any other time, as some have discovered to their cost. But never mind that. This is the book I brought for you. The *Gentleman's Magazine* for 1745."

"But I know that," she said, "I know where it comes from, too. So you've been down in the stacks. I didn't know you were interested in the eighteenth century. I thought you, like Mr. Dodds, were only concerned with such things as the *Drug Trade News,* and Advance Paper, No. 50-PRI-18. What were you doing down there?"

He held the book on his knee, placing his right hand on it to flatten down the pages. He did not immediately reply, but the corners of his mouth were twisting up as if her question amused him. It was all the more startling then that the gaze he suddenly turned on her was reflective and hard.

She said, "I like your hands. I always did, long before I liked you."

He looked away, then moved his hand to clasp hers. "Well," he said, "we'll not talk of the forty-five, then. Though I wish I'd been there. I'd not have turned back at Derby, by God, by God, by God."

"You sound more like my heroes every minute. You should have lived then. It would have suited you. You wouldn't have needed to—to——"

"To what?"

"Oh, put stencils on people's faces. Your madness would have been right. *Monsieur le fou*——"

"*What* did you say?"

"I—I don't know. It just seemed to suit you. Are you angry now? I'll call you Tom Wharton, then."

"Ah, my damned fanatical face—I've not forgotten that. It came so strangely from Miss Smith of the Location Department, a nice, prim little girl, whom really I'd never bothered to notice. That was the first time I looked at you. I liked the eyes, I remember. We're becoming dangerously anatomical. We get off here. Come——"

They walked from Canning Town down Silvertown Way.

They stopped at a café and ate sausages and chips; they stopped again at the 'Admiral Nelson' and drank beer. And so at last they crossed the humped bridge, and leant over the railing to stare at the Royal Albert Dock, which stretched before them in tranquil, moonlit beauty.

"Ah," she said on a sigh, "what a pity we cannot get down to the dockside. It would be wonderful to lie there and——"

"And?"

"—watch the ships."

"And why shouldn't we?"

"It's *verboten*, strictly, strictly *verboten*. The Port of London Authority would never permit it. Look. There's a policeman at the gates. He'd think we were saboteurs."

"Would he? He'd not be so far wrong. Do you think a policeman will stop me? It never has yet. Wait here. Stay exactly where you are."

He came back, some five minutes later, smiling, very pleased with himself. "Come with me," he said, "and we will break the Port of London Authority into little pieces. We will sabotage the ships and blow up the Royal Albert Dock as far as the Memorial. Good God, is this the spirit that has made I.L.D.A. what it is? You should be ashamed of yourself, whey-faced girl. If I say you can come, you can come."

"It's an extraordinary story—that train-load of Jews," said the sergeant, unable to keep his reluctant eyes from the pages before him. "You have to hand it to the fellow, swine as he is. The Maquis got wind of the coming of the deportation train. Our friend here boarded it, and got the load of them—they were all in the truck behind, some fifty odd, of every nationality, terrified, hysterical—and waited till they came to a point where the train had to slow down. He said, 'If I say you can jump, you can jump.' And jump they did. And, what is more, thirty of them got away. The others were shot, but I dare say that was preferable to what was waiting for them. The nerve of it. Well, he's got a fair nerve now, and a fat lot of use it's going to be to him."

They lay on the dockside. The policeman, when they came through the gates, had been talking to a colleague; he had not looked up as they passed. ("Did you bribe him?" asked Barbara. "No. I told him a story. Don't worry. It's all right.") On the hoarding at the back of them was a forbidding notice of the Port of London Authority, informing them of the penalties they would have to pay.

"We might be sent to prison," said Barbara.

"I'd get you out. I'm an expert prison breaker."

There was not a soul in the world. Before them in the still bright August night lay the two phalanxes of ships, ghostly white, shadowed, frail, made of sugar, so that it seemed one could balance them on the palm of one's hand—ships of phantasy, to sail out into a twilight world. The air lay heavy with the heat, only the water, a couple of yards below them, swirled in the fast current, rippling the moon's reflection towards the horizon.

They lay there for a while in silence. Then he took her into his arms. Perhaps he felt the shudder that ran through her, perhaps he chose deliberately to misunderstand it. "Are you afraid of me?" he said.

"Yes," she said slowly. "Yes. But I don't know why. Why am I afraid? Can't you tell me? Oh, it's not what you think. I'm not so silly as all that—at least, I don't think so. But I want to be with you so much, I'm so happy to be close to you, and yet it's true I am afraid, and I don't know why, and it worries me terribly."

He said in a sudden harsh voice, "I think you and I are beginning to know each other too well. It happens. Sometimes one's mind is like a radio, and once in a while the receiver is waiting to pick up the message. I shouldn't like that to happen for the sake of either of us. If we can't think in privacy, what in God's name is left to us? Do you know what I am thinking now?"

"No! Of course not." Then, "Mark. This murder——"

His hands tightened with such violence that she cried out. She turned to look at him, and he as sharply averted his head. The next instant he had raised his hands to her face, gripping it, flattening the hair across her cheeks, distorting her features. "Oh, damn murder!" he said. "Damn, damn, damn murder. Why the hell must you talk of murder? We have the world and the seven seas and the Queen's Navy before us, we are kings with all the luck in the world, we lie here in the moonlight, and you—you talk of murder. Shut up, you damned little fool, shut up, shut *up*." He kissed her savagely each time he said it. She could feel him shaking, hear his gasping breath, and the sweetness and the terror blended so that she closed her eyes, deafened by the pounding of his heart.

Then he released her as suddenly as he had seized her. He flung himself back on the dockside, his hands beneath his head. He said, "You hold too high a conception of the sanctity of human life. You see life as something whole, entire. But I have seen it in its disintegrated parts, with the sinews twisted, the bones broken, the blood unsheathed, and then you know the body is nothing. Compared with that, murder is the ultimate peace. Though," he said, suddenly grown calm, "I have been fortunate there, too. I found at the very last, when I thought I could endure no more, that the mind can detach itself from pain. It did not save me, but it saved a great many others." He laughed, without mirth. "Oh, Barbara, how damnably humiliating it was. Like being whipped. And when the ecstasy of non-pain is over, how you hate, how you hate. Your reason goes in a passion for revenge."

"Did you get your revenge, Mark?"

"Yes. I suppose so."

"And was it so satisfying?"

He reflected. "It was a little—surprising. Oh, at first there was a magnificent feeling of power, a kind of grand, religious, 'That'll larn you, you so-and-sos.' But then, it was such a mess. One felt one could have been tidier. Ah, my darling, we're treading in each other's thoughts. It's not good. It leads—— I don't know where it leads. Will you comfort me a little? Sometimes, just occasionally, I wonder if the luck always stays."

She comforted him and loved him, pushing down the fear that pulsed like fever within her. And so for a long time they lay there, embraced, silent, and at last, still.

But he said at last, his voice rough again, "It's no damned good. You're still thinking of it. Your thoughts are cold in mine."

Barbara stirred. The faint shiver crept through her once more, though the night was warm as midday, though Mark's arms were round her and her head on his shoulder. She said, in a kind of desperation, "I think it's perhaps that there's always with me an odd feeling that something I heard—some small, unimportant thing—just does not fit in. I don't know if you read detective stories?"

"Never," he said curtly. "They bore me."

"Well, I do. And always it is the one small fact that's out of keeping which holds the clue to the whole thing. I wish I could remember—something someone said. Perhaps it was Greta—Greta—— The odd thing is I feel almost as if it were you. Something to do with you, your office. Oh, I don't know. I suppose it doesn't matter."

He turned towards her, his face above hers. In the clear

moonlight she could see each engraven line, the line from nose to chin that might have been laughter, the line between the brows that might have been anger. It was the face of her hero, past, present and future. It had changed a little, but perhaps that was because a small, dusty cloud had slid across the moon. The cloud had shadowed his face, too, so that it looked down into hers, hard, bleak, immobile. His arms tightened so that he hurt her. But she did not move. They were still alone in the world. The water lay deep and dark at their feet.

"Can you not remember?" he said, his voice a little slurred. "Are you sure you cannot remember?"

(An echo of childhood—— The story of Bluebeard—— *Eh, alors, madame—— Vous n'en savez rien? Vous êtes entrée dans le cabinet! Eh bien, madame, vous y entrerez, et irez prendre place auprès des dames que vous y avez vues——*)

"Are you sure you cannot remember? Answer me."

She muttered, her breath catching, "I'm sorry, but you're hurting me. I can't talk. I'll try to remember."

"Try," he said, and laid his cheek against hers.

Something rippled in the water. A small piece of wood, caught in the current, whirling past them down the river, until it was out of sight.

"I'm cold," she said. Her teeth were chattering. "Oh, Mark, I feel as if something were walking over my grave. It's no good, I can't remember. How fast the current goes."

For a second he looked away from her into the water, his eyes following the moon's trail, flickering past the green-slimed wharf edge to the horizon where the sugarships blended small and fragile with the sky. Then he looked at her and smiled, a brilliant smile that lit his face. "Then," he said, "it's not important. I'm glad. I didn't want it to be important. Darling, dear, dear, darling, I don't want to talk of murder to-night. Murder is omega, and this is only the beginning. Don't watch the river. Would you drown us there? The Thames runs softly, Barbara, and you remember nothing, and I will keep you warm——"

His arms held her tightly again, his mouth came down on hers.

She said suddenly, moving her head to one side, "I—I am really cold. I don't know what it is. I want to go home, Mark."

He neither moved nor answered; his weight held her down. She said again, bitterly ashamed, "I'm sorry. I—it's not

that I'm being—it's——— But I can't forget. I can't. I wish to
God I could. But it's as if murder is all around me. It's so
cold. Like the river. So deep and so cold and so—so final.
Please take me home. I don't want to be hysterical, but I'm
afraid and—and———"

She thought he would be blazingly angry. He would be
justified. But he only looked at her in a way that was new.
His face had grown sad, almost bewildered. She loved him
most dearly, so that the love swelled in her throat, so that
her tenderness almost broke her. He moved away a little,
rubbed at his eyes, pushed his hand through his hair. Then,
without a word, he jumped to his feet, and held out his
hand to help her up.

When they came to the main road, he hailed a taxi. He sat
close to her, his arm casually on her shoulders, their knees
touching. He said, "It is as if our minds follow parallel
lines—not the same line, yet going in the same direction.
Are you still cold?" Then, without a pause, "Office again to-
morrow. I have a feeling I shall not be very popular. But
people will just have to learn to mind their own business."

She said, with gentle mockery, "I think they will have
learnt. And all for a microfilm."

"Ah," he said—she could see the sudden whiteness of his
teeth—"all for a microfilm, and the world well lost. Still.
Still. I think, don't you, that the post-room will be more
careful in future? I think, too, that Mr. Rills will be more
careful." His voice caught and died. He made no sound, but
she felt the tremors of laughter running through his body.

She said, almost angrily, "Have you no pity for him?"

"Pity? Oh, pity—no. None whatsoever. He had his little
moment, after all. And he made full use of it. And now the
moment's passed, and I'm having mine. But then, perhaps
you're right. He's not worth the ammunition. If only he wasn't
so afraid. It invites one so. However, to-morrow I shall receive a further lecture from everyone, and then I shall go
round apologising. I shall even apologise to Rills. I'll wait
till he's in the canteen with everyone there———"

"Mark!"

"But surely you would wish the apology to be public?"

She could still feel the laughter shivering through him.
She sighed. She turned to bury her face in his shoulder.

"You're very sweet," he said absent-mindedly. "But that
Miss Langdon—do I have to apologise to her, too?"

"Certainly."

"Very well. If you say so. 'Miss Langdon, God damn your

eyes, I'm a beast, and a revolting, disgusting beast into the bargain.'"

"She spoke up to you," said Barbara, "and in a way that many would not have dared."

"Oh," he said, "surely I am not as formidable as all that?" She could see in the dim light that he was smiling. "Do you find me so formidable? Do you?" And he gave her a little shake.

"Yes."

"Well, I've not noticed such marked respect this evening. Is this where you live?"

"Yes. Thank you, Mark. It's been wonderful."

"You must come again some time," he said. "It's been a pleasure meeting you."

"But I mean it."

"Shall I come in with you?" he said.

"Oh, I—— My landlady——"

"Ah, of course. The landlady. We mustn't upset the landlady. She must be a dragon, indeed."

"There is no landlady," said Barbara miserably.

He was not smiling now. He bent down and kissed her very gently. "You're wrong," he said, "there's always a landlady. Always. I think I love you. Perhaps it's right there should be. Do you love me, too? You must not. Hold on to your landlady, who will keep little girls out of mischief—foolish little girls. Good-night, Barbara. My regards to your hero. What is he doing now?"

She did not answer. Mr. Andrews, at this moment, was nothing. She wanted to say, 'Come in. Come upstairs. Don't leave me.'

The taximan said wearily, "If you'd be so good as to settle up with me, sir. It's past one o'clock."

"So it is," said Mark, "so it is." He paid the driver. From the "Thank you, *sir*", he must have tipped generously. He stood for a moment looking at her as she fitted the key in the lock. She said wretchedly, "And to-morrow is I.L.D.A. again——"

His face seemed in the lamplight to have grown a little grim. "Yes," he said, "I.L.D.A. again. And again, and again. Good-night."

And, without another word, he walked swiftly away.

She stood there for a long time, until he was out of sight.

BARBARA learnt the news the moment she came in; indeed, she knew that something had happened before she entered the doorway. The policemen were back on duty; there was that strange atmosphere charged with disaster that she had learnt to recognise. Even the Press was back again, even the little group of peering bystanders. 'Mark,' she thought, 'Mark.' She came up to the telephonist's window. "Who is it?" she said, not What is it? but, Who is it?

"Oh, Miss Smith——" The telephonist had been crying. She was a thin girl, with a long, narrow face, who never showed emotion. "It's Mr. Wilson. I've asked for my cards. I can't stand it any longer. We shall all be murdered."

"Mr. *Wilson?*"

"Yes. Isn't it wicked? Such a nice boy. Always so polite. Never shouted on the phone, like some I could mention. Mr. Purley found him last night. After you'd all gone home. In the stacks he was. With his neck broken." She was crying again. "I—I told Mr. Ridley I was going. I wouldn't stay here another day if they doubled my salary——"

Barbara turned away without a word. She walked up the stairs. On the second floor she met Mrs. Bridgwater, her face blubbered with tears. She did not seem to see Barbara, only ran down to the first floor; her high heels tapped towards Mr. Latimer's office.

Barbara walked into the general office without taking her coat off. She did not even say good-morning, but sat down at the nearest desk, staring ahead, her hands folded in front of her. She had not thought she could be so scoured by grief for someone whom, after all, she had never known well. She thought of Mr. Wilson, so very young and sometimes so very foolish, but always good-tempered, always courteous, the only member of the staff—with the possible exception of Mr. Dodds—who was on good terms with Mark Allan. It had been so different with Mrs. Warren. There was no excuse for her murder, but she had been, after all, a rather horrid old woman. And Jack Wilson, a young boy, nineteen, with the world before him—to lie in the basement with his neck broken, and all because he had played the detective and unearthed something bigger than he realised.

"It's such a waste," she said aloud, "such a wicked, abominable waste."

No one replied. She saw that Miss Langdon was crying, and so was Greta. She did not wish to cry herself, but for the first time she began to understand Mark's views on revenge. This time the murderer must not escape. She raised her head, filled with a bitter, enveloping anger, and saw the door open.

Mark came a little way into the room. He stood there, with his hands in his pockets, facing the condemning eyes.

Mr. Rills sat silent and shivering in his room. He felt very ill indeed, what with yesterday's shock and humiliation, and now with this appalling news. He was sincerely sorry about young Wilson, but his main thoughts were concerned with the possibility of his being the next victim. He had never faced life successfully; he could not face death at all. When the door opened, and Mark Allan came in, he turned so ghastly a colour that it seemed as if he might faint. He half rose to his feet, but his knees would not bear him. He stared up, parched, paralysed, speechless, though murder, if indeed this were murder, wore a resigned, contemptuous air that did not entirely suggest assassination.

Mark, too, had been told the news by the telephonist, and he, like Barbara, had made no comment, only walked up the two flights of stairs to Mr. Rills's room. He stood there now, looking down at Mr. Rills. He was gaunt and hollow-eyed; he had cut himself while shaving, so that a thin scar ran from the corner of his mouth to his jaw. He said abruptly, "I've come to make you my apology."

Mr. Rills said nothing.

Mark waited for a moment, then the familiar derision flickered into his eyes. "I can hardly," he said, "offer you the satisfaction of a gentleman, for that term would not apply in either case, but I'll admit, if it pleases you, that my behaviour was ridiculous and rather disgusting, and you'd better file this apology on record, for it's the last you will ever receive from me. I gather it's not accepted." His face twisted into the half-smile that Mr. Rills so detested. "I suppose I can hardly blame you. If I say that I hope it taught you some manners, that shouldn't detract from the apology. Be-

cause you have the breeding of a guttersnipe doesn't neces-
sarily mean that I should have the same. Still," he added,
"it's a pity it happened. And I'm sorry. That's all."

Mr. Rills preserved his silence until Mark's footsteps vanished down the corridor. Then, alone in his room, he burst into
a torrent of speech. "You swine," he cried, glaring up, bang-
ing his fists on the desk, "you lousy, filthy, bloody swine. You
think you can bully your way through life, don't you,
humiliating people, beating them up, killing them? But you'll
be sorry for this. I'll see," shouted Mr. Rills, "that you regret
this to the end of your days."

And then he remembered Jack Wilson, whose days were
ended for good and all, and somehow his personal humiliation dwindled into unimportance. He huddled there, a miserable, ashamed and self-tormented young man, who wished
he were dead, if death could only come without dying.

The general office looked at Mark with weakening disapproval. They were not old enough to be proof against his
looks and charm. His gaunt air of exhaustion, coupled with
the scar across his jaw-bone, made him almost irresistible.
"He looked smashing," said Greta afterwards, "just like a
film star."

Barbara was not proof, either. She would not look fully
at him, but she wondered with sudden irrelevancy why last
night she should cling to a virtue that at ten in the morning
seemed not to matter a damn. Then she remembered, and was
shocked by the egotism of her thoughts, and regretted last
night more bitterly than ever.

Only Miss Langdon seemed completely unimpressed. When
Mark came over to her and said gravely, "I owe you an
apology, Miss Langdon," she merely replied, "You certainly
do. But you're wasting your time. I'm not interested in your
apologies. You don't mean it, anyway. I expect," she added,
"you're really enjoying being in the limelight."

Mark's eyes widened, the eyebrows shot up. There was a
pause, and not one of submissiveness. But he only made her
a little bow, and then turned towards Barbara.

She flushed scarlet beneath his gaze, then she saw that
Miss Langdon's judgment was perfectly correct. He was enjoying himself, and he was enjoying himself hugely, playing the
contrite penitent with his tongue in his cheek. He began, "I
must apologise to you, too, Miss Smith——" but she interrupted him, saying almost on a sob, "Oh, please don't. Please."

"It seems," he said, "that I am become a kind of wandering

Jew, compelled to walk from room to room until at last my apologies are accepted. Am I so completely unpardonable?"

"Yes!" said Miss Langdon, and at that his composure suddenly broke, as if his nerves had cracked to pieces; the exhausted face twisted into a white, murderous rage, and he whirled round on her, his fists up.

He must have seen the horror on the faces staring at him. He opened his mouth, then shut it again. His effort at self-control was as palpable as if he had wrenched his mind round like a stopper. He walked out without a word, and Barbara, not caring now who saw her, ran after him, to seize hold of his hands. "Mark," she said, "Mark, you must forgive her. You must forgive us all, and yourself, too, for this is so shocking, so dreadful, that we are all nearly out of our minds."

He said quite calmly, "Are you not forgiving me, either?"

"You must know," she said, "that I'd forgive you anything."

"Even last night?"

"Perhaps," she said, "it is I who should be forgiven."

He inclined his head a little. There was a rather wry smile on his lips. "Well, that's as may be. There are other nights, after all. The sergeant's back. And, by God, he's on the warpath."

"How could anyone kill so young a boy?"

"One can kill anything if one has to. I don't suppose it's agreeable, but it's always possible. I'm going to my room. I've done my duty. I've apologised to everyone, and I haven't meant a bloody word of it, except to you. To-morrow we go out, you and I, and we're going out if the whole world dies. After all, Barbara, it might be for the last time. Life in this establishment has become strangely precarious. You're a nice girl, for all you're so proper, and I really like you very much indeed. I mean that, you know." Then he broke into a sudden roar. "Why the hell couldn't he listen, the damned young fool? Why had he to interfere? He was only a baby, after all." He made a despairing gesture. "You see. I'm simply not speakable to this morning. For God's sake, let us all do some work."

But of course no work was done. Miss Holmes, as shaken as the girls, came in to say without assurance that the work must go out, whatever happened, and that she expected them all to be typing hard next time she saw them. They gazed at her. They said, "Yes, Miss Holmes." And the moment she left the room, they fell back in frightened, awe-struck conversation.

"Of course," said Miss Langdon, "it's that Mr. Allan. I said to Eric last night, 'Eric,' I said, 'the man's a murderer. You've only got to look at him.' Of course, I'm very sensitive about these things. It's queer, actually. I seem to have a kind of sixth sense about what people are thinking."

"If that is so," said Barbara, raising his head; she had returned to her seat at the desk; "you'd better take warning by it. For if you say that again, I shall get up and murder you. Yes! Murder! That's what I said. For you don't know, do you? I may have done the murders. Any of us may have done them." And the thing in her mind that she had pushed down for so long began slowly and slimily to creep up from the depths of her inner self. She thrust wildly back at it, but the effort was too much. Suddenly everything crowded in on her—Mr. Wilson alive, Mr. Wilson so dreadfully dead, hands that had hurt her, the river running at her feet, a face grown wary, hard. She bowed her head upon her outstretched arms and wept bitterly, not caring that it was Miss Langdon who put a hand on her shoulder, Miss Langdon who hurried to bring her a glass of water.

Sergeant Robins said to Mr. Latimer, "I don't see any point at the moment in interviewing all your staff. I gather that the young man took great pains to do whatever he wanted to do in secret." Then he cried out, as he had cried to Police-Constable Hall, the day before, "If only people would tell us. Believe me, sir, half the things that happen in the world could be avoided if only people didn't have the idea that they must keep things to themselves." He went on more quietly, "He was found at a quarter to six. He must have died some time between twelve and three. Can you give me any idea of the movements of your staff during those times?"

"It's virtually impossible," said Mr. Latimer. "Between twelve and one half the staff would be out at lunch, and between one and two the other half. There'd be very few people about. Mr. Allan had gone home. He took the afternoon off. Mr. Dodds—I think he lunches between twelve and one, and Mrs. Bridgwater between one and two—— The trouble is that the librarian staff never stays in one place. They are always going down to the stacks for one thing or another. Do you know what the poor boy can have found out? He was such a nice lad. We all liked him."

"I have a pretty good idea, sir."

"It's a shocking business," said Mr. Latimer. It had been his task to break the news to Mr. Wilson's family. He said, "I know one doesn't ask these things, but have you no idea as to who—I mean, we can't go on like this. We are all looking sideways at each other. Two of the girls' parents have rung up to say they are taking them away. You can't blame them. Good heavens, if one can't go downstairs these days to fetch a book without—— It's a nightmare. It's not possible." Then, because he was a man unaccustomed to strong emotion, he apologised and mopped at his forehead.

"There will be no more murders, sir," said the sergeant rather grimly, "and there will shortly be an arrest. We are only waiting for one small piece of evidence. But there will be no more murders."

In this he was, perhaps, rather over-optimistic.

He sat in Mr. Latimer's room for a long time, with the open file before him. His emotion was spent now. The murderer may have been a great many things in his time, and some of them were magnificent, and some of them were vile, but now the leaves of his life were being opened one by one, and from those leaves came an image like the photostat he had watched being made. At first the page was blank, and then one dipped it into the developing fluid, and slowly there evolved the lineaments of a man who had done strange and inconsistent things, who had saved the lives of some and broken the lives of others, who had brought salvation and damnation in his train. He ought, thought the sergeant, to have been born into another age, been one of those soldiers of fortune, or whatever the name was. He'd have enjoyed himself plotting and fighting, and perhaps in the end he'd have settled down to respectable citizenship. Well, now he'd settle down into the hangman's rope, and it was a pity for him that the times did not permit the grand, farewell oration he would have loved.

He heard the knock on the door and said, "Come in." So vivid had been the image in his mind that he thought to see the person in the doorway; so harshly bright a conception had he created of the murderer's character that he would not have been surprised to see him armed. But, when he saw who it was, he rose to his feet.

"Good-morning," he said. "Do you know, I half expected to see you. You'd better come in and sit down."

Mrs. Bridgwater sat down in a huddle, collapsed way, as if her knees would no longer support her. She looked hopeless, bedraggled with weeping, and frightened nearly to death. Even the magnificent body seemed to have sagged, and her face, when she raised it to the sergeant, was that of a sick, old woman. She gave him an abject look, put a cigarette in her mouth, then opened the match-box the wrong way, so that all the matches fell to the ground.

He stooped to pick them up for her, but she burst out crying, so that the cigarette, too, fell from her lips.

"Come," he said briskly, "you must pull yourself together, madam. What is all this about?"

"I should have told you before," she said, not looking at him, but staring at the carpet, fingering the spilt matches that now lay on her lap. Her accent had slid away from its carefully cultivated purity into a flat, genteel, half-Cockney whine.

"I expect you should," he agreed. "But at least it's something that you're telling me now."

She spoke at last in a quick monotone, so low that he had to listen with the utmost intentness to catch what she said. She did not look at him once, but all the time her hands were playing with the matches, and a muscle in her cheek flickered up and down. "I saw the body, you know——" she began.

Sergeant Robins was genuinely startled. "Mr. Wilson's?"

"No. No, no, no." A fresh outburst of tears. It was entirely natural, indeed inevitable, but the sergeant, who had not slept much lately, had a sudden and violent desire to shake her. But he waited as patiently as he could, and at last she went on, "Hers—— It was while Mr. Latimer was locked in. I heard people running about, so I came out of my office. I went into the packing-room. It's next door but one to mine. And I fell over a sack. It opened. She was there. So I tied it up again," said Mrs. Bridgwater, as if this were the most natural thing in the world, "and that's how I cut my hand, you see, because the string's very tough, and I have a delicate skin."

"You did *what?*" He realised that he was shouting, and checked himself with an effort that swelled the muscles of his neck.

"I tied it up again," she repeated in a little girl voice, then suddenly, shrill, spiteful, "Why not? I hated her. She told Henry. She was a beastly woman. She only envied me because I was young and pretty and everything she had never been. I wanted poor Mr. Dodds to get away with it. But now with Jack—— That's cruel and dreadful. I wouldn't want anyone to get away with that."

"You wanted *who* to get away with it?"

"Mr. Dodds. It must have been Mr. Dodds." Her eyes were beginning to shift beneath his gaze, and he saw slowly coming to the surface a terror so shocking that she herself would not admit to it. Her voice rang out, almost in a scream. "But of course it was Mr. Dodds. You're so *stupid*. He's quite a sinister man, you know. And there's only him and—and Mr. Allan on this floor, and, after all, it must have been someone near——" Then the terror broke, and she began to shriek, "It couldn't have been—— It's not true, it's not true. Why, we were friends—— He kissed me—— He—— Oh, God," whimpered Mrs. Bridgwater, "I nearly told him, I nearly told him. If he'd been kinder, I would—— He'll murder me, too, he'll murder me, too——"

"Mrs. Bridgwater," said the sergeant sternly, "you should have told me this a long time ago. If you had told me, Mr. Wilson might now be alive." He surveyed her with a bitter distaste that no officialdom could hide. "However, it's too late to do anything about that. I want you to go home. I shall send a plain-clothes man with you. And I want you to stay there and not return to the office until you've heard from me." He added—he simply could not restrain himself, though this was the kind of thing termed exceeding one's duty—"You have been an extremely silly woman. You are fortunate to be alive. Will you please go immediately I have arranged for an escort. I will explain to Mr. Latimer. I don't think I need say to you how important it is to hold your tongue. You have held it long enough, unfortunately; for your own sake, you'd better continue doing so."

She left the room. Her teeth were chattering. She walked upstairs to her office and, as she reached the fourth floor, met Mark Allan on the landing.

"Well, Mona?" said Mark, and Mona Bridgwater immediately turned up the whites of her eyes and tumbled to his feet in a dead faint.

"And poor Mrs. Bridgwater——I saw her going along to the sergeant's room this morning," said Greta, rolling off envelopes in Barbara's room. "Perhaps he scared her. Anyway, she fainted, and she had to be taken home."

"Oh?" said Barbara.

"She fainted in front of Mr. Allan, too. I wish I could faint in front of Mr. Allan, don't you? I do think he's smashing, and I don't really think he means to be rude, it's just his way of talking."

"And what happened after she fainted?" demanded Barbara.

"Oh, Mr. Allan called for Mr. Purley, and they gave her some sal volatile. Mr. Allan didn't pick her up, or anything. I thought they were such great friends," said Greta. "You're great friends with him, aren't you, Miss Smith?"

"I—I suppose I am."

"Do you remember," said Greta, giggling a little, "the time he got in such a temper with me? I'll never forget him coming out with his hands all wet. He looked so white, too, and the water trickling on to the floor. But he gave me a smashing box of chocolates afterwards. What's the matter, Miss Smith? You're not going to faint, too, are you? You look awfully queer."

"No. I'm not going to faint. I wish—— But I'm too tired to think any more, and too miserable. I wish it were time to go home."

"What you ought to do, Miss Smith," said Greta, who seemed remarkably untouched by the violence about her, "is to go to the pictures. I suppose you're going home to work at your silly old novel. You only overtire yourself, and then you faint in the office."

"I haven't fainted in the office," protested Barbara, beginning to laugh.

"Well, you soon will do. Why doesn't your boy friend take you out like he used to? He looked ever so nice. What paper does he work on?"

Barbara told her, adding, "I don't see him any more, you know. But, if it interests you, I'm going out to-morrow."

"Smashing! Where are you going? Is he nice?"

"Well, I don't know if you'd call him *nice*. And," said Barbara, "I don't know where I'm going. I don't know where I'm going at all."

She walked with Mark along to the garage. "I didn't bring her up to I.L.D.A.," he said, "I thought it would cause too much attention. Besides, the old girl's in a temperamental mood, and has to be cranked up to start, and altogether our exit would have been as quiet as if we were going on our honeymoon." He added, "How is your landlady?"

She could not reply to this, nor would she meet his eyes. But presently she said, "Doesn't it seem shocking to you that we are going out like this? He only died two days ago. He must have been killed soon after you left. I would be typing, we would all be busy——"

"If," he said in a rough tone she had not yet heard from him, "you are going to go on like this, we are not going out at all, and you can sit by yourself and weep to your heart's content. Do you think I wish to drag a hearse about with me? This was planned as an evening of pleasure. If you want to cry on my shoulder, you can do so, but it'll be for some other reason, and it'll be when I choose it. Wilson's dead. Dead as mutton."

"Mark!"

"Dead, gone where the good niggers go, like a million others. We all have to die. Were you in love with him?"

"Darling, don't be silly."

"Well, then? Why should you mourn for him? He was a nice boy. All right. There are plenty other nice boys. The world is full of nice boys, and some of them survive. But you don't have to weep over them. Well? Are you going to cry your eyes out all evening? I cannot stop you, but you are not doing it in my company."

Barbara said faintly, against the blare of his words, "I'll not weep. Are you going to rate me all evening? I suppose I cannot stop you, either. Are we going to quarrel?"

"Probably," he said, then, "No. Why should we? Ah, for God's sake. You remind me of Mona."

"I hear she—she fainted," said Barbara. Her voice was a little choked, for Mark's anger appalled her.

"The silly bitch. I left her to it. I've other things to do than pick up fainting women. Except," he added, looking down at her, "when it suits my purpose, and then of course it can be quite pleasant."

"Perhaps she had a rough time with Sergeant Robins."

"Oh?" said Mark. "I didn't know she had been talking to Sergeant Robins. Perhaps he's accused her of the murder. I must ask her to-morrow."

"She won't be here. The doctor says she must rest for a few days."

Mark made no comment on this, but she felt, without looking at him, a swift change of mood, and then suddenly his arm came round her shoulders. "What a bastard I am. Look. Here's the garage. I'll introduce you to her ladyship, and we'll go, and I'll be nice to you, and you'll be nice to me, and we'll stop bickering like an estranged married couple, and you shall talk of young Wilson to your heart's content, and of Mrs. Warren, afterwards, if you wish. Get in. I must get in first, because the right-hand door doesn't open. At least it does open, but it falls off. I'll just crank her up."

This he did energetically, and the engine roared into life with the noise of a jet plane. He was a first-class driver, as she could recognise, though she knew nothing about cars. But he drove fast and without courtesy; he took risks with the utmost dexterity, and seemed to take a perverse delight in exasperating the smaller and more modern cars that crossed his path.

He did not speak for a time. She watched his hands on the wheel. Then he said reflectively, "I suppose some time I should really get a licence."

She turned to stare at him. "Do you mean to tell me you're driving without one?"

"But of course!" His tone made her remark an absurd impertinence. "Good God, I've driven all over France, cars and lorries and vans and jeeps. You don't expect me to take a test here, do you? They've got a confounded nerve to expect it."

"Suppose you get involved in an accident?"

"I won't," said Mark, shooting between a lorry and a small car, and removing his hand from the wheel to wave a derisive salute at the driver of the latter, who was shouting abuse at him. "It's a question of judgment. I have an accurate eye. I always had. It was necessary in my profession. I'm not, of course, referring to schoolmastering."

"Schoolmastering!"

"Did I never tell you I was a schoolmaster? Quite a good one, too, though I am not a very patient man— Damn your eyes, why can't you look where you're going? These sports cars are a bloody nuisance—I taught physics. I didn't mind the boys, but I didn't like my colleagues, so I became a librarian instead, and don't care much for my colleagues, either. Still, one has more privacy."

"You never speak of what happened to you in the war."

"There's nothing to speak about. Perhaps there'll be another war soon."

"You sound as if you wanted it."

"Do I? Oh, Herr Krupp and I have a great deal in common. We are both bandits at heart. Why not? Sometimes I suspect that since then I have slowly died."

"Mark, there's a zebra crossing. That woman and child——"

"Ah, to hell with them. One woman more or less, one baby more or less, one librarian more or less, what's it matter? We'll all be blown to smithereens within the next few years, and your quaint honour turned to dust—highly

radio-active at that. And now what is the matter? She's all
right. I didn't kill her, and the child will grow into a probably revolting man. I've given her something to talk about—
the devil went straight at me, and on a zebra crossing, too,
hope he rots in hell. Don't suppose she'll say that, but she'll
think it. As if it matters whether one rots in hell or on earth.
If you don't unblink those genteel and reproachful eyes, I
swear I'll ram the car into that number thirteen bus, and
kill the whole blasted lot of us."

It was that strange excitement again, it struck her like a
blow, stirred her to hysteria. She suddenly raised her clenched
fist and beat it against the side of the car.

"What the devil do you think you're doing?" he demanded.
"Are you trying to destroy the car? Are you trying to destroy
us?"

"No," she said, speaking almost as if she were in pain.
"No. I was just wondering why I endure you. You shout,
you bluster, you roar at me, you insult me, and sometimes I
think you are mad."

"But so I am—though only nor'-nor'-west, to use my
friend, Dodds's, favourite quotation. Though sometimes the
wind veers round, sometimes it blows from all quarters of
the compass. I'll tell you why you endure me. Shall I?"

"Your vanity," said Barbara coldly, "will no doubt answer
for you."

He broke into a splutter of laughter and mimicked her.
"So my vanity will answer for me, will it? Wait till we get
out of this car. Just wait. To-day is V-day, and I'm not
being put in my place by a female novelist. We'll pass this
bus——"

"You can't——"

"Can't I!" He drove the car at full speed through what
seemed to be an incredibly narrow space and turned off the
Strand, down to the Embankment. "We'll stop here a while.
The band is playing. I am sure you'd like to listen to the
band. We will rest in the shade of His Grace the Duke of
Buckingham, who has baptised the whole neighbourhood. I
will kiss you in George Street, kiss you twice in Villiers Street,
clasp you in my arms in Duke Street, and what happens in
Of Alley—*ce n'est pas dit dans la chanson*. I'll not continue
the analogy, or you'll run away, back to your landlady."

She felt as if she were walking into the teeth of a full
gale. She looked into his triumphant face as he stopped the
engine. She said, "Yes. I can understand now why you liked
the war."

He was whistling between his teeth, as she had heard him whistle before, "Pom-pom-pom-*pom*—— Oh, it was something," he said, "to wake up and know you were still alive. How fresh the dawn seemed, how clean the sea wind. But we'll not talk of war. It wouldn't suit your genteel ears, for you'd expect heroics, and I'd give you muck."

"What is that you're always whistling?"

"Oh, it was our signal. By a fellow called Ludwig von Beethoven. Aren't you educated at all? Come into the gardens, and I'll educate you. What are you laughing at? When I want you to laugh, you cry, and when I want you to be serious, you laugh. What is all this? Are you making fun of me, by any chance?"

"That I wouldn't dare," she said. "There should be a notice in all lifts, and all cars too, I suppose: 'No laughing.' Or, if one is educated enough to understand, *Défense de rire*. Do you speak French?"

And then, because she knew he was going to behave abominably, because she did not care at all, because her gentility was in fragments before the blast of his vitality, she laughed in his face and, when he threatened her, laughed the more. When they came into the gardens, she lay down on the grass beside him and let him take her in his arms, though half the world was there and, for all she knew, half the staff of I.L.D.A. also.

"We'll imagine," he said at last, "that this is the last time we'll ever spend together. I am a hero going to the wars. I may never come back. There is, after all, no notice up, *Défense de s'embrasser*—I do speak French, incidentally. In fact, there are no notices up forbidding us to do anything at all." He fell silent for a moment, then he said, "If I were really going to the wars, Barbara, if really I might never come back—it's possible. Who knows what will happen? The I.L.D.A. motto should be, 'In the midst of books we are in death.' You're afraid again. Oh, God," he said, "I shouldn't be with you. It's dangerous, dangerous. But I don't give a damn. I want to stay with you. May I, Barbara? Shall we stay together to-night?"

"Yes, Mark."

He drew in a little sobbing sigh. For the briefest of seconds the look flashed across him that she had seen before—reflective, calculating, hard. It was not a lover's look. Then the next instant it was replaced by an expression of the utmost tenderness. He held her very close; she knew that danger was

close, too, but she held it to her heart, and it was as if the
rhythm of its beat went pom-pom-pom-*pom*.

And as she thought this, he said, "It's my war-song. But I
told you——"

She did not answer. Some instinct told her not to answer.
She was very afraid, then he kissed her, and the fear sank
back. He said, catching at her hands, "Well, there's now no
need to scandalise the neighbourhood. I think that old lady's
gone off to fetch a policeman. We'll go before she comes
back, otherwise the report will doubtless go straight to the
Yard, and then the sergeant will know we've done the murder in collusion."

They drove on for a while, then Mark said, "I want some
cigarettes. I won't be a minute." He drew up by the pave-
ment outside a public-house, stepped across Barbara's knees,
and climbed out.

She let her head fall back against the car seat. She closed
her eyes. The fear was rising until it was a cold wind of
panic. She fought against it. There was no reason, no reason—— It was not because they were going to spend the
night together, and yet it was a little that, too, as if she had
pledged herself to lie with danger, as if with her own hands
she had directed the sword towards her breast. Soldiers of
fortune are not agreeable people to make fools of. She had
no wish to make a fool of him, but she had to hide her
fear, because that was part of her fear; if he knew how afraid
she was—— She shuddered, put her hands up to her face.
He must not see her like this. He must not be angry with
her to-night, because to-morrow he would be away at the
wars.

"Nonsense!" she cried aloud, and jerked herself up. And,
as she did so, the car, which was parked on a slope, stirred
beneath her, then started slowly to glide down the road, gathering momentum as it went.

She had never driven a car in her life. She knew nothing
at all about it. The phantom fear was succeeded by one all
too founded in reality. She clutched at the wheel, then
screamed at the top of her voice, "Mark!"

He heard her. He came to the door. Then he sprang
after the car at full speed, leaping on to the running-board
by the door which would not open. The car was now gathering speed, zigzagging from right to left, as Barbara's unin-
structed hands turned at the wheel. He hung on; he shouted,
"Put on the foot-brake and pull the hand-brake tight."

But she did not know where anything was. The car sped

to the main road, where two streams of traffic were moving past. 'Oh, God,' she thought, 'in a few seconds we'll be there, and it'll be slaughter, with the cars piling up on us.'

"The extreme right!" he shouted, then she heard clearly, "God damn this ruddy door."

She was beside herself. The world was black with terror. Mr. Andrews would, no doubt, have coped admirably, but his creator was lost, plucking frantically at the various levers which seemed to have multiplied themselves by twenty; she still mechanically turned the wheel, miraculously sliding past other vehicles by a hair's breadth.

There was a great splintering of glass as Mark crashed his arm through the window. He tried to reach the brakes, but it was impossible. They were just on the main road. To the right of them was parked a small car. He glanced at this across his shoulder, then, catching at the wheel, wrenched it to the right so that the Humber rammed into the other car's running-board.

The car stopped with a jolt that seemed to send Barbara's teeth through her head. Half a dozen yards distant lay the main road. She looked up dizzily at Mark. His face was alight with excitement. Then she saw that his arm was dripping blood. He came round to her side, pushed her over into the driver's seat without ceremony, switched off the engine, and sat down beside her. He said, "I think for future occasions you should really know where the brakes are. Now this——"

"For God's sake," she said. "You might have been killed."

"We might have been killed. So might a great many other people. It would have been a fine massacre, for no one would have had time to signal to the car behind. Why, it might have gone on for miles and miles."

"Mark, do something about your arm, instead of talking. You'll bleed to death."

"I'll go in and ask them for first aid. It seems that I also have to make a very uncomfortable apology and pay out a considerable sum of money. Our bumper is our own affair, but this running-board is not, and I doubt if it will ever be the same again. You come with me. Your pale face will carry more conviction than my arm!" He put his sound arm round her. "You were very frightened, weren't you?"

"Oh, God, scared to death. I feel—I must stay here for a minute——"

"Well," he said, "with the best will in the world, I can't

pick you up in my arms. It'll have to be under one arm,
I'm afraid, and that won't look so dignified. Hang on to me,
my darling, keep your eyes moving, count twenty, and you
won't faint."

She thought that it should be she who should support
him, for the blood was running down his sleeve. But he
seemed hardly to notice it, and this shamed her, and helped
to steady her.

He rang the bell. While they waited, he said, "At least,
you tried to steer it. I can't give you full marks, but I think
you deserve five out of ten." He bent his head to kiss her,
and she saw that he was delighted with himself and the situation, that the emergency seemed to have released in him such
good spirits that it was as if he were exhilarated with
drink.

He told his story to the householder, and the condition
of his arm, and the colour of Barbara's face were such that
the story could not be disbelieved. She went with him to the
bathroom to bandage him up. It was difficult to get his jacket
off, but he seemed to ignore the pain, though she exclaimed
when she saw the bruised condition of his arm and the ugly
gash upon it.

He started washing his arm at the basin. He would not
let her help him. "I don't like being fussed over," he said
quite irritably. So she sat on the edge of the bath and
watched him as he rolled up his shirt-sleeve and deluged
his arm with the running cold water—watched the broad
sweep of his shoulders, the line of his neck and jaw, watched
the dark hair that fell across his forehead.

"Do you know," he said, speaking clearly through the
noise of the taps, "I haven't enjoyed myself so much for
years." And he swung round on her, his smile wide and
enchanting, his eyes alight with exultation. His hands and
wrists were dripping wet. Barbara looked down at them.

You did photostats with three trays. You dipped the paper
in each in turn. You wetted the tips of your fingers, not
more.

His hands and wrists were dripping wet.

A small, dark room. A long table. Beneath the table a
squat and crumpled body, with protruding tongue, eyes wide
and sightless. An ugly, unsightly remnant, stuffed half-way
into a sack. And then a foolish little girl, a little girl in
love, a silly little girl, asking silly little questions, refusing
to go away. Three yards and a half-open door between the

alive young girl and the dead old woman. Safety so near. Danger so near.

His hands and wrists were dripping wet.

Oh, there were a hundred explanations. He had upset a tray. He had washed himself at the sink——

He had looked dreadful. Like Boris Karloff. To kill in cold blood is, after all, something of a shock. It had not yet become routine. It had not yet become inevitable.

The water had trickled on to the floor. It was trickling on to the floor now. He would have had to wash himself. The dead——

A hundred explanations.

And—one eighteenth-century volume. Hard looks, calculating glances. Hands that suddenly tightened. A kiss so harsh that it burnt the flesh. And the sweet Thames running softly, with a spar of wood being carried out to sea, carried out to sea——

A hundred explanations.

But then, of course, she had always known, always——

He said, "Tie this knot, darling, will you? I want to kiss you most urgently, and I can't with yards of bandage trailing round me."

She tied the knot. Her hands were steady. She held up her face to be kissed.

He put his sound arm round her. (He must have carried the body in his arms.) He touched her rather gingerly with the other, wincing as he did so. "I do not suppose," he said—the current was flowing from him to her in a hundred, thousand, million volts—"I do not suppose anything like this has ever occurred in this bathroom before. People just probably take a bath, perhaps with their shift on. We will leave our aura of wickedness. Let us in God's name pollute this spotless atmosphere of pure white tiles and unsullied towels. Damn it, I have to pay the bloke fifteen bloody quid, so we might as well have our money's worth. It'll serve as an aperitif. And if you cry out, I can turn the taps on to drown the noise——"

She let him kiss her and fondle her. She said between kisses, "I love you with all my heart," and then a shudder swept through her, a sick, cold shudder that twisted her stomach and twisted her heart, so that it was like the approach of dissolution, it was like the coming of death. Beneath his hands her body grew cold and small. Her eyes slid down to the strong hand beneath her breast. Her breath caught in her throat. She closed her eyes.

She opened them again to meet his, staring into hers. They had grown blank, and then the blankness was succeeded by incredulity, anger, and then pure, disbelieving horror.

He did not kiss her again, but he did not move, his face an inch away from hers, his hand against her heart. They were both utterly still. And in that stillness their minds opened wide to each other. No more was there a secret between them. And so for a long, eternal minute they stayed in the neat, white bathroom of a neat, white house while the occupant, outside in the street, wondered why the devil people should choose to ram their car into his.

He gave a deep sigh, as if of pain. His lashes came down. She saw that they were long for a man's. He said, as if to himself, "Oh, my God——" But he still did not move, neither did his hand. And then she saw that his look was changing, was becoming again probing, calculating, menacing, hard, as if the thought of self-preservation were edging into his mind. He released her and stood back. She thought her love and fear and unhappiness would destroy her. She looked full at him. Then slowly she shook her head.

He said pleasantly, "Well, Barbara, I suppose our gentleman may want to be taking a bath." A faint smile twisted his mouth, a smile of bitterness, affection, and always the something else that was neither. "I think perhaps I had better take you home."

She whispered, "Yes."

"After all," he went on casually, as if he were making polite conversation, "it would be a little difficult with one arm out of commission. You would have to be so accommodating, and I should hate that. Besides, for the first time—— It would have been the first, wouldn't it?"

She could not answer that. Her head sank down. The sense of bereavement, of loss, was utterly unbearable.

He did not continue. He only said, "Your guardian angel has proved most efficient."

They walked back to the car in silence. The engine started easily, as if the violent jolt had set it in order again. They drove back to Barbara's flat, and during the drive, which lasted for three-quarters of an hour, neither spoke a single word, except for once when he asked her if she would like a drink. She said, "No, thank you." Then the silence was absolute; yet their thoughts spoke continuously, like the con-

stant blare of voices in a radio-cab; their love and their
hate and their fear were as a tangible cord between them.

He stopped outside her door. He leaned back, his hands
lightly on the wheel, and regarded her. "Well," he said, "I'm
sorry, and all that. I hope you're not angry with me. You
are at least saved from what they say is worse than death.
I wonder if it is. What do you think?" Then he laughed.
"Of course, you might ask me up for a cup of coffee. Though,
I suppose, there's always the landlady——"

"You can come up, if you wish," said Barbara.

"Can I? Can I?" Then, "No. It's—it's too late. Much too
late. Besides, my arm is giving me hell, and I'm tired. Thank
you all the same, my dear." The half-smile flickered again.
"In the circumstances, I appreciate it."

Her thoughts cried out to him, 'All right, come. I don't
care. Perhaps you'd better get it over. I don't think I can endure the waiting, and I think you like me enough to make it
quick. You'll only go home and think it over, and then you'll
know that you dare not leave me, lest I grow hysterical,
talk in my sleep, confide in my best friend. You'll not dare,
you are long past the stage when you could take such a risk.'

He looked, surprisingly, as if he wanted to laugh. She was
certain he read her thoughts quite clearly. The bond between
them was an iron-forged chain. The walls of their minds
were down; there was nothing now but the truth. But he
only held the car door open for her then, stepping out after
her, leant forward to kiss her cheek, then her forehead, and
at last her mouth. "Do you know," he said, his lips against
hers, "I was once nearly drowned? I was only a hundred
yards from the shore. But the current was too strong for me.
Every time I swam a yard forward, the sea caught at me and
threw me three yards back. How near the shore seemed.
And what a paradise—a stretch of yellow sand, with the
sun blazing down. And always driven back and back with
bursting lungs and muscles screaming damnation. But I was
resolved not to be beaten. The moment when my feet at last
touched the hot sand—— Only that, you see, Barbara, was
a long time ago. And the current can be so confoundedly
strong. Good-night. You're a nice girl. I said that before,
didn't I?"

She said, "I love you very much. I suppose I always will.
It's a pity."

"Yes," he said, "it's a pity. Well, I'll see you in the morning. Good-night, Barbara. I'm very sorry it should have turned
out like this."

"Good-night, Mark."

She sat in her room for a long time. Then at last she dialled Charles's number. She held on for several minutes. There was no answer. She lay back on her bed. She did not sleep. And so the night passed.

THE sergeant said to Police-Constable Hall, "Hudson lost him when he came back. He saw him walking along with the little Smith girl, and then they leapt on to a moving bus, and there was such a jam of traffic he couldn't even get the number. But he went straight to Liverpool University. It's closed officially, but apparently that only means they are stock-taking, and there were people working in the Library. He went in. He seems to have had a long talk with them. I've no doubt at all he got what he wanted, but that, of course, is something we can never prove. He wouldn't in any case have been fool enough to take the microfilm away. As for Mr. Ludwig, that is just too bad for Mr. Allan. We have traced Mr. Ludwig. He banks at the Westminster, and Mr. Allan at Barclays'. Mr. Ludwig's account is a most interesting one, with very large entries, indeed, paid in at irregular intervals by Mr. Ludwig in person. There is no doubt, I think, at all. Allan is, after all, a distinctive-looking type, and he doesn't seem to have disguised himself with a false beard or anything. And do you know," said the sergeant, looking very angry indeed, "that nearly all Mr. Ludwig's money is paid regularly to France, via the Bank of England. All above board, and all—the Bank of England checked this, because he had to fill in forms, with reasons for sending money abroad—to widowed females and their families, whose husbands were killed in the Maquis. If only," he went on, now quite uncontrollably furious, "people would be consistent. Here's a cold-blooded murderer—nothing on God's earth could have been more cold-blooded than his killing of that boy—and yet he seemed to have shouldered the responsibility of some twenty families. Twenty! Smuggles in this filthy stuff, which ruins and destroys, involves himself in the dirtiest racket imaginable, kills when it pleases him, and yet—— I am thinking of resigning. If I'm not pushed." Then he added, "That little Miss Smith looks half-dead this morning. I wonder—— I swear she knows something she

191

shouldn't. Why murderers have this extraordinary attraction
for women, I have never been able to understand. You'd think
something would warn them. But no. They insure their lives
and hop into baths. They go away for week-ends with them
at the first meeting. They accompany them to deserted
copses, and they endure every symptom of arsenical poison-
ing, and ask for more. It beats me. He's a good-looking devil, I admit, which is more than you can say for many
murderers, but even so—— Anyway, this gentleman has
come to the end of the road now, and he'll find it's a blind
alley, with something waiting for him which he won't like.
Do you know, when that child was talking to him, he must
have had the old woman's body next door. It's not a nice
thought. No wonder he was in such a state. And what a piece
of luck for him about Mr. Latimer. Is that incredibly stupid
woman being watched? I can't feel she'd be much loss to the
community, but one more murder, and I'm for it, and quite
right, too. I wish I knew what had happened to Miss Smith.
She's dead scared of something. Ask her to come here, will
you?"

Barbara came in, in the state of apathy and despair which
had lain upon her since last night. She had not slept at all.
She could not. Her memory trundled along like the wheels of
a train, grinding out monotonously foolish things she had
thought to have forgotten—— A murderer walking beside
you. The hard look which came so suddenly. Hands that
hurt—— Moments in which her life had held by a line thin
as a spider's weaving. Other things, too, which had once
been sweet to think of, and which now rose in her throat like
vomit. How afraid he had been that she would remember.
She could understand that. She could understand now a
great many things. It would have been easier to think, 'He
is a murderer. He never gave a damn for me. He made use
of me, loved me for expediency's sake, kissed me into obliv-
ion, would have slept with me to bind me irrevocably.' But
it was not like that. People were never in one piece, and this
did not astonish or anger her, as it did Sergeant Robins. He
had given a damn for her. He would even give a damn for
her while he killed her. Why not? He had loved her in his
own way. The bond between them, which must now destroy
them, was not a bond so easily forged. And even now it was
there, though she knew, and so did he. Of course he would
have to kill her. She thought that he would not want to do it.
She remembered his outburst of fury after Jack Wilson's

death. But he would be compelled; he would never be safe
while she was alive, and he would not see that he would
never be safe again after she was dead. The chill of terror
laid its finger on her. She was utterly unhappy, but she did
not want to die. Yet she was so tired, so tired. The fear
brought the sweat out on her, but, even if Mark had stepped
before her with his arm raised, she could not have cried out,
so drained was she of life.

She barely glanced at the sergeant. She slumped into a
chair.

He said, "Are you not feeling well this morning, miss?"

"I'm all right."

"Miss Smith," he said, "I want to ask for your help. I
wouldn't say this to everyone, but you are a sensible girl.
There is a very dangerous person here. You know that."

She said nothing.

"You do know that, don't you?" he insisted.

She shrugged. A man standing there, hands bound, looking at the wall, face white, expressionless, blood running
down the cheek—Pom-pom-pom-*pom*—— She said, *"Je ne
comprends pas."*

"I *beg* your pardon, miss?"

"Je ne com—I—I——" She gave him a wild look, half
rose from her chair, then sank down again. "I'm sorry. I—I
think I'm not—not very well."

"I can see that," said the sergeant sympathetically, and
thought, 'She looks as if she's due for a nervous breakdown,
or something. I wonder if I ought to send for a doctor.' He
went on, "I won't keep you long, miss. It's just this. I thought
as you're a writer, and trained to observe, as one might say,
that you might have seen some small thing which could help
us. It might seem quite unimportant to you. Is there anything you could tell us?"

"No."

"A moment's strangeness. An odd trick of feature or behaviour——"

"I don't know. I don't understand what you mean."

"You do know something."

"I don't understand what you mean. Why can't you leave
me alone?" *Je ne comprends pas.* Then she cried out, "Don't!
Don't! You're killing him." Then, her face quite white, "Am
I going mad? I think I'd better go. I'm sorry. I don't know
what's happened to me."

She saw, in the nightmare, that he was standing over her.
She managed to smile at him. She said quite calmly, "I'm

all right, really. I'm sorry. Only I didn't sleep very well last
night. I'll go and do some work. That'll be the best thing
for me."

He said again sternly, "You do know something. Why
won't you tell us? Don't you see that it is dangerous for
you to keep this knowledge to yourself? That is why that
poor boy died. He found out something, and he thought he
was clever, and he didn't tell us. Do you——" His voice
rang out in the rage of despair. "Do you want to be murdered, too?"

"I don't care," she said. "It wouldn't matter very much."

"Then you have nothing to say to me?"

"No. Nothing."

As she was by the door, he said sharply, "Do you know
who the murderer is?"

She turned her sunken, shadowed eyes upon him. "No."

"Are you sure?"

"Yes."

"Very well, then. But if you change your mind—— I
mean, if you think there is something I ought to know, will
you promise to come and tell me immediately?"

"Yes."

"Even if it seems ridiculous and trivial?"

"Yes."

"God help us all," said the sergeant when she had gone.
"She ought to be shut up in a home. It makes me sick. Give
me Hudson's report again, will you? I've got to get hold of
one of those microfilms. And keep on Allan's tail if he goes
out. Though I bet we don't find a damn thing, anyway. If
only he'd drop half a pound of cocaine—— What a hope.
Perhaps the police at the other end will have some news for
us. Meanwhile I want men on duty at all the exits. I'm not
running any more risks, and I've an idea that things are
going to begin to happen——"

The office had fallen into routine again. The work piled
up, and the work had to go out. It was very horrible, but
rather exciting. One was frightened to stay, but it was stim-
ulating to have one's friends pursuing one for details. The
telephonist had left. There was a new one from the agency,
a young man with an excessively refined and drawling voice.
He was only staying for three days, and it had been difficult
to persuade him to do that. He had answered a call from
Mark's line; he had said in his drawl, "Really, if you shout
so, I cannot understand a word." To which Mark had replied

as might have been expected, and the young man had turned a fiery red and at once given in his notice. Mr. Latimer, to whom this was reported, begged him to stay for three days, and said nothing to Mark at all.

Mr. Rills was working harder than he had ever worked in his life, and shut himself up in his room, from which he hardly stirred. Mark Allan was also enclosed in his office; no one had seen him that morning, but his footsteps could be heard pacing up and down. The rumour went round that he was in the worst possible temper; his privacy was completely ensured.

Mr. Dodds, on the other hand, wandered about, irritating everyone with queries about this periodical and that; he came down five times to the Location Department, until Miss Holmes was nearly driven mad. On the fifth occasion, he looked in on Barbara.

She did not raise her head to greet him. She was typing her forms, more slowly than usual, but with a dogged concentration.

He came and stood by her desk. He said, "Why don't you go home?"

"Why should I?" she answered, without a smile.

"If I answered you truthfully," he said, "you would be extremely angry. I will say then that you look pale and tired and far from well, and, if you were my daughter, I should take you home in a taxi, tuck you up in bed, and ring for the doctor. Isn't that sufficient reason?"

"No." Then she said very slowly, "Mr. Dodds. Do you think it is possible to know another person's mind? Do you think the bond of telepathy can be so strong that one knows not only what is going on now, but what has happened long before? Or perhaps you think I am going mad. I am beginning to think so myself."

She saw him settle into what Mr. Rills, in happier days, had termed his Hyde Park posture. He said, with the comfortable air of a man who likes to talk and knows he does it well, "I don't think you're mad at all. I know very well that can happen. But it's unusual, of course, to telepathise what is past. It must mean that the past is always present in the—the other person's mind. Tell me—and I'm not meaning to be impertinent—are you very much in love with this person?"

"I don't know," she said, "I don't know. But I am completely bound to him. I do not know how I shall do without

him. He is always there with me, all that he thinks is in
my mind. I see nothing but him and what he sees."

"And what exactly do you see?" he asked, looking at her
very steadily.

She answered in a dull, toneless voice, "A room. A man
with his wrists tied. Pain, dreadful pain, ugly voices, and
then—*Je ne comprends pas. Je ne sais pas.* I cannot rid myself of it, and all the time there is a phrase of a tune that
goes through my mind, like muted drums. The sergeant
thought I was mad just now. Perhaps he was right."

"And your novel?" demanded Mr. Dodds abruptly.

"Oh, that! I'd forgotten about it. I shall never finish it."
She gave him a wan, desperate smile. "Mr. Andrews is no
more. I can't bear even to think of him. I feel I shall never
write again, but I don't suppose that's true, because writing
is like malaria, it never quite leaves you, and it comes back
at the most inopportune moments. But my—my soldier
of fortune——" Her voice cracked. She looked down at her
typewriter, began to rub the shift key with her finger. "What
is wrong with soldiers of fortune, Mr. Dodds? What is lack-
ing in them? Why are they as they are? They can be so
charming, and yet——"

"They are egotists," he said. "They are not safe. And
they know they are not safe. To attain safety they will sac-
rifice the world. It is not entirely lack of heart. It is, I believe, a kind of inner compulsion. Barbara. Take my advice
and go home."

"I can't. Truly, truly, I can't."

"I wish you would, you obstinate, pig-headed young
woman," he said. He looked genuinely distressed. "At least,
take care of yourself."

"I can't do that, either. I don't even want to."

Mr. Dodds gave her an expressive look and went towards
the door. There he paused. He said, "I'm an old man. I can't
run after you all the time to see if you're all right. But at
least don't tempt Providence too far. There is no point. It
may seem the end of the world to-day, but it won't neces-
sarily seem so to-morrow. This won't go on very long now,
you know."

"What do you mean?" Her face had blanched.

"Oh, my dear child, how can it? You must know—we all
know—that the course is nearly run. Barbara, take my advice.
Go home. I'll give you the money for a taxi. I'll explain to
Miss Holmes——"

"I am not going home."

He heaved a deep sigh. But he did not say any more, and, when he had been gone for sufficient time to allow him to reach his own room, Barbara pushed back her typewriter and rose to her feet. She moved stiffly, like an automaton. She felt so ill that she wondered if her legs would carry her. She wanted at that moment with passionate urgency to run up to Mark's room, to say, 'Let me be with you, even if you're going to kill me.'

But she did not. She walked into the lift, which was waiting on her floor, and pressed the button marked 'Basement'.

She stepped out into the stacks. She glanced neither to right nor left. She walked across to the shelves where Mr. Wilson had stood only three days ago, where Mr. Wilson had fallen only three days ago, to lie there eternally in his twentieth year. She moved her head slowly to look about her. Like Mr. Wilson, she had switched on the one light; she stood in the flare of brightness, surrounded by the dark. She turned her eyes to the shelves of the *Gentleman's Magazine*. Her heart jolted as she listened to the singing silence. Her ears were open for the faintest echo of a footstep, the faintest slithering sound such as that a person could make who was moving softly towards her. There would be some indication, surely—a rustle, the sound of breathing. One could not appear without sound. Not on those stone flags, not with those echoing walls. Mr. Wilson did not expect anyone. She did. She knew the person would come. But not just yet, not just yet. Long ago, when she was a child, she had played hide-and-seek. She remembered now how she had hidden and waited for them to find her. The excitement had grown into an agony; when at last she heard the running steps, she had not been able to endure it; she had cried out, 'Oh, find me, please find me, I am here, here, here.'

'Here, here, here,' echoed the walls. She flung her hand across her mouth. Had she really spoken? Was she going mad, after all? The radio message was flickering in her mind, *Je ne sais pas, je ne comprends pas, je ne sais pas, je ne comprends pas,* a confusion, hideous sounds, then, *'Raus! "'Raus,"* she whispered. *"'Raus——"* Why that, what does it mean? She turned sharply. Time was running short, so short. She bent down to examine the gap in the row of volumes. She had forgotten the sloping floor, or perhaps she was a little dizzy, for she nearly lost her balance, and only saved herself from falling by clutching on to the nearest shelf. She heard the clatter as something fell to the floor.

She looked down at it. She picked it up. It was a micro-film.

She stood, staring at it for a long time. She did not examine it, only twisted it round in in her fingers. It was nothing. It was like a photographic spool. For this, then, young Mr. Wilson had died.

Then she heard the footsteps. There was nothing furtive about them at all. They were normal, brisk footsteps, making a great noise on the stone stairs. But she recognised them immediately. In a panic she reached out her hand and switched off the light.

But it was worse in the dark. The footsteps had arrived in the basement. It seemed as if he hesitated; there was a step, a pause, another step, a pause again. Then the steps came up to her. The stuff of his shirtsleeve brushed against her arm. He stopped dead. Then, shamefully, she began to whimper, "Mark! Oh, Mark, don't, don't. I'm so frightened."

There was another pause. Then the light flooded down as he pressed the switch. He was standing almost against her, his eyes fixed on hers. They both blinked in the sudden light. Then she could see that he looked as usual, rather surprised, a little amused. And then she saw that he did not look as usual at all. For a change had come upon his face, and the change was as that that comes upon the countenance of the dying, as the shadow of non-living slowly spreads. A handsome face, strong, intelligent, with humour, but there was something missing, and with that something humanity had fled. Perhaps the current was now running too fast. Perhaps his feet would never again step on the yellow sand——

He said, "What on earth are you doing here? And in the dark, too. Is this an assignation? Are you being unfaithful to me? I.L.D.A. seems to have grown into a hotbed of the more sultry passions."

She did not answer. Her gaze fell to his hands, strong, beautiful hands, that she had always loved. He saw this and flung them up, fingers outstretched, as if in a gesture of capitulation; thus held, they were only an inch away from her face, her throat. In a kind of desperation, she bowed her head so that her cheek brushed against his palm. A brief flash of anger came into his eyes as if he did not want this, had not expected it. The next instant he had flung his arms about her, was holding her to him so that she was nearly suffocated, was kissing her frantically, as if he would never stop.

"Mark," she muttered, "Mark, Mark, Mark, Mark——"

as if there were some power in his name, as if by speaking it she could compel him to her will.

Her arms came up to clutch at him.

Then he saw what she held in her right hand.

He released her. She saw his mouth go down a little at the corners. She saw the tautening of his jaw muscles, the sudden tension of his whole body. But he only said, coolly enough, "Mine, I think. May I have it, please?"

She handed it to him without a word.

He looked at it briefly and slipped it into his pocket.

"Well, Barbara?" he said. "Well?"

(*"Et alors, madame? Vous êtes entrée dans le cabinet! Eh bien! madame, vous y entrerez, et irez prendre place auprès des dames que vous y avez vues. Il faut mourir, madame, et tout à l'heure. . . .*)

She said, and her voice came from a great distance, as if she were about to faint, "Is the current so very strong, my darling?"

"Current?" said another voice, a testy, recognisable voice. "The things people talk about! I make no apologies. If you wish to hold the kind of conversation you are apparently about to hold, you should go somewhere else. I am looking for a periodical. I am perfectly entitled to look for a periodical, and, if you must turn the stacks into Hampstead Heath or wherever it is that young people now conduct business that used, in the old days, to be done in decent privacy, you must expect to be interrupted. If you wish, I will suggest to Mr. Ridley that we have an official courting-room. The stacks are for books, not for erotica. Mr. Allan!"

"Adsum!" said Mark.

"Of course, you were a schoolmaster once," said Mr. Dodds. "I had forgotten. I'm not sure if I'd care to tread the academic path under your guidance. One would never know where one would end up." He turned fiercely on Barbara. "Well, Miss Smith? Have you no work to do? Have you no novel to finish? Go up to your own room and be thankful you're not my daughter, for I'd starve you on bread and water for a week, for this ridiculous vulgarity. You and Mr. Allan can finish your conversation some other time. I am old-fashioned enough to believe there is a time and place for all things."

Mark had made no comment during this tirade. She thought he was not even listening. His fingers were clenching and unclenching; his face was still and cold, with despair in every line. Only at this point did he turn to her. He said, "Good-bye, Barbara."

She could not answer. It was all drifting away from her, and the walls were drifting away, too. There was no comfort any more, no warmth, no love. She turned blindly towards the stairs. Through the mist of grief and fear and loneliness she heard Mr. Dodds's brisk voice saying, "Well, as you are here, Allan, you may as well help me over this matter of the *New Ireland Review*. Cork University College have it, but won't send it out. It'll have to be a microfilm. Now if you——"

She did not hear any more. She crept up the stairs, clinging on to the railing, and came at last to the ground floor.

And then she saw what she had not seen before. There were policemen everywhere. There were two on guard at the door. There was another by the telephone desk, where the refined young man was plainly enjoying himself. She saw another couple going up the stairs. She thought, 'They must be certain at last. And he does not know.' The need for action cut through her misery, so that suddenly she came alive again. He must be told. Soon he would go up to his own room. He would use the lift; he would not see the policemen. And even as she thought this, she heard the sound of the lift rising from the basement. She ran up the stairs. She was so engrossed in her own thoughts that Miss Holmes's voice struck her like a blow; she started guiltily, flushing.

"And where have you been, Miss Smith?" demanded Miss Holmes. "We have been looking for you everywhere." There was alarm rather than reproach in her tone, but Barbara misinterpreted it and, being in no state to withstand any kind of attack, began to stammer excuses.

"You are not looking well," said Miss Holmes accusingly.

"I am perfectly all right——" Suppose they arrested him now. 'Suppose he suddenly appears between those two policemen who went upstairs, struggling, fighting, caught by something that even he could not evade'——

"I want you to come into my office," continued Miss Holmes, "and sit down for five minutes."

"But I—I——"

"I'm not having my staff fainting all over the place. I suppose you want me to be accused of neglecting you. Come on, Miss Smith. There's a cup of tea waiting for you."

This was something quite unheard of in the annals of I.L.D.A., but Barbara, led along to Miss Holmes's office, could only protest, almost weeping, at this kindness which was such a cruel torture. She had to go into the office. She had to sit there with a cup of tea before her, the sight of which made her sick. She had to listen to a long talking-to; it was meant to be kind and friendly, but she could not endure to sit still, and always she was listening for the sounds that she dreaded, so that her replies were incoherent, and the cooling tea slopped into the saucer.

When at last she was permitted to go, she ran without ceremony up to the fourth floor.

Greta was dispersing the midday post. She delivered a bunch of letters on each floor. It was a task she enjoyed, for it involved movement, and she hated sitting still. She walked down to the ground-floor and then up again, singing gaily as she climbed the stairs, her face alight with excitement, her black hair tousled across her forehead, her operetta skirt swinging blithely about her hips. Mr. Ridley on the first floor, and Mr. Latimer. The post-room. Mr. Rills on the second floor, and the Reference Room. And up past the Location Department on the third floor, to the fourth, where there was a large bundle for Mr. Dodds, a couple for Mrs. Bridgwater—only she was away, poor thing, had a sort of collapse or something—and a nice little lot for her smashing Mr. Allan, whom she had quite forgiven for his former rudeness, which was, after all, in the best film tradition. Mr. Dodds was out at lunch, so she left his mail on the desk, then she tripped along, still singing, to Mr. Allan's room and knocked on the door.

She heard his voice saying, "Come in."

She entered, beaming. "Post for you, Mr. Allan." She said then, "I say, have you hurt your arm?"

He made a weary, contemptuous gesture with his other hand. He looked, she thought, rather ill. Of course, everything had been very trying lately. She said, "I think you work too hard."

"Possibly," he said, the wide, light eyes flickering up at her.

"Oh, well," said Greta, "work doesn't kill anyone, so they say. And here's some more for you."

She was an energetic girl, and she laid the letters down before him with an exuberant slam, knocking various articles on to the floor as she did so. She did not see the murderous spasm of irritation that tightened his features. She cried, "I am a clumsy girl, aren't I?" and stooped down to pick them up.

"One pencil," she said, "one ruler, one paper-weight, and one of your silly old microfilms, Mr. Allan. Nothing broken, no harm done—I say! There's a lot of powder or something on the floor." She raised her great, dark eyes to his. She was smiling. "Your microfilm's all unscrewed, or something. I didn't know you kept things in the middle of them. What a good idea, simply smash——"

Then she saw the look on his face as he rose to his feet and came towards her.

Greta was strongly-built young woman, with an excellent, primitive, sense of self-preservation. Mr. Allan's hands came round her throat so that she could not scream, but she could kick, and kick she did, and then her eyes, shifting wildly from side to side, fell to the bandaged arm. She grabbed this, twisting it and digging into it with her nails, so that her fingers pressed upon the open gash. He gave a sudden hiss of pain, and the dreadful pressure on her throat eased for one second; in that second she screamed at the top of her powerful lungs.

Barbara, running up the stairs, heard that scream. She flew towards Mark's door, pushing it open with such violence that it flung back with a crash. She saw that Greta was standing against the wall. Mark, with one hand swinging at his side, had his other arm crooked round her neck, so that he slowly bent her head back and back. His face was that of a surgeon performing some intricate operation, intent, expressionless.

She cried out, "Mark! You can't. It's too late, it doesn't matter any more. They're here——"

He raised his eyes to hers, and in that second his arm relaxed its hold. Greta wrenched herself from his grip. Clutching at her neck, she looked from him to Barbara, gave a faint whimper, then burst into hoarse, howling sobs.

They heard her running down the stairs, sobbing frantically as she went.

He stared at her. He said slowly, "You damned, interfering little bitch." And then, unbelievably, the smile caught at his mouth. He might never in his life have contemplated murder. He said, "Do you know what you have done?"

"I've done nothing," she said, her hand going to her own throat. "Nothing——"

He came close to her. His hands came down on her shoulders, the thumbs stretching upwards to her neck. Then he wrenched her hand away. "What have you told them?"

"Nothing, Mark."

He studied her intently, then said with angry bitterness, "No. Of course you haven't. I'd know if you had. You couldn't lie to me, and I—I suppose I can't lie to you either. Not any more, not any more. You're not the betraying kind, are you, Barbara? Oh, well," he said, releasing her, sitting down on the edge of his desk, as if he had all the time in the world, "perhaps it's as well you came. She's a blasted little imbecile, but I didn't really want to kill her. I'm so tired. Where are my cigarettes, in God's name?"

"Mark," she said, struggling to speak clearly and distinctly, "I think they know. There are policemen everywhere."

He glanced at her, then reached out for the packet of cigarettes. His hands were steady as a rock.

Her voice, despite herself, began to soar up. "Mark! Greta will go downstairs. She will go into her office. She will tell the girls. They will tell Miss Holmes, and she will ring down to the sergeant. That gives you ten minutes at the outside. You must do something. You must——"

"Ah," he said, brushing aside with a gesture the whole of Scotland Yard. "Let the b——s wait. You're a nice girl, though. I always liked you. I thought I'd have to kill you. I didn't want to, you know. But we'll forget about that. We've had good times together, haven't we? Come here. I want to kiss you."

"Mark, for God's sake. They'll be up, any moment. There—there's the fire-escape."

His eyes fixed on her with an abrupt, ugly intentness. "Ah!" he said. "There's the fire-escape, is there? The fire-escape. What a clever, clever little girl. The fire-escape, and two nice gentlemen waiting there for me. Two nice gentlemen in nice blue coats and nice bright buttons. What size bloody fool do you take me for? You wouldn't be trying to decoy me, darling, would you? You wouldn't be leading me into a pretty little trap?"

"Oh no, no. Oh, Mark, my darling, they're coming. I'm sure I hear them."

"Well, so what?" He rose swiftly to his feet and moved towards her. She stumbled back, her breath sobbing, her hands fluttering feebly at him. "So you don't want to kiss me now? You weren't always so prim, my girl." Then he roared out, "God damn you! What is this? So you won't kiss me. You've grown too good for me. The landlady doesn't let you kiss murderers, I suppose. You're all the same, all the same. Damned edge-of-the-bed virgins, the whole bloody lot of you——" His voice changed. His eyelashes were flickering up and down, his head turning from side to side. "Don't cry. Ah, don't cry. I didn't mean it. I tell you what, Barbara —stop crying now, there's a good girl—when I'm safe, I'll send for you. Then you can come and join me. We'll have a magnificent time together, you and I."

She could hear the footsteps now. "Mark! They're coming——"

One could dread the wild beast in the forest, the leopard crouching on the bough. But one could not bear to see it hunted, killed. She was frantic. She struck at him with her clenched fists. "Why don't you go? Can't you hear them? Are you quite mad?"

"Now, now," he said soothingly, catching at her hammering hands. "Don't panic so. Keep calm. I've got out of worse messes than this. The main thing is to keep cool. Once before they thought I was finished." He laughed. "But I wasn't, as they were to discover. There's always a last reserve."

But he, too, had heard the footsteps. His eyes turned to the window, then to the door. "Do you know," he said in a calm, yet surprised voice, "I think the old she-devil's done me after all. Who would have thought it? Who would have thought it?"

The sergeant must be on the floor beneath.

Mark looked for a moment at Barbara. "I'll tell you something, my dear," he said. "This is the wrong age for me. It's too civilised, and it's too dead, oh, God, how dead, how dead. And life doesn't matter a damn, unless you're living. Not a damn, not a bloody damn. If I am to be half dead, clamped down in dullness, I'll not live at all. There's nothing to live for. No adventure. No risk. No excitement. Ah, Christ, would you have me go to work, come back from work, breed children, and till the garden in my spare time? I'd sooner be torn to pieces." His face stiffened. The running steps were almost on him. He sprang to the door, knocking Barbara aside as he did so, and leapt on to the back stairs that led to the roof.

She heard the hissing whistle between his teeth, that phrase that she would never be able to hear again without turning sick and faint. She ran after him, saw that he was standing on the far side of the roof, outlined against the sky. The sergeant came panting after her. He was a stoutish man; his face was scarlet with exertion. There were two uniformed men with him.

Mark stood and laughed at them. He stepped back until his heel touched the railing.

"Now, sir," said the sergeant, "why don't you come quietly, and save us all this bother? You can't get away, you know. All the exits are guarded. Come along, sir, now."

He still laughed. He did not even glance at Barbara. It was as if he had forgotten her existence. For a brief second his eyes turned to right and left. There was no way out. Only the four-floor drop. He stepped back a fraction more, and at that Barbara screamed. At this, he did look at her. But there was no recognition in his eyes. There was no indication that once he had kissed her, laughed with her, made love to her, held her tightly in his arms. His gaze was wide, very bright. He smiled, as if this were the one point of time for which he had been waiting. And in the bottomless depths of her horror and despair, she could understand that this was his stage, and he the great actor waiting for his cue. Yet even at the last they must be together; his thoughts were turning in her mind.

They spoke to her. It was his voice, 'I am undefeatable. I have beaten love, and beaten death, and beaten the world. They thought they could beat me, but they did not live long enough to know better. Clever, clever, clever—the old woman, too. So clever, and then lying on the floor, with her fat neck broken . . .'

"*I think, Mr. Allan, there is something I must talk over with you.*"

"*And what is that?*"

"*You're engaged in rather a dangerous business, Mr. Allan. I am not, of course, referring to the seducing of other men's wives——*" That laugh—God, that laugh. But you stop laughing when your neck is broken.

"*This wouldn't be blackmail by any chance, Mrs. Warren?*"

"*Some might call it common justice.*" The laughter again —giggle, giggle, giggle, like an hysterical schoolgirl.

"*Well, well. And what, may I ask, do you know?*"

"*Something the police will be interested in. Very, very interested in, Mr. Allan.*"

"*Ah! I see. And how much do you want?*"

"*Oh, I don't want money.*"

"*I said, How much do you want?*"

"*I don't want money. I want justice.*" But she had stopped laughing.

You shall have it, lady. Just wait. "*So this is pure high-mindedness, is it, Mrs. Warren?*"

"I don't approve of drugs. My husband was a doctor. He told me what their effect was."

He had mimicked her. *"You don't approve of drugs——"*

Frightened now. Not so gay. Not so sure of herself. She had moved back. And he moved with her. The black eyes had dilated. Only for a second. But he could smell the fear on her. There was a shimmer of sweat on her forehead. Her lips were out of control. He stood with his back to the door.

"I think I had better warn you"—he laughed. He knew that tone, desperate bluster with the terror shivering through—*"that I am not to be trifled with."*

"Naturally not." Very amiable. *"I see that I am sunk, then."* He had added idly, *"Not that I am really to be trifled with, either."*

Beginning to lose her head—the great Mrs. Warren. Didn't seem to want to laugh any more. His hands were hanging loosely at his sides. Then a sudden screech, *"If you dare to hit me, I'll summons you."*

"If I hit you, old girl, you'll never summons anyone again."

Furious at the coarseness of his tone, the disrespect of the appellation, but how afraid, how wonderfully afraid. Rank fear from every pore of her. He had come slowly up to her. Mouth opened to scream, then the whimper, fading away, *"No! Don't! No, no, no, no——"*

Her squat, strong hands flew up, with some half-formed intent to protect her face. And his flew down. A useful blow. It had served him well before. He had smiled at her. She had not laughed again, never again. Clever. Clever. They would never have known. But that foolish little boy. Well, that was a pity. Like killing the baby. But there it was. One hadn't always the choice.

Someone was talking. Someone was crying. Some idiot was saying, "Now, sir, now, sir, now, sir." Ah, to hell with the lot of them. He looked boldly round, his eyes wide, his mouth split in a smile. A silly, fat little man coming towards him. A silly, frightened little girl, face grey-white, tears pouring down, mouth an O. "Mark!" she was crying, "Mark, Mark, *Mark*——" Mark, Mark, clever Mark. Always the lucky boy. He surveyed them all for the last time. Fanatical—who had said that? And damned. He turned his head a little sideways. He bestowed a broad, enchanting, derisive smile on the sergeant, who rushed towards him, then stepped back against the railing, and for the one second leant back, farther, farther——

If I say you can jump, you can jump.

Then he executed a neat half-circle in the air and disappeared.

There was no sound, no cry, nothing but the hiss of a weight cleaving the air. Only a long time afterwards was there the thud as the body hit the paving-stones four floors below.

She came out of I.L.D.A. She was shuddering from head to foot. She was devoured with grief, grief for Mark, grief for herself, grief for a world that could turn a man into a jungle wolf and thence to a dead thing that lay motionless in the courtyard below.

She paused outside the gateway. She was half out of her mind. Nothing seemed real any more. She had not the strength to go any farther. She heard steps coming towards her. She raised her head, moved her hands a little to ward off the shadows that fell so blackly about her.

Charles's voice said to her, "One of the girls from your office rang me. She said you'd saved her life. She thought I should come and take you home. I thought so, too." And with an old-fashioned gesture that came oddly from him in his jacket and flannels, he offered her his arm.

She took it in silence. They walked up to the main road. As they came to the crossing, Charles held her back for a second. An ambulance tore round the corner, screaming past them.

Then at last she began to cry.

XII. SHADES AND SHADOWS. 515.7

IT seemed for a while as if I.L.D.A. would never again recover its former academic calm. There were policemen everywhere, doctors, ambulance men, journalists. There were black, flaring headlines in the newspapers, photographs. Mr. Ridley sent in his resignation to the Committee; it was not accepted, and he afterwards withdrew it, for indeed he could not possibly be said to be responsible for what had occurred. Two of the girls left. There was great difficulty in replacing them, and also in finding a new telephonist, though the refined young man agreed to stay on for a while, now that Mark Allan was no longer there to curse him on the line. Miss Holmes went frantic while the forms piled up; everyone huddled in corners with everyone else; no work was done at all.

And yet, in a matter of days, I.L.D.A. was back to normal. Mr. Ridley was still there, and some of the colour had returned to his face. Mr. Rills was heard to make an indecent, spiteful witticism at the expense of Miss Holmes; Miss Holmes was heard to rate him soundly. A new young man replaced Mr. Wilson. He was, indeed, rather like Mr. Wilson, only he did not share his predecessor's enthusiasm for Newbolt and Kipling; he preferred the more modern poets, and quoted them extensively, sometimes shocking the girls who heard fragments coming down the corridor. His entry into I.L.D.A. was sweetened by Mrs. Bridgwater, who had now returned, looking precisely as she had always done —large and splendid and blonde, talking a great deal about her art, and saying insistently how happy she and Henry were, considering they were an old married couple. At least, as Mr. Rills remarked, she appeared to be still married. She was very kind to Mr. Nesbit, the new young man, and mothered him in a delightful manner; he fetched and carried for her, though she told him he was a silly boy—"and really, Jim—I may call you Jim, mayn't I?—you must have better things to do with your time than run about for an old mar-

ried woman like me." Mr. Nesbit had apparently nothing better to do with his time, and assured her of this many times a
day. "One does like to be kind to these young lads," remarked Mrs. Bridgwater in the canteen. "After all, it's a difficult age, and, though perhaps I should not say this of myself,
I really do understand the difficulties of adolescence."

"That does not surprise me at all," said Mr. Rills, for his
tongue had been unleashed again with a vengeance, now
that the person who terrified him was gone for good and all.
"Try fainting at his feet some time. That should make his
adolescence even more difficult."

Mrs. Bridgwater went an ugly yellow-white. She left the
canteen immediately, and she and Mr. Rills were not on speaking terms for a week.

Mr. Dodds, of course, was precisely as he had always
been, and still drove the Location Department into fury by
his handwriting and his incessant queries. Miss Langdon had
left, and was replaced by a full-time girl who had not even
heard of the murders, and showed no interest when they
were mentioned to her.

The microfilms and photostats were taken over by a Miss
Cullen. Mr. Latimer had said privately to Miss Holmes that
he felt it better that a woman should take over the department. It caused great disappointment. "She's not a patch
on our smashing Mr. Allan," said Greta, and, when her
colleagues gazed at her in open-mouthed astonishment, giggled vaguely and said, "Oh, I'm sure he didn't mean to kill
me. And he was so handsome."

It was only too true, from all points of view, that Miss
Cullen was not a patch on Mark Allan. Barbara hated her
with a sick revulsion that had little to do with reason. She
never came near the room if she could possibly avoid it,
and the sight of Miss Cullen, sitting primly at Mark's desk,
made her sick and faint so that she had to steady herself by
leaning against the wall. But then Miss Cullen was not in herself a very attractive personality—a little woman of uncertain age and uncertain feelings, with a girlish bob and a
thin, sour face, who wore jangling beads and ill-fitting twin
sets, whose voice was thin, cold and refined. She was told
about her predecessor. Mr. Latimer felt it to be his duty. She
said, "Oh. Well, I've really no patience with that kind of
thing," and, having thus dismissed drugs, lust, suicide and
murder as dregs that should be poured down the sink, did
not mention the matter again. Even Mr. Latimer was slightly
surprised. She insisted, however, that she needed at least

two typists to help her with the work that Mark had done single-handed; she was a martinet to work for, but liked to brighten the day by telling regularly two funny stories; she insisted always on a pause before relating them. They were never very funny, but her girls used to giggle because the situation was.

Barbara hated Miss Cullen from the depths of her lonely and unreasonable soul. Looking at her, she would think, despite herself, of the Elizabethan pirate who had scoured I.L.D.A., thrown it to the ground, and himself after it. And then her fancy, comforted perhaps by Mark's own, would picture the two working together, and she could imagine what Mark would have said and thought of this genteel, flat-chested person, and for a second laughter, and genuine laughter, would rise in her throat.

And so it went on. Greta sent up a request for a 'Beginner's curse on engineering'; Peggy asked for Volume II of *Revista Medicale, Cordoba,* instead of Volume XXI—and the department rocked in the scandal. Barbara, whose work was not so careful these days, sent off to Nottingham University when it should have been Nottingham Public Library, and Miss Holmes raised her voice like the Israelite prophets, as if the end of the world had come. It mattered again that one could not trace a history of Italy in the eighteenth century; it mattered that this university was open and that closed; it mattered that a certain public library would on no account lend to a certain chemical firm. The highlights of the week were someone slipping on the new linoleum, a gushing remark from Mrs. Bridgwater, a virulent one from Mr. Rills. It was incredibly funny that Miss Cullen should ruin a photostat, and Mr. Nesbit's new American tie provoked a storm of argument and interest. Life was the office and the office was life, and except in one person's mind and heart, Mark Allan was almost forgotten.

"It's very strange," said the sergeant to Mr. Latimer in their last interview. "We pieced things together. It seems a shocking thing to say, but it looks as if he started this in fun. Of course, it got most dreadfully out of control. But he never touched the stuff himself, and he never seemed to profit much by the money, most of which he gave away. He lived quietly enough, he didn't seem to drink or riot around. There were women, of course, and plenty of them, too, but not the diamond and mink kind at all, and what he wanted from them he got easily enough, and didn't have to pay for.

It was like a boy playing a game. Of course, once he had killed it was a different kind of game. Perhaps he enjoyed that, too, though I think it turned his mind in the end."

Mr. Latimer asked, with difficulty, "Did he recover consciousness?"

"He never lost it," said the sergeant flatly. "He died in the ambulance, of course, but he was perfectly conscious when we picked him up. One wouldn't have thought it possible. But he was. And he never said a word. He never made a sound. The men gave him morphia, of course, but that didn't happen at once; he must have been in the most shocking pain, but he did not so much as moan, only looked at us. It is a common belief," said the sergeant, "that we have no feelings, but I cannot rid myself of that look. It was as if he had detached himself from his agony and was looking down on us, almost with satisfaction. I suppose he felt he had diddled us, after all. Who does his work now, sir?"

"A Miss Cullen," replied Mr. Latimer, staring out of the window. "She is plain, middle-aged and very refined. She is not popular. But I have come to the conclusion that exciting members of the staff are not a good thing. She will certainly never excite anyone. She is a perfectly able woman. She could not do anything against the law if she tried." He added in a burst of confidence, "She clears her desk every night and puts a pot plant on it."

"Not quite Mr. Allan's line," said the sergeant before he could stop himself.

"No," said Mr. Latimer. "Not quite Mr. Allan's line."

"And—and the little Smith girl?"

Mr. Latimer sighed and looked unhappy. "She's taken it very hardly. Very hardly indeed. She is leaving us in a few days' time. She is changing her job, which I think is the only possible thing to do. This place must, I think, be haunted for her." He uttered the last words half apologetically, for he was not a fanciful man.

"Isn't there a young man?"

"There was, but I'm afraid—I had hoped that—— He fetched her on the day of—the day this all happened. But it seems it's not working out, and I believe she doesn't see him any more." He added, more robustly, "But after all, she's young and resilient, and who knows what will happen in a couple of years' time? There are always other young men. She'll forget. She's a sensible girl, after all. At least, I used to think she was."

"The trouble with people like Mark Allan," said the sergeant after a pause, "is that they communicate their own excitement. It's like eating some exotic dish and then being offered bread and butter and fish and chips. But women will never learn, never learn."

Mr. Dodds came into Barbara's room. The newspaper headlines were long forgotten and filed away. The name of Mr. Allan was never mentioned these days, and Miss Cullen nibbled away in her little hole, watered her pot plant, told little jokes, and primmed her mouth, where once had lain the centre of existence.

He looked at Barbara and she at him. He said, "I understand you're leaving. I think I should like to talk to you."

"I'll get you a chair," she said.

He smiled at her. "Oh no. I like to talk while standing up. I believe our friend, Mr. Rills, has had some words to say on that. You're looking better."

"Oh," she said, "one goes on living, you know. At first it doesn't seem possible, but one does." Then, "Tell me. When did you—did you know?"

"Oh, I always knew. There is, after all, such a thing as instinct. You knew too, didn't you?"

She did not answer. For a second she closed her eyes. "There was no proof," said Mr. Dodds, looking away from her. "But you see, he was the kind of man who could kill. The only one here. Rills is too cowardly. Mr. Wilson, poor lad, wouldn't have harmed a fly. I could not see Mr. Latimer and Mr. Ridley committing a murder, except perhaps in academic combination, for the good of the Library. As for the women—well, everything is possible, but it really wasn't a woman's crime, for your sex do not as a general rule, in the history of crime, hit people in such a scientific and warlike way. But Mark Allan—no, Barbara, I will mention his name, and you should mention it, too, if only for the reason that it would delight him to be so discussed—Mark Allan was right. He fitted in in every particular. You, of course, fell in love with him and could not see that, but I, who wasn't so blinded, saw him as someone who would kill quite detachedly, if necessary, and do it very efficiently, too."

"He wasn't really bad," said Barbara, with the utmost difficulty, for she could still hardly bear to think of Mark, much less talk about him.

"Bad!" repeated Mr. Dodds. "What does that mean? Bad—wicked—evil—they are all labels and mean nothing whatsoever. I am no more fitted than anyone else to sit in judg-

ment. But he was ruthless, you know, and dangerous. He had
some very good points. We all have. But you never saw him
properly, because you loved him and glamourised him, and
saw him as attractive and good-looking and charming, and,
indeed, he was all of these things—pity he didn't make
better use of them. You were, if I may say so, completely
foolish about him. When I found you down in the stacks——
Why did you go? Why in heaven's name did you go? You
must have known he'd follow you."

"That's why I went," said Barbara. "I couldn't wait any
longer. I couldn't bear it. I wanted it over and done with. I
was terrified of him, but I couldn't be without him. I thought
if he killed me, I wouldn't suffer any more. You're making
me cry. I thought I had stopped crying."

"Well, it's time you did stop," said Mr. Dodds. "I may
say that I am not a violent man. I do not commit murders.
But I didn't trust you an inch. You ruined my entire morning's work. And when I found you down in the stacks, I
could have beaten you. You say you wanted it over and
done with, but I don't believe you really wanted to die. And
you nearly did die. He knew you knew. I think he knew,
too, that you would not deliberately give him away, but you
quite misunderstood his character if you think that would
have counted with him. You knew. You were a source of
danger. That was quite enough. He would not have dared
to let you be, however much he wanted to. It was against
his code of living. The Maquis man is never safe. Oh, I dare
say," added Mr. Dodds, "that he may have loved you in his
own way, but he had travelled a long road, and it was not
the kind of road where love was important any more. Love,
after all, is sanity, and he was no longer sane. When he
said good-bye to you, he said good-bye to sanity for good
and all. I am sure, however, he would have killed you very
prettily. You would never have known what was happening,
if that is any consolation to you."

"You are very cruel," she said. She was crying helplessly
now, not troubling to dry her tears.

"I am not meaning to be," he said gently, "but it is surely
time that you spoke his name again, and thought a little
clearly. You have been walking this office like a ghost; one
hardly dared look at you. Talk about it now. Be honest
with yourself. He was honest, in his own way. He would have
hated all this mourning. He wouldn't have had any sympathy with your tears at all. Isn't that so?"

"Yes," she said, "it's true. And I would like to speak now.

I can to you. I did at first, to Charles, but that was different. I was out of my mind. I would have spoken to anyone, to a stranger in the street. I did go down to the stacks on purpose. And I didn't want to die. But I was so afraid and so tired. Of course, I didn't know I'd find the microfilm, but that didn't really make any difference. I'm a coward, you see. And so much had happened. We—— There was this strange link between us. I suppose there still is, even though he's dead. We knew each other's thought. I *know* how he felt. I *know* how he murdered Mrs. Warren. I know that in the end he did not think of me at all. But that doesn't matter. Only—only I've been—been haunted by the feeling that in the last moments I did betray him. If I hadn't gone up——"

"Miss Holmes," said Mr. Dodds gravely, "would have had to ring the agency for another typist."

"You're laughing at me. How can you?" She gave a sudden hysterical choke of laughter, confused with her sobs, then rested her head against her arms, struggling to control herself.

"Would you really have sacrificed Greta? I don't think so, Barbara. But I'll settle this one misery for you. You didn't betray him. I did. After I came up from the stacks, I went straight to the sergeant and told him everything I heard. You see, I listened, I followed you, I heard the whole conversation. And I make no apologies for it, either. I was frankly growing tired of murders, and I was growing tired of Mark Allan, too. And when I saw his face as he looked at you—— Did you not see it?"

"Yes."

"I have never seen a warning flare so plainly. Then I knew he had left the civilised world for ever."

She cried out passionately, "Oh, would you sit in judgment, after all? What do you know about him? What can you know? You wander about with your periodicals and your silly queries—— I beg your pardon, I didn't mean to be so rude. But after all, the money that he got for this he sent away—to people in France. He was apparently a good schoolmaster. And he saved the lives of refugees and airmen and friends in danger——"

"And ruined the lives of many more. Not to mention cutting short the lives of at least two people, one of whom was utterly harmless and very young. I see," said Mr. Dodds, "you have been studying the newspapers. They painted a most romantic picture, and the photographs would have en-

sured a contract in Hollywood, had he been 'alive. The clergyman's son turned commando. The hero of somewhere or
other. The saver of Jews. Legions of Honour and all that,
kissed on both cheeks by the President of the Republic——
How he must have laughed! But the trouble with soldiers of
fortune is that they must have their adventure. And in the
modern world the type of adventure they choose is always
aginst the law. You do not surely hold a brief for a man
who imports drugs, of all things. Why, he didn't even take
them himself, which would have been some slight excuse. He
did it for pure devilment. He sent the money away. He only
wanted the excitement. And no doubt he had some genuine
feeling for the families of his former comrades. It would all
connect up with the one part of his life when he must have
been entirely happy. Then he could be as he was—fighting
and twisting and daring death, withstanding torture with
incredible bravery, killing, snatching people out of danger,
using up all his muscle and wit and brain. No swords these
days, Barbara, but wit will serve, and of that he had plenty,
though I think it left him a little time before the end. But
then he had gone too far; the mind can only endure so much,
and perhaps the thought that he had to kill you was the final
straw. He was, after all, very fond of you. And you were excitement, too. Carrying on a love affair in I.L.D.A., kissing in
office time——"

"Mr. Dodds!"

"Well," said Mr. Dodds, looking for once slightly ashamed
of himself, "my office is, after all, next door but one, and I
have the common share of curiosity. But we'll leave that. It
isn't, after all, my province. Only a great deal went on in
that office, at one time and another, what with Mrs. Bridgwater and—— I see she is fully recovered. She gets on very
well with young Nesbit. I suppose it is part of his education.
But to get back to Mark Allan——"

"Please don't," said Barbara, beginning to cry again, "for
I think I cannot stand any more. It hurts so to think of him,
and I remember—— I don't want to remember. I did love
him so dreadfully."

"You employ the past tense," said Mr. Dodds. Then he
said very kindly, "My dear, you are very young, and I am
sixty-five. You don't learn so much in a long life as old people
choose to imagine; it is often a case of 'the longer thou livest,
the more fool thou art'. But you do learn one thing, and
that is that everything passes, everything passes as time

goes by—love, grief, loss, ambition. This will be forgotten, like everything else."

"I don't want to forget it," wept Barbara.

"That," he said, "is always the trouble." Then, "I understand you are leaving us."

"Yes." She had stopped crying. She looked away from him.

"Not to get married? The young man who used to call for you——"

"No. It wouldn't do. He is so nice, and kind and gentle. He has been extraordinarily understanding. But you don't love people for that, it's nothing to do with it. I did think," said Barbara, "that perhaps we could make a go of it. But it wouldn't be fair on him, and it wouldn't be fair on me, either. So we—we have just decided that it's no good, and it's all been quite friendly and—and terribly depressing. Because he doesn't really understand, and I can't explain it to him. Perhaps, later on—— But I don't think so. No. I'm taking up a new job, as research assistant. I shall like that. And I couldn't stay in I.L.D.A. any more. It has too many ghosts for me. Even to go up to the fourth floor makes me quite sick. When I leave it, I might feel happy again."

"So we shall soon," said Mr. Dodds, in a prosaic manner, "be contributing to Miss Smith's leaving present. What do you want?"

"Oh!" Then for the first time for many days she laughed. "A shroud, do you think? A nice pair of plumes? Or simply a large pile of monogrammed handkerchiefs to dry my tears?"

He looked at her for a moment. "You'll recover," he said. "It hurts like the devil. I know that, old as I am. But you're on the way to recovery now. And next time you fall into tears and despair, just think of the gentleman you are weeping for, and imagine how he'd probably clout you over the head for such damned stupidity. After all, he wanted excitement, and he got it, and he ended in high drama just as he would have desired. Stop crying, Barbara, and write your novels; to mourn too hard for a person is always such a poor tribute."

She stood by the window, staring out, for a long time after he was gone. She had no longer any desire to cry. There was a confusion of images and sounds about her—the great thudding, Pom-pom-pom-*pom* of the opening of the Fifth

Symphony, the grass-lands and vineyards of France, the joy of life and the excitement of death—on the run, out to hit first, always alert, jubilant, exultant, triumphant——

A world to live in. A world to die in.

And here—— Books from Manchester University, Willesden Public Library, the Hannah Dairy Research Institute. Periodicals from Bibliothèque Nationale, France; Biblioteca Nazionale, Italy;—Berlin—Warsaw—Helsinki. Reading material for students, writers, professors, engineers, the man in the street. For home reading, for library reading, for long extension. Books on how to cure bacon, how to make clothes, how to pick locks; books on Alexander, Lucrezia Borgia, criminals, priests, scientists, heroes. The thin threads of reading, running through I.L.D.A., picked up in the Reference Room, the Location Department, the Microfilm Department. A typing and a stamping and a filing and a packing, and you have before you the '45 as it really was, or the most modern work on thermodynamics. You pays your money, and you takes your choice.

He had said, *We are both bandits at heart.* He had said, *The current can be so confoundedly strong——* He had said, *I think I love you. Do you love me, too? You must not—— Good-bye, Barbara——*

And now he was dead and gone, his lust in ashes, and his body in dust, and the adventure ended. Murder was something in a book—a chapter, a few words strung together, nothing. And a man was like a chapter, read, closed, finished with and forgotten. The harsh words, the loving words, the blows, the kisses, the ecstasy, the fear, were turned back into pulp.

And the girls sunned themselves on the roof in lunchhour, for the September was exceptionally mild. And in Mark Allan's office sat Miss Cullen, neat, censorious, corseted and refrigerated, unaware of the sardonic ghost who, in the evening's whispering hours, might cast his grim, derisive shadow across her prim gentility. If a cold wind blew, she would merely shut the window. If a word such as could only be tolerated in the classics brushed against her ear, she would merely shake her head. If a hand slid softly across her beaded throat, she would merely say that these starched collars could be quite tiresome. Murder and passion and suchlike were not quite nice, must be ignored. And so Miss Cullen sat there, chattering like a mouse, her eyes agleam with self-righteousness, her mouth with its prominent teeth pursed up. Her little paws gathered the microfilms into her hoard; she nibbled up life in gobbets.

The violent ghost brushed past her, and she was unaware.

And Barbara covered her typewriter, put on her coat, and stepped downstairs into the September evening.

MURDER...
MAYHEM...
MYSTERY...

From Ballantine

The Queen of Suspense... RUTH RENDELL